# OH SO OSCAR

## FOREVER LOVE BOOK THREE

## CHARLIE NOVAK

# A NOTE FROM THE AUTHOR

While Ilias and Oscar's story is still full of fun, fluff, and steam, their story also contains some heavier moments.

As part of this, this novel contains discussions of grief and loss including the past loss of a parent and the past loss of a partner.

Please feel free to skip this novel if either of these topics will cause you any distress.

*For everyone we have loved and lost.*

# CHAPTER ONE

*Oscar*

"I HAVE TO SAY, Mr. Moore, I'm very impressed, and I don't use those words lightly." Madelyn Rossi, the legendary editor-in-chief of *The Traveller* looked over her desk at me and fixed me with a smile that was both terrifying and impressive.

"Your piece on eco-tourism and conservation in Sri Lanka was beautifully written. I think our readers will enjoy it."

"Thanks," I said, trying not to appear as nervous as I felt. I still wasn't over the fact that I'd managed to land a full-time staff writer position with one of the most prestigious travel magazines in the world.

I'd been reading *The Traveller* since I was fifteen and dreaming of faraway places. To now be contributing was a dream come true, and one I desperately didn't want to fuck up.

"I'm glad you liked it. I really wanted to bring some nuance to the piece. I think it's important for our readers to be aware of these things. As long as we don't sound too... preachy. The local community knows the issues they face better than I do, and I wanted to make sure I brought their voices through."

I wasn't sure it was the right choice of words or whether I'd be able to get my point across without sounding like an ass, but Madelyn nodded and looked down at the spread laid out across the desk.

"Indeed." I wondered if she was going to say any more or if that meant I was dismissed. "So, what are you going to write next?"

"Well, I have a piece to finish on the Seychelles, but I'm still discussing options with Marcus." Marcus was my direct manager, and I'd known him for several years before I'd started working at *The Traveller*.

He was the one who'd first helped me get my foot in the door with some freelance work, and he was also the one who'd encouraged me to apply for the staff writer position when it had opened last summer. I owed him a lot, but luckily, he was one of the nicest and most genuine men I'd ever met.

"What are the options?" Madelyn sat back in her chair, and it felt like I was being interrogated.

I took a sip from the glass of lemon water I'd been offered when I'd first arrived for our meeting, using it to buy myself a second to gather my thoughts. I'd been bouncing a variety of ideas around with Marcus for weeks, but at that moment, one in particular stuck out. Marcus hadn't been convinced Madelyn would go for it, but it was now or never.

"Ideally, I'd love to do a series focusing on LGBTQ+ holidays, specifically resorts and destinations that welcome LGBTQ+ couples. While straight-presenting couples have the world as their oyster, same-sex couples have to put so much more thought and work into their travel because, if they don't, their lives could be at risk. I'd love to showcase some destinations where they can feel welcome and experience the holiday of their dreams, especially if it's a romantic trip or a honeymoon. I've seen so many articles about luxury honeymoon destinations and packages, but most of them aren't suitable for queer couples."

Madelyn hadn't cut me off yet. In fact, there was something resembling a smile curling the edge of her lips. I'd come this far, so I decided to continue, laying everything out on the metaphorical table and hoping I could reach any kind of warmth that lurked under her icy exterior.

"A lot of my family, myself included, come under the rainbow umbrella, and several of them are starting to settle down. I hate the idea of them not knowing where they can go or what they can do if they want to go away together. And while a lot of travel agencies now offer LGBTQ-safe packages, I'd really love to see it celebrated. *The Traveller* is the leading travel brand in the world. Think about what a piece like this would say to our readers, or at least our UK readers. Many likely have queer friends or family or are queer themselves. And I want… I want to show them the beautiful parts of the world where we can be who we are. Where we don't have to hide our love and worry that even looking at our other half could end our holiday before its even begun. I want to showcase the best hotels and the best destinations, vetted by us, and put queer travellers at the heart of the piece. *The Traveller* is a brand people trust, and I want it to represent all our readers, not just a select few."

Now that I'd said it all, I wondered if I'd gone too far. I'd always been out at work, as far as was possible, but I'd never shouted about my queerness from the rooftops. For a lot of my travel, I'd never mentioned it because, as I'd just told Madelyn, it wasn't safe.

I was lucky, in a horrible way, that I was masculine presenting and nobody ever questioned my sexuality if I didn't mention it. I brushed off comments about having a wife or a girlfriend by saying I was too busy, and because I was a man, people accepted it without question.

"I think," said Madelyn, "that sounds like an excellent idea."

"Really?"

Madelyn chuckled, and it softened her for a second. "Yes, really. It's something I've been thinking about myself. My niece got engaged to her girlfriend at Christmas, and we had a similar conversation over lunch recently. It was difficult for me, but mostly because... well, selfishly, I'd never considered the issue before. I made suggestions of places she and Chelsea could go on their honeymoon, and she told me how many of them just wouldn't work due to local laws or safety concerns. Some of the resorts might look the other way, but that doesn't make it an ideal situation."

I nodded, suddenly aware that *Madelyn Rossi*, the

woman who had once made the director of The Garden hotel chain break down with a single look, was being open with me. I should have felt honoured, but instead I was frozen in fear because now the whole project felt intensely personal, and I knew Madelyn was going to take a keen interest in what happened. And if she didn't like it...

I tried not to think about that and instead nodded sympathetically. "It's hard. I've definitely hidden parts of myself away while travelling, and it's bittersweet because there are so many places I'd love to share with a partner, but I just can't."

"All the more reason to find some places you can," Madelyn said. "I'll speak to Marcus and ask him to get you and your partner a press trip. We've just had an invitation from a locally owned boutique resort in Hawaii that prides itself on being a diverse and inclusive destination. I'll let you and Marcus review it and see what you think. We'll start with one and see how it goes."

That all sounded amazing. Except for one thing. "Partner?"

"Yes. Since this is a series aimed at couples it makes sense for you to take your partner, and I'm assuming you wouldn't have pitched such an idea if you were single."

Bollocks.

Madelyn stared at me, her eyes narrowing, and all the blood drained from my body. "Is that a problem?"

"No." I swallowed. "Not a problem at all. I'll... er, I'll just have to check whether he's free. He's... he's a free-lancer and a photographer, so his diary is a bit all over the place."

My tongue was knitting a web of lies, and I hoped Madelyn believed them. I didn't have anything resembling a relationship in my life, but I wasn't going to let that get in the way of the opportunity, and I wasn't going to tell Madelyn she'd been wrong. That would sink my career faster than a lead balloon, and I didn't want to be out of my job less than a year after I'd started it. I'd worked too hard to get where I was to throw it away so carelessly.

"Oh? A freelancer? What does he write?"

"He's a travel writer," I said, my brain desperately hopping between all the men I'd worked with. "We've been on a couple of the same trips, but he's better known for his photography. His pictures are... They're incredible. He makes the world come alive through his lens."

"Perfect. That means we won't need to send a photographer or have you take any pictures."

That was a damning observation of my photography skills if ever there was one. Still, I hadn't been hired to take pictures, so it shouldn't have bothered me.

Except now it meant I had to convince the man I'd described—a man I was barely friends with—to come with me on a romantic press trip and pretend to be my partner. If he didn't dismiss me immediately, he'd definitely laugh in my face.

Then again... the last time I'd seen him, in Singapore, he'd taken to teasing me, and I hadn't been able to make heads or tails of his actions. I'd barely been able to get him off my mind either.

"Sounds great," I said. "I'll talk to Marcus."

And with that I scurried out of Madelyn's office before I could dig myself into an even deeper hole.


"You did what?" Marcus was staring at me, open-mouthed and holding his giant mug of coffee in mid-air.

It was later that afternoon, and we sat in his tiny office with the door closed while I recounted my entire meeting with Madelyn.

"I panicked! She asked for my ideas, so I gave them to her. I didn't think she'd say yes." I groaned.

"I didn't know you had a boyfriend," Marcus said. He looked hurt, and I realised he thought I'd been keeping secrets from him. This was my moment to come clean and tell him it had been a lie, but I couldn't do it. If I told Marcus, he might tell Madelyn, and then I'd be in deep shit. It would be better to try to keep the façade up for as long as possible, even if it meant digging myself into an even deeper hole.

"It's very new," I said. "We're just figuring it all out. That's why I didn't tell you. He and I are both super busy, and we're still at that early stage where everything is a bit... up in the air."

Marcus nodded. "This job is hard on relationships. You have to take the wins where you can. And taking this trip together sounds like it would be great for you. It'll give you some time together."

"But we'll be working. It's a press trip. Those itineraries are always packed."

"Not necessarily." Marcus grinned, and I felt the bottom

drop out of my stomach. The hole I was standing in was suddenly three feet deeper. "I'll get the hotel to set up a couple's press package. Tell them about the article, get them to do an itinerary of their best activities for couples. You know, romantic hikes, a spa day, dinner on the beach. That sort of stuff." I stared at him. Marcus sipped his coffee.

"You pitched this as something focusing on safe places for LGBTQ+ couples to be themselves and be open about their relationships, so it's going to be focused on shit for couples to do that. That okay?"

"Yeah, why wouldn't it be?" I asked, wondering if I'd blown my cover already.

"Because you're staring at me like a rabbit in headlights."

"I just wasn't expecting Madelyn to take such an interest or for this to get the go-ahead so quickly," I said, which was nine-tenths of the truth. I hadn't been expecting any of this at all, and the weight was already starting to press on my shoulders.

"You're talented, you work hard, you have good ideas, and Madelyn likes that. And you're not afraid of her."

"I am. She's terrifying."

Marcus laughed, the joyous sound bouncing off the walls of his office. "She is at first and when you screw up, but if you do a good job, she'll tell you, and if she takes an interest in you, it means she thinks you've got talent. Madelyn will be impressed by the fact you didn't just pitch her some puff piece. You went in there and pitched her something personal, something from the heart but that also fits the brand."

"I didn't do it on purpose," I said. At least I didn't think I had. "I just threw out the idea I really wanted and told her why it was important."

"Are you even listening to yourself?" Marcus asked. "You did exactly what I just said." He grinned and shook his head. "I'll get you some dates for the trip. All you need to do is send me all the details for your other half—name, passport details, etc. I'll get Vanessa to book everything for you."

"Okay, cool. When do you need it?"

"End of the week."

I nodded. That gave me three days to convince my supposed boyfriend to rescue me from my own incompetence. "That's fine. I'll send everything across."

"Great," Marcus said, taking another sip of his coffee. "So who is this mystery man anyway? Someone I know?"

"It's Ilias Verrati."

# CHAPTER TWO

*Oscar*

Sitting on my bed in my tiny studio flat in South London later that evening, I wondered how the fuck I'd gotten there. The day had been a blur, and I really wanted to forget it had happened, but unfortunately, I now had to get hold of Ilias and convince him to be my fake boyfriend for a week-long trip to Hawaii.

This was like the setup for a really bad romcom or one of those ridiculous Hallmark Christmas movies my siblings had made me watch last year.

I stared at Ilias's Twitter profile, which was currently filling my phone screen. I didn't have his number, and it was the only way I could think of to get hold of him. And that did not bode well.

I'd been partially honest when I'd told Madelyn about him. I had met Ilias when we'd been on a couple of the same press trips over the past few years, but while we'd chatted when we were together and followed each other on Twitter, we weren't close.

In fact, there was something about Ilias that always got under my skin. I didn't hate him—I didn't know him well enough to hate him—but he... both intrigued and irritated me for reasons I couldn't put my finger on. Part of me hated the fact that he was the first person my brain had suggested, but he was the only person who'd fit the brief, and the idea of spending a week with him pushed on something inside my chest.

Flicking open the messenger, I tapped out something I hoped didn't sound too ridiculous.

OSCAR *Hey, hope you're well. I have a photography opportunity for you for a presser to Hawaii. Would you be interested? It has a few complicated side details, so maybe give me a call? I'm in London right now too if you want to meet up to discuss.*

I added my number at the end and hit Send, wondering whether I'd even get a response. To distract myself, I looked through some of the ridiculous videos and messages that had popped up in our family group chat over the past couple of days.

My stepbrother Eli, who was a drag queen, had sent us some snippets from his latest tour. I chuckled as I watched part of his comedy routine, which focused on the incident last year when his older brother Richard had punched him in the face just after he'd found out Eli was dating his best friend, Tristan. I hadn't been there, but I had seen a video, and it made me laugh every time I thought about it.

Richard was older than me by about nine months, and we'd been seven and eight respectively when our mothers had gotten together and created a huge, blended, queer family. The pair of us had gotten along fine, but I wouldn't have said we were close. Richard could be a bit of a tool, and these days, I found it easier to avoid him as much as possible. Eli, on the other hand, fought fire with fire and had never been one to back down from an argument with his brother.

I opened another video my baby brother, Finn, had sent me of a ferret in a chef's hat doing a little dance and lost myself in a stream of mindless scrolling. Eventually, I heaved myself off the bed and strolled to the kitchen, peering into my tiny fridge and wondering whether I had anything edible. Not much, so takeaway it was.

I ordered a bento box through Deliveroo, collected my laptop, and began reading through the details Marcus had sent me on the resort. Given the time difference, we probably wouldn't hear back from their marketing team until tomorrow at the earliest about whether they were interested in our offer, but it wouldn't do me any harm to read up on the place.

I'd just pulled up the website and been bombarded with photos of crystal-clear water, lush tropical flowers, and stunning mountains when my phone flashed with a call from an unknown number. I assumed it was the Deliveroo driver because my studio could be a pain in the ass to find.

"Hello?"

"Hey, Oscar. Thanks for your message. I'm fascinated by your offer, so here's your phone call." The voice was rich, warm, and familiar, and I could picture the man it belonged to with absolute clarity.

"Ilias, hi… I didn't expect to hear from you." Fuck, that made me sound like an asshole, but luckily, Ilias laughed.

"So you sent me a message asking me to call you without expecting a response? What sort of man do you think I am?"

"A busy one?"

"Luckily for you, I'm back in London and completely and utterly bored," Ilias said, and I heard a note of amusement in his voice. "So stop being a tease and tell me all about these complicated side details."

"Right… so…" Fuck, I actually had to ask him to be my fake boyfriend now. I'd wondered all afternoon if I could just get away with telling Madelyn and Marcus that Ilias was busy, but since Marcus *knew* Ilias, that wouldn't work as it was bound to come up in conversation at some point. At the very least, I had to tell Ilias what the fuck I'd said in the hope he'd save my skin at a later date by pretending we'd had some sort of fling.

This was already more complicated than it needed to be, and I'd barely begun.

"I'm waiting… on tenterhooks, believe me."

"Sorry." I swallowed. "I had a meeting with Madelyn Rossi today." Ilias let out an impressed whistle, which I tried to ignore. "She, er, she liked the last piece I wrote, so she was asking me about new pitches. And I told her I wanted to do a piece focusing on LGBTQ+ safe destinations and resorts that welcome queer couples."

"That sounds fun and sorely needed. But I'm still fuzzy on the complex details part," Ilias said.

"I'll get to that."

"Tease."

"I... I'm not teasing," I said. I hated when Ilias did that. It all felt so... unnecessary. Ilias chuckled, and my skin prickled. This was why I hadn't wanted to work with him. In small doses, I could cope with Ilias, but if I was stuck with him for a week, he'd probably drive me crazy. "Anyway, to cut a long and boring story short, they're putting a press trip together to St. West Hualālai on Hawaii's Big Island for me, and I need a photographer. I was wondering if you'd be interested?"

"A free trip to Hawaii with you? Sounds like fun." There was a pause. "What's the catch? I'm still not hearing anything I'd consider to be complex details." I was sure Ilias had already figured it out, but he was pushing me to ask him outright. And I needed to because if this was going to work, I was going to have to communicate with him or risk everything going arse over apex before we'd even started.

"Er... well... because I pitched this as focusing on queer couples, they want to send people who fit... you know, for a genuine experience. And, er, there was some confusion, and Madelyn now believes I have a boyfriend, specifically you... so it would be a press trip for us... as a couple." Every word felt like it was stumbling out of my mouth, and I had no idea if I was even making sense. There was another long moment of silence broken only by the thudding of my heart against my ribcage.

"Run that by me again," Ilias said, his voice still rich with amusement. "You told Madelyn Rossi we were together, and now she wants to send us on a couple's press trip to a luxury resort to review it? I'm not sure whether to be flattered or confused."

"You can say no," I said hurriedly. "I can tell them we broke up or that you're busy."

"And turn down a free trip? Why would I do that?"

"Because this is ridiculous. You can't possibly want to pretend to be my boyfriend for a week just for a presser? You can't be that desperate."

"Are you calling me desperate?" Ilias teased. "I'm flattered you thought of me. Was there a particular reason you decided to make me your beau? Were you that charmed by our drunken conversation about butterflies in Singapore?"

I'd forgotten about that, and the memory sprang to mind, fresh and vibrant, bringing with it an unexpected sensation of warmth. I frowned. "I just... I'm not sure."

"Sorry, but I need more than that," Ilias said. "If I'm going to be your boyfriend for a week, you need to charm me."

"But you just said you'd go!"

"I know, and I will, but I want to know why you picked *me*. Come on, charm me... I want to be wooed."

"You're insufferable," I said. "I should have told Madelyn it was a misunderstanding."

"You and I both know Madelyn Rossi does not like being told she's wrong."

"I should have blamed myself."

"True, but you didn't," Ilias said with a note of sickening sweetness that turned my stomach. He had a point, and I was stuck between a rock and a hard place. If I called this off, the truth was bound to get out somehow. I didn't think Ilias would go around telling everyone what I'd done, but then again, how well did I actually know him?

"Fine, my brain chose you because... because you're a good photographer, and you're funny, and you're queer—which I know because you told me in New York when we bumped into each other there last September—and you're... handsome." I said the last word quietly because it was the one I didn't want to admit out loud.

I kept telling myself I'd subconsciously picked Ilias because he fit the brief, but it was impossible to deny that he was good-looking. He had a beautiful smile that seemed to light up a room and dark eyes that were speckled with green. I only knew that because he'd sat right next to me at the rooftop bar in Singapore, and it had been impossible to miss the flecks of colour in the sunlight.

He was charmingly handsome, and he knew it. There was something in the way he carried himself that screamed that he knew how beautiful he was. During our brief inter-actions in the past, I'd seen him charm every pretty man that strolled past, and all of them had fallen into his arms.

I think that was what grated on me the most—how boundlessly self-assured and self-confident he was. Ilias knew he was handsome, charismatic, and talented, and he wasn't afraid to use those skills like he was weaving some kind of magic spell. I wasn't sure if I was in awe of his charms, or worse, jealous he hadn't attempted to use them on me. Not that I wanted to jump into bed with him, but it was more the principle of the matter.

"You think I'm handsome?" Ilias asked. "I'm flattered."

"You're welcome."

"And you're right. I'm a good photographer too. We'd make a good match." I could hear him grinning, and I hoped I'd done enough to convince him. "Why don't we meet for lunch tomorrow, and you can tell me all the details."

"Sure," I said. "That's fine. Where do you want to meet? Do you want me to send you the trip itinerary first?"

We hashed out a time and place to meet, and Ilias gave me his email address so I could forward anything Marcus had sent me before we said goodbye. I stared at my phone, wondering what the fuck I'd just agreed to.

My dinner arrived two minutes later, and I ate it while scrolling through the pictures of the hotel. It did look beautiful—exactly like the place I was looking for. I could imagine strolling along the golden sandy beach hand-in-hand with someone I loved, or climbing through the jungles and up mountainous peaks together, wondering at the beauty of the natural world, or spending the evening surrounded by candles under a million stars.

It was somewhere I'd want to share with someone special.

And now I was going with a man I hardly knew, even if I was inexplicably drawn to him.

# CHAPTER THREE

*Ilias*

I woke to the sound of breaking china and a large amount of screaming.

"Not already," I groaned, rolling over in bed and burying my head in the pillow. It couldn't be later than seven. "I need to get out of here."

"Ilias!" My brother's voice was like a foghorn through the bedroom door. "Can you come down?"

"Yeah, yeah," I said into the pillow. "I'm up."

"What?"

I twisted onto my side and sat up before yelling. "I'm up!"

"Good. Watch out when you come down. A mug broke on the kitchen floor." I heard him stomp down the stairs, and I sighed, figuring if I didn't get up, Dominic would be back and probably armed with small children.

I loved my nephews, but I did not want to be jumped on

this early in the morning. The little clock on the bedside table said six forty-five, and I cursed under my breath as I swung my legs out of bed.

As much as I appreciated my brother and his wife giving me a place to stay whenever I was in London, I wished it came with a side of peace and quiet. Still, it was cheaper than finding my own place and easier than moving back in with my parents, who'd hover and obsess over my every move, so I could suffer through another few weeks of early mornings until I escaped on my next trip.

Throwing on some joggers and an old hoodie, I pottered down the townhouse's two flights of stairs until I reached the spacious, open-plan kitchen that took up the back half of the house. My sister-in-law loved cooking and entertaining in her free time, so they'd spent a fortune making it the heart of their home.

I heard the chaos before I even entered, but that was what happened when you had four boys under five all trying to have breakfast at the same time.

"Morning," I muttered, sliding around the edge of the large table that filled the centre of the brightly lit room towards the coffee machine on the counter at the far end. It was one of those ridiculously fancy ones that looked like it belonged in a coffee shop rather than a home kitchen, but I wasn't going to complain.

"Morning, Ilias," said Louisa, Dominic's wife, who was trying to simultaneously feed their eight-month-old twins, Sam and Matti, drink her own coffee, and explain to Nico—who'd just turned three—why he couldn't have Oreos for breakfast. "Sleep well?"

"Not bad, thanks." I slid a mug into place and began making myself a drink, watching as one of the twins leant over the side of his highchair and dropped something squashed and beige into Louisa's mug. I shook my head, grinned, and quickly began to make her a fresh one.

"Here." I offered her the new coffee, and when she frowned, I added, "That one has unwanted additions."

"Oh, thanks. I swear, I need eyes in the back of my head."

"Where's my brother?" I asked, walking over to the table and sitting on one of the long benches next to the twins in their colour-coordinated highchairs. "He can do something."

Louisa smiled. "He's helping Teddy get changed. He spilt orange juice all over himself."

"Was that what the screaming was about?"

"A little," Louisa said before turning back to her second child, who was still whining and on the verge of a full-blown tantrum. "No, Nico, you cannot have Oreos for breakfast. You can have yoghurt and strawberries or Weetabix."

This was a familiar argument, which Louisa always won, so I just sipped my coffee and took over with the twins. I was getting pretty good at it now, even if they'd both started to reach the age where they were making grabs for the spoon and were happy to mash up whatever they could get their pudgy little hands on.

More shouting heralded the arrival of Teddy, the oldest of the four at nearly five, in a fresh t-shirt, followed by my oldest brother, who looked like he hadn't slept in years.

"Morning," Dominic said as if he'd forgotten that he'd yelled through my bedroom door barely ten minutes ago. "Sleep well?"

"Until the screaming started," I said as I scooped more baby porridge onto a spoon.

Dominic shrugged casually. "Just be grateful they don't wake you up at five."

"Who was up at five?" Dominic pointed at Nico, and I chuckled. The boy was an adorable hellion with more energy than any physical being should possess. Dominic had been muttering about enrolling him in some form of sport as soon as he was old enough, just to try to get some of the energy out. I didn't want to point out that all that was going to do was make him fitter.

"Uncle Ilias," Teddy said, sitting down on the kitchen bench next to me with a piece of toast and jam on a blue plate covered in sharks, "can we go see the sharks at the weekend again? Please."

"If I'm not working, sure, we can go and see the sharks again." Ever since I'd taken him to the London Aquarium six months ago, Teddy had become obsessed with all things shark.

It had made it easy to buy Christmas presents for him since the whole family had just bought him shark clothes, shark toys, shark books—which he insisted on having read every night—shark crockery, shark everything. And now, whenever I didn't have weekend plans, Teddy and I would hop on the Tube and spend the day at the aquarium. He'd happily spend hours in the shark tunnel, his nose nearly pressed to the glass, watching them.

Teddy beamed at me. He had jam all around his mouth already. "Thank you."

"You're welcome," I said, reaching for a napkin to clean him up before the stickiness spread.

"What are your plans for today?" Louisa asked, having finally convinced Nico to eat yoghurt. "Are you working?"

"Yes. I've got a meeting at lunch with a writer for *The Traveller*. He wants to talk to me about a press trip he's going on. He's looking for a photographer to go with him, and he reached out." I knew I was making it sound more formal than it probably was, but I'd learnt a long time ago that I had to make everything sound serious or nobody believed I was actually working.

As soon as someone in my family got even a hint that I might have some free time, they volunteered me for something. I'd had to learn to draw firm boundaries or I never got anything done, and half the time, I worked out of coffee shops instead of my bedroom at the top of the house.

If I was available, it was easy for Dominic or Louisa to ask me to pick up Nico from playgroup, or to get Teddy from preschool because the nanny was ill or on holiday, or to watch the kids for a bit while one of them was at an appointment or working late or because they wanted a date night, or to pick up some shopping, or whatever else they could think of.

And because I lived here for the tiniest amount of rent possible, I always felt guilty saying no.

So I'd learnt to remove myself from the situation because if I wasn't in the house, they couldn't ask me to nip out. Obviously, I was still around for emergencies, but it gave me time to concentrate and get work done. Which I needed to do because as a freelancer, I lived from job to job, and not getting work done meant I didn't get paid. And I quite liked having money.

"That sounds nice," Louisa said. "Where's the trip to? Anywhere fun?"

"A locally owned, boutique hotel in Hawaii."

"Seriously?" She grinned at me. "You get to go to all the nicest places."

"Perks of my very poorly paying job." I sipped my coffee. "Which I wouldn't change for the world," I added hurriedly before Dominic could say anything.

Being the oldest of my three brothers, he tended to be overprotective, and because I was the only one of us who'd ended up in the creative sphere, his focus was on me rather than anyone else.

"As long as you're happy," Louisa said. Out of the corner of my eye, I caught her pulling a face at my brother.

"I am." And I was. I loved my life. I got to travel and take beautiful photographs of all the places I visited. I got to see mountain ranges so tall they disappeared into the heavens and oceans so clear and crystal they seemed to stretch out into infinity.

I got to explore the nooks and crannies of crowded cities, finding paths off the beaten track that only the locals knew about, spending late nights in tiny bars and restaurants with the best food I'd ever eaten, listening as people shared their lives with me. Give me a run-down restaurant shack filled with sizzle and spice over some fancy Michelin-starred place any day.

And when all was said and done, I'd have a lifetime of memories to look back on that didn't involve being crammed into the Tube every morning or sitting at an office desk and counting down until the end of the day, drinking bad coffee out of a chipped mug while answering pointless email after pointless email.

I'd have lived a free life. Which was all I'd ever wanted.

Louisa asked me a few more questions about the trip before the nanny, Astrid, arrived, then it was time for the chaos of getting everyone ready for playgroup and nursery and work and whatever else was going on that day.

I finally managed to make a break for the safety of my bedroom, planning on a quick shower before I got down to business. I had some photos that needed editing and submitting and another article that needed polishing, and I needed to schedule some posts for my Instagram account, which had a surprisingly big effect on my ability to get jobs.

But when I sat down at the small yet beautiful desk Dominic had added to my room, I found I couldn't focus.

There were two questions running round and round in my mind, and I didn't have a satisfactory answer to either. Why had Oscar picked me? And why the fuck had I said yes?

Oscar and I weren't close, and although I considered us friends, it was in a very loose sense of the word. Sure, we'd had in-depth conversations late at night over drinks while overlooking beautiful cityscapes, but they were always about random things like where to find the perfect chilli crab, noughties sitcoms, and butterflies. They gave me a fragmented view of him as a person but nothing more.

It was why I'd teasingly pushed him last night. I needed to know why he'd picked me.

His answer hadn't been satisfying though. I knew I was talented, funny, and charming. I'd always been good with people, and my charm was a skill I'd honed over the years when I realised it would get me places.

Being queer seemed to fit the brief, given the type of trip, so it didn't really feel like a plus but more of a necessity. Oscar had said I was handsome too, and egotistically, I knew that. But there was something about the way he'd said it, like it was something he didn't want to admit, that gnawed at me. Did he not want to find me attractive? If so, why not?

I assumed he didn't already have a partner, otherwise he wouldn't have asked me, so I could rule out not wanting to be attracted to me for that reason. And if he didn't like me, he wouldn't have asked me to save his ass, so it couldn't be that either. The whole thing had me spinning in circles and the only way I was going to get answers was by asking him directly.

But the one thing I couldn't ask him was why I'd agreed to the trip.

Sure, the trip would be fun. I'd never been to Hawaii before, and the hotel looked beautiful, but I didn't think I'd said yes just because of that. Especially given the added "complications" of having to pretend to be Oscar's boyfriend.

Why the fuck did I want to do that? I hadn't been a boyfriend person for years. Not since...

I shook my head, refusing to follow that train of

thought. That subject was dead and buried. Quite literally in fact.

I sighed and looked back at my laptop screen where I'd subconsciously pulled up the hotel's website. There was a banner of photos scrolling lazily across the homepage, each one more beautiful than the last.

The only reason I could think of, and the only one that made sense, was that Oscar intrigued me.

# CHAPTER FOUR

*Ilias*

CINNAMON & Clove was a tiny café and bakery in Fulham that I'd never heard of before Oscar had suggested it. The outside was painted terracotta orange with bright lettering adorning the fascia and a scattering of bright metal tables spilling out across the pavement surrounding it, each one filled with people enjoying the April sunshine.

I saw Oscar through the window and stepped inside to join him, the heavenly smells of freshly baked goods and rich coffee filling my nose. He sat facing the door as if he wanted to keep an eye out for me, but he was currently scrolling through his phone. It gave me a moment to look him over.

His dark hair was longer and fluffier on top than it had been the last time I'd seen him, but the faded sides still bled neatly into the carefully trimmed stubble that highlighted his strong jaw. He still carried a lingering tan from his last few trips, and it suited him. The bronze of his skin was highlighted by the simple white t-shirt he was wearing that skimmed over his shoulders and wrapped around his biceps. Oscar wasn't muscular per se, but he was toned.

A smile played across my lips because if I was handsome, so was he. We'd make a perfect couple—at least in pictures.

"Hello, beloved," I said, sliding into the chair opposite him and shooting him my most charming smile. Oscar looked up at me and grimaced, his thick eyebrows knitting into a frown as he put his phone face down on the table. "Too soon for pet names? I'll make a note."

"Hey. Thanks for coming." He didn't return my smile, and it made something inside me flicker. Although I didn't know Oscar well, I had discovered he was great fun to tease —gently of course. And stupidly, like a small child, his coolness made me want to react the opposite way. I knew this meeting was a serious one, but the situation was farcical, and we should at least be able to joke about it. Besides, Oscar sounded cute when he was bordering on exasperated.

"Of course. I'm not turning down an opportunity like this." I grinned. "I'm not sure what part of it is better—the luxury hotel or the fact that I've suddenly acquired a boyfriend. A cute one too."

Oscar grunted. "It's not…"

"Not what?"

"I was going to say it isn't like that, but it is." He sighed. "I'm sorry, I shouldn't have dragged you into this mess."

"It seems a little late for that, especially considering the email you sent me earlier."

"Did you read it?"

"Not all of it," I said. "But what I did read sounded lovely. Especially the part about the couple's massage. And the dinner on the beach." Oscar winced, and I could partly see why.

The St. West Hualālai was part of a small, locally owned chain that had seized upon the idea of being featured in *The Traveller* with gusto. They'd happily put together an all-inclusive press trip along with what look liked some bumph about their diversity and inclusion policy and why they were happy to welcome and support queer guests.

It seemed a little like their marketing team might have landed on the idea of allyship as a way to make money, but I was trying not to be that cynical. Especially because I was glad we were heading somewhere locally owned rather than a massive resort chain.

"Yeah, well, they want us to have the full experience they give to... couples."

I opened my mouth to ask a question about the way he'd said couples, but we were temporarily interrupted by a smiling waitress in a bright pink t-shirt who'd come to take our orders. I decided on a delicious-sounding roasted beetroot and halloumi salad with pomegranate seeds and thin slices of fresh peaches, a peanut butter-caramel sour-dough doughnut for afterwards, and a large cappuccino.

"I hope," I said as the waitress disappeared behind the counter, "that we'll get a chance to explore. The hotel and excursions sound great, but I do love to have a good nosy. You find all the best places that way."

"I hope so too," Oscar said. "I'm sure we can find at least one free afternoon to go exploring. Not that we have to go together... If you want to go by yourself, that's fine. I just..."

"Don't worry, I won't leave you behind. It'll be our little adventure." I smiled at him again, and this time Oscar's lip twitched, which I considered a minor victory. There was a moment of silence, which stretched out just long enough to become awkward.

"So... do you want to walk me through all the details?" I continued. "We should talk about our relationship as well. I want to know everything. Have we been dating long? Who asked who out? Are we in love, or is it more sexual? Have you met my family? If so, that's definitely a sign of something serious. They're an... interesting bunch. Very loud."

And that was the polite way of putting it. My family was a chaotic hurricane of drama, centring largely around my nonna and my grandma, who hated each other and started cross-family feuds whenever possible. Everyone else was continuously caught in the middle and forever changing sides, so it was impossible to know who was mad at whom on any given day.

Oscar chuckled. "Mine are the same. Do you have many siblings?"

"Three brothers, all older. And about twenty cousins. Plus eight nephews and four nieces," I said. "I'm the only one of my brothers who isn't married."

The waitress reappeared with a tray and slid our food onto the table. The salad looked amazing, and I picked up my fork ready to dig in, hoping we could move past the awkward part of the conversation about me not being married.

"I have five siblings," Oscar said, looking at the enormous ciabatta sandwich stuffed with homemade pesto, heritage tomatoes, rocket, and mozzarella. "Four brothers and a sister, and I'm the second oldest. Technically, I'm only related by blood to my sister and the second youngest brother, but I've known the other three long enough that they feel like family, especially Lewis—the youngest—because he was only two when our mums moved in together."

"You have queer parents?" I knew I sounded rude and that my mouth was hanging open, but I'd never met anyone near my age with queer parents. It was cool.

"Er, yeah. My mum, Eleanor, has known my stepmum, Miranda, since they were kids, and when my dad died and Miranda got divorced, they just... realised they were in love with each other."

"Oh. That's so sweet."

"Yeah, I guess it is." Oscar didn't look convinced, and I wondered if it was a sore spot for him. I didn't want to press him for further details though, so instead I said, "I'm sorry about your dad."

"Thanks." Oscar nodded, giving me another of his rare half smiles.

"Are any of your other siblings queer?"

"Yeah. All of them except one. The oldest, Richard, is straight. The rest of us are all…"

"Gay as fuck?" I grinned and stabbed one of the pieces of roasted beetroot and a piece of halloumi. The salad had been the right choice, and I was going to have to try recreating it in Dominic's kitchen. It was either that or come back here. It would be a lovely place to work.

"Something like that. We're all under the umbrella somewhere. But none of them are married yet. A couple have partners…" He frowned again, then shook his head. "Although I've just realised my sister Jules and I are the only single ones left."

"Just wait," I said, trying not to roll my eyes. "As soon as one of them settles down, the rest of them will, and then it'll be weddings and grandchildren and the endless nagging about why you're still single."

I jabbed my fork into another piece of beetroot with more force than necessary and watched as it went spinning across the bottom of the bowl. "Although, since your family is mostly queer, they might be different."

"Speaking from experience?" Oscar asked.

"Yes." This was my sore spot. I loved my family, even if I didn't always like them, and the constant questions by my grandmothers, aunts, uncles, various cousins, and even my brothers was starting to drive a wedge between us. They'd accepted me being gay, but they hadn't accepted the idea of me being single past the age of twenty-five. It was like I was some shrivelled piece of fruit that was rapidly heading past its sell-by date.

Sometimes I wished I was a rotten tomato or something

just so I could throw myself at them to make them be quiet for five fucking minutes.

The only people who were on my side were my parents, who hadn't gotten together until they were nearly thirty, and my cousin Zoë, who had her own reasons for avoiding my family.

"I'm sorry," Oscar said. "That must suck." He gave me a little nod, then picked up his sandwich and continued. "So details... Let's start with the basics. Let's say we've been dating... eight months. Since New York." He took a huge bite and looked at me, waiting for me to react. I was just stuck on the fact that he'd changed the subject away from my family without wanting to know more. It made my chest flutter.

"Eight months sounds good," I said, trying not to let on how much he'd thrown me. "I suppose I charmed you with my winning ways? Convinced you how wonderful and sexy I am."

"Something like that. I mean, we've sort of known each other for a while, and dating in this job is hard. It would make sense."

"That is the most unsexy thing I've ever heard come out of your mouth. Dating for *practical reasons*." I shot him another smile as I rolled my eyes in the most melodramatic way I could. "But fine, we can go with that. I'm still going to tell anyone who asks that you were won over by my bountiful charm and vivacious wit."

"You do that," Oscar said, and this time, he actually smirked at me.

Oh my fucking God. So there was something underneath the grumpy façade. That was very interesting. It made me want to flirt harder to see if I could get more out of him, but if I pushed too much, he was liable to just clam up, and that would be even worse.

"I will." I scooped up the last few bits of my salad. "Did we have a first date? Was it romantic?"

"I don't know. I don't think that matters." Oscar took another bite of his sandwich, and I had the urge to roll my eyes again. I couldn't tell if he was being deliberately obtuse or just poking me, but either way, it was annoying.

"Of course it matters! We need to sell this fantasy. You have to commit to it," I said. Then I thought for a second while I chewed. "Our first date was at Lola's. It's this tiny Cuban restaurant in Washington Heights run by Nina and her husband Eddie and named after Nina's abuela. The food is incredible, and it's one of those places that you'd walk right past if you didn't know it was there."

"That sounds amazing." Oscar was staring at me, and it felt like I'd said something that had struck a chord with him.

"It is. Next time you're there, I'll send you the address." He nodded. "I'd like that."

There was another pause, but this one felt less awkward. I took a long sip of my cappuccino and reached for my doughnut. "Basic details are sorted, then. What about things like PDA?"

"We'll be working, so we'll need to be sort of professional," Oscar said, frowning again. "But I guess I'm not opposed to things like hand holding. Or cheek kisses."

"Any more?" I asked. "Are you okay with hugs? Kisses?" His frown deepened. "Just the occasional one. And I won't use tongue. It'll be very teenage first date but without the awkwardness."

"Um... yeah, fine. We can do that."

I wanted to ask why he had objections to kissing me, but I could get to that later. "Good. It'll be fun, I promise."

Oscar hummed as if he didn't believe me, and I was almost offended. Then he opened his mouth and did it for real.

"As this is a press trip, and we're supposed to be dating, you can't go round flirting with everyone and going off with whoever takes your fancy. I don't want to wake up and find you sneaking back in from some all-night fuck fest with a twink you found at the beach."

"Excuse me? Do you really think that little of me?" I glared at him. This was just fucking typical—when it was all going well, he had to go and accuse me of being a slut like it was the worst thing in the world.

"How dare you be so judgemental! You said yourself that dating in this job is hard, so what if I want to have a little fun? Are you the sex police or something?" Oscar was starting to look a little contrite. Good. But it wasn't enough. I wanted him squirming.

"Do you really think I would go to all this effort to help you out and then leave you for some rando?" I asked.

"Er... well..."

"Because that's what you just said, and I can't believe you wouldn't extend me the basic courtesy of believing that I could act like a professional. You owe me big time for this shit, and I'm doing you a favour. The *least* you can do is not act like a pretentious, stuck-up dickhead who judges people for their choices, choices which are, coincidentally, none of your fucking business."

"I'm sorry," Oscar said. There was no hesitation to his words, and no insincerity either. "That was wrong of me. I shouldn't have done that."

"No, you shouldn't. You should never judge people for their romantic or sexual choices as long as everyone involved is consenting and of age and nothing illegal is being done."

"I know." He nodded. "You wouldn't be the first person I've heard that speech from."

"Really? Are you a pretentious, judgemental twat with other people too?"

"No. It wasn't about something I said… it was…" He thought for a second, then shook his head. "One of my brothers said it about another situation. Not involving me. It was one of them. They're fine. It was nothing bad. They were just making a point about something." He grimaced as his eyes met mine.

"I'm really sorry, Ilias," he continued. "I'm so nervous about this trip, and I'm worried I've dragged you into this hole I've dug, but I shouldn't be taking my worries out on you. I shouldn't have thought less of you."

"No, you shouldn't. But I accept your apology," I said as I pulled apart my doughnut, watching the peanut butter and caramel ooze onto the plate. "If you say it again though, you'll be on your own. We'll have the messiest, most public non-breakup-breakup ever. There'll be screaming and plate throwing and everything."

"I think I'd deserve that." Oscar looked down at his dessert, which looked like a pastry twist brushed with jam and covered in icing and slivers of almonds. "Are you sure you still want to do this?"

"Why wouldn't I be?"

"Because of what I just said. You must think—well, I know you think I'm a colossal dickhead."

I thought for a second while I ran a bit of dough across my plate to mop up the caramel. The truth was, I still wasn't sure why I was agreeing to the trip. There were hints that Oscar and I could pull this off, that we might be vaguely compatible or at least able to fake a bit of weak chemistry. But there was still so much about each other we didn't know, and we'd already managed to have one argument.

But there was something about him that pulled me in like I was on the edge of a gravity well and couldn't escape. I couldn't see myself backing out even if I wanted to.

"It's fine," I said. "A rocky start doesn't mean a rocky ending. Besides, my hopes are up now. You'll have to work a lot harder to dissuade me from a week in paradise."

"Okay, then. If you're sure."

"I am."

I wasn't sure I believed it though.

# CHAPTER FIVE

*Oscar*

AS I PASSED through security at Heathrow, I couldn't shake the sickening dread that was churning in my stomach. It was too late to turn back now, but with every step I took towards this ill-advised adventure, I felt acid burning my throat.

It had been two weeks since my disastrous lunch with Ilias, and although he'd accepted my apology for acting like a wanker, I still felt guilty for what I'd said.

If Eli, Finn, or Lewis had heard me, they'd have chewed me out without a second thought. My brothers were very serious about sexual freedom and consent, and none of them would have been impressed by my behaviour.

I still didn't know why I'd said it. I'd tried to rationalise it by telling myself I'd just been looking out for our arrangement, but even to me that sounded like bullshit. Every way I tried to frame it just made me sound like a selfish twat, which, when I sat down and thought about it, I realised I was.

But that still didn't explain *why* I'd said it.

The only thing I'd come up with was that I was jealous, but I'd dismissed that immediately. I wasn't jealous of Ilias giving other men attention. I just... didn't want him to do it in front of me. That was as far as I'd gone down that line of thought before I'd squashed it.

Despite my apology, I was surprised Ilias had still agreed to this. The out had been right there, but he hadn't taken it. It was another thing I couldn't explain. We'd talked every few days since, but it all felt superficial—just exchanging information for the trip and the barest pleasantries about our days. I almost missed Ilias's ridiculous flirting.

Collecting my belongings from security, I headed towards departures, checking my phone to see if Ilias had arrived yet. We'd agreed to meet there two hours before our flight, but so far I hadn't heard from him. The concourse was packed, and I turned my gaze across the crowd, hoping I might be able to catch a glimpse of him.

"Hello, darling," Ilias said as he slid out of the crowd, walking up to me and pressing a kiss to my cheek. My heart skipped as I felt the brush of his lips against my skin, and a waft of soft cologne filled my senses. He smelt like vanilla and peaches. "Have you been waiting long?"

"Er, no." I swallowed and shook my head. "There was just a bit of a queue to get through security."

"I think I got lucky because they opened a new lane just as I got there so I sailed straight through." Ilias shot me another of his brilliant smiles. The ones that made my stomach twist and my heart race.

He was wearing a black t-shirt with a stylish-looking jacket over the top that perfectly complimented his olive skin along with a loose pair of caramel-coloured trousers that looked ridiculously comfortable, and he had a fashionable carry-on bag slung over his shoulder. I'd never managed to look that stylish while travelling, but Ilias made it look effortless.

"Good timing, then," I said. "Do you want to get a drink or something? I don't think we'll get a gate for a bit."

"I don't suppose your business expenses will stretch to the champagne bar?" Ilias asked, but it was easy to tell he was teasing. I grinned.

"Sorry, you're on your own there. But I can get you a coffee if you'll accept that?"

"I suppose." He winked at me, then turned and headed towards the bustling Starbucks on the far side of the room. I followed him quickly, but every step felt like I was walking across uneven ground. I'd been expecting awkwardness or bristling politeness, not this. It was like nothing had happened.

Maybe Ilias had really meant it when he'd said he'd forgiven me.

We grabbed two coffees and found somewhere to sit and chat for an hour before we were summoned to our gate on the other side of the terminal. The flight was an afternoon one, and it would take just under eleven hours to reach San Francisco. Then we'd have two hours to hotfoot it through immigration, collect and recheck our bags—since apparently the airline wasn't going to do that for us—and get to our second flight, which would land us at Kona International Airport on the Big Island at about ten at night local time.

It would be nearly nineteen hours of travel in total, and that was without any delays. It wasn't the longest journey I'd ever taken, but it was still going to be rough.

My jetlag had gotten better over the years, mostly because I'd abused my internal clock to the point where it just accepted sleep as sleep and meals as meals, but I did my best to help it where I could. I just hoped there was nothing too arduous scheduled for our first day to give me time to relax and adjust to the change in time zone before I had to start working.

"I assume we're in cattle class," Ilias joked as we sat by the gate. He was peering through the little glass divider at the first-class lounge, watching as people sipped cocktails and expensive coffee in their little bubble of luxury.

"Sorry, yes. Vanessa usually tries to get us good seats though. But if you've got an issue, I'm sure you can take it up with Madelyn."

"Ha, ha, you're hilarious." Ilias gave me a deadpan smile. "I'd rather tell my grandma she uses too much salt in her cooking, and that her pot roast is bland and dry." He shuddered. "It would probably be less painful."

I laughed. "Cattle class it is then."

"By the way," Ilias said, his deadpan expression morphing into a knowing smirk. "You are now sworn to secrecy about my grandma's cooking. That's a family secret."

"Am I going to meet your grandma, then?"

"Probably not, but even so, I have to make sure you're not going to rat me out."

"Is it that bad?" I asked, and Ilias nodded.

"Yeah, it is. But you can't tell her that because she's defensive about her cooking. I think it's because Nonna is Italian, and her cooking is amazing, and my grandma gets jealous, even though her cookies are the best thing I've ever tasted. I think it's the amount of butter in them." He sighed. "My family is this huge cross-continental mash-up —Greek, Italian, American, British, and even a little Irish, although I'd never say that to an Irish person because nobody in my family has actually been to Ireland in a hundred years. Anyway, they're loud, and interfering, and *everyone* has an opinion and thinks they're right. Facebook was the worst thing ever invented because it allowed them to stalk each other across the world. It was why I deleted it two years ago. I got sick of my every move being watched."

"Don't they follow you on Twitter?"

"Only a few of them," Ilias said. "Mostly because the rest of them don't know it exists."

I chuckled. My family was nosy, but they weren't that bad all things considered and we'd always been given space to be ourselves. We had a lively family group chat, but that had arisen out of a desire to communicate, not force or necessity.

"That sounds intense."

"It is." Ilias shrugged and stretched. "But it is what it is. I avoid the drama as much as possible, but somehow it always finds me. At least being away for the week will mean I get some peace and quiet."

Part of me wanted to press because I was curious, but something in the corner of my eye was drawing my attention. We should have been boarding by now, but there was no sign of any staff. When we'd first arrived at the gate, there hadn't been a plane in front of us, but that hadn't registered as a problem because often we were boarded through one gate and shuttled out to a plane elsewhere. But now there was a sinking feeling in my stomach.

"Something's wrong," I said. "We should be boarding right now."

Ilias checked his watch, which looked like one of those beautiful, top-of-the-line smart watches, and frowned. "Yeah we should. But there wasn't anything about delays on the boards or the flight information. I watched it all last night."

"Me too." I looked around, trying to see someone I could ask. We couldn't afford to be delayed for long, otherwise we were going to miss our connection.

There still weren't any staff around, and when I checked the flight information on my phone, there was nothing listed. All we could do was wait and see what happened. It still irked me, and I shifted uncomfortably in my seat. I hated delays, even though they were part and parcel of my job.

"Ladies and gentlemen," said a muffled voice over the tannoy, and I noticed a man wearing an airline uniform standing behind a nearby desk. "We apologise for the delay. Due to inclement weather, the incoming flight has been delayed in its arrival and will be landing shortly. Once the plane has been cleaned and refuelled, we will be able to depart. Once again we apologise for the inconvenience."

As he spoke, the enormous nose of an Airbus appeared behind him as if it had been waiting for the right moment. At least now we had a plane, which was something.

"Bollocks," Ilias muttered under his breath. "That sucks. How long do you reckon it'll take to get it sorted?"

"I'm not sure. Maybe an hour?" I glanced at my phone and realised our departure time was about to come and go with us still stuck in the lounge. "Unless there's some sort of miracle and they can get the flight time down, we're going to miss our connection."

"Fuck!" Ilias sighed. "They'll have to put us on another flight though, so that's something."

"Yeah." The sinking feeling in my stomach was getting heavier. "I'm going to call Marcus and let him know."

Since it was a Monday afternoon, I knew he'd still be in the office, and although he couldn't do anything, it was better to keep him informed. Plus, he could get Vanessa to let the hotel know we probably weren't going to get there tonight.

Marcus swore when I told him. "Fuck's sake! Thanks for letting me know. Keep me posted. I'll let Vanessa know, and she can work her magic with the airline."

"Cheers, I appreciate it." I wasn't sure exactly what magic Vanessa was going to work, but thirty minutes later, when we were still sitting in the departure lounge watching the plane be refuelled, an email popped up on my phone with a hotel booking for tonight in San Francisco and details for a new flight to Kona tomorrow morning.

It came with a cheerful note from Vanessa telling me not to worry about the delay, that these things happened and everything was sorted and reminding me to keep all my paperwork and receipts for later. I wasn't sure what had happened behind the scenes, but I was very grateful that it had.

Ilias noticed me tapping out a response. "Everything okay?"

"Yeah, just an email from Vanessa."

"What about?" He sounded a little snarky, and I realised he'd been getting progressively quieter and snappier over the past hour. Despite his calm exterior, it seemed the delay was getting to him too.

"The flight and tonight," I said as I relayed all the details. "It's a bit of a pain, but it's not too bad. Honestly, Vanessa is a lifesaver. I've heard about her doing this for a couple of other people, but I've never had a delay this bad."

"This is not a bad delay," Ilias grumbled. "Sleeping overnight in the airport is a bad delay. This is easy in comparison. You just had to make one call and someone fixed everything."

"Hey," I said, trying not to give in to the urge to snap back. "Don't take your frustration out on me."

"Tough. You're my boyfriend for the week. You have to listen to me grumble."

"If you were my boyfriend, I'd tell you to shut up," I muttered. I felt Ilias's eyes boring into the side of my head. He said something quietly that I didn't catch, but when I turned to him to tell him to repeat it, an announcement came over the tannoy that we would be starting to board soon.

"Fucking finally," Ilias said. "And don't tell me to shut up. I'm allowed to be frustrated with this fuck up just like you are."

"You don't have to take it out on me though."

"Believe me, I'm not."

"Why are you being an asshole?"

"Has it occurred to you that I'm stressed?" Ilias asked as he raised his eyebrows and shot me a pointed glare. "Even though you've said it's 'all sorted', I'm not used to that shit. I'm trying to tell myself that I don't have to worry about missing my connection or trying to find an airline rep to sort out a new flight and maybe somewhere to sleep or some food vouchers. You know what freelance life is like. It's endless worrying about money and other shit. So don't get arsey with me just because you now have a cushy job that sorts that shit for you."

He went to grab his bag to storm off but I grabbed his wrist, holding it tightly. A shock zipped across my skin and made my breath catch.

"Ouch," Ilias said. "Fucking static."

"I'm sorry," I said, not letting go of him. "I should have considered that. I've only been in this job nine months, and I guess I've already forgotten all the shit that comes with freelancing."

"Forgotten or suppressed?"

"Probably both."

Ilias let out a dry laugh. "I'm not surprised. I'm sorry

too. I'm being a dick. I just hate shit like this." He gestured with one hand. "But thanks for sorting it."

"I did fuck all. If it wasn't for Vanessa, I'd be panicking too."

"I'll remind you to get her a present or something."

"She likes fridge magnets." I smiled as I remembered her talking to me about it once when another journalist, Ailette, had brought her one back from New Orleans. "She puts them on the mini-fridge in the admin office."

"That's really sweet," Ilias said. "We'll have to find her a nice one."

He was smiling now, and seeing it made something warm spread across my chest. It felt... better. But I didn't have time to think about it because airline staff had started to arrive in the lounge, and it wasn't long before we were finally queueing up to board.

As usual, Vanessa had gotten us good seats—a little pair nearer the back but not so close to the toilets or the staff area that we'd be disturbed—and we settled in for the flight, which finally departed nearly three hours later than scheduled.

Ilias and I both had headphones, so we alternated quiet conversation with films and random episodes of TV until we were fed, and after that Ilias produced an enormous hoodie out of his carry-on to pull over his t-shirt. It swamped him, but in a cute way rather than a ridiculous way, and the fact that I'd noticed that pulled at something inside me.

It didn't take long for Ilias to drift off, but I couldn't sleep. I felt like I was in over my head and in danger of drowning. I had no idea what I was doing, and it scared me. This was just supposed to be a professional arrangement—pretend to date for the week or at least long enough to fool Marcus and Madelyn, and then go back to being...

What would we be?

I supposed it would be friends. We'd started as acquaintances, but since we'd grown closer already, it would be impossible to go back to that. Still, I liked the idea of us ending up as friends. It would be nice to know someone in the same boat who understood what this life was like and why certain things were impossible.

Settling back into my seat to watch another film, I felt something brush against my shoulder. I glanced over and realised Ilias had shifted his position so his head was lolling to the side. I smiled to myself because he looked sweet with his long dark eyelashes brushing his cheeks and his soft, relaxed mouth. This close, I could see a smattering of freckles across his nose.

As I watched, he shifted again to rest his head on my shoulder, one hand finding my arm. I froze, not sure if I should move him or not. Would it be awkward for him if he woke up and realised he'd been sleeping against me?

Ilias let out a snuffly little snore, and his grip tightened on my arm. He still smelt like vanilla and peaches. I decided to let him sleep. There was a good chance he'd move again before he woke up.

And it wasn't like I had to tell him he'd been cuddling me.

· · ·

It was seven thirty that evening when we landed in San Francisco and dragged ourselves off the plane, our connection well and truly missed.

As predicted, the queue to get through immigration was long and slow moving, and even though both Ilias and I had Global Entry, it still took a couple of hours to get through and collect our luggage. I felt awful for the smattering of other passengers who'd also missed connecting flights and now had to hang around in search of someone to speak to.

I was getting Vanessa a fridge magnet and a box of cupcakes.

Luckily, the hotel we'd been booked into was barely a five-minute taxi ride away, and it had a small restaurant. Ilias offered no protestations when I shoved us both into a taxi and headed straight for the hotel, which was simple but clean and functional with friendly staff who checked us in quickly and offered to let the restaurant know we'd be straight down after we'd dumped our bags. I accepted their offer, even if I didn't really feel hungry. I knew I needed to eat something, and doing something mundane like sitting in the restaurant would help me adjust.

"What floor?" Ilias asked as he climbed into the lift in front of me, wheeling his giant suitcase in front of him. He seemed less stressed now that we'd arrived, and that pleased me.

"Six." I stepped in behind him as Ilias pressed the button. "Room 622. Are you okay with getting some food after we've put everything down? I realise I answered for both of us when they asked."

Ilias nodded and shot me a wry smile. "Taking charge already? How naughty. Usually I'd ask for dinner first, then I'd make you work for it. I'm not that kind of man." I rolled my eyes, and Ilias snorted.

"Actually, I'm starving, so if you hadn't suggested dinner, I'd have just gone without you. Do you think they'll have burgers? I feel like I deserve something absolutely decadent after today."

The lift came to a shuddering stop, announcing our arrival on the sixth floor, and the door slid open. "I'm sure they will," I said, climbing out of the lift with my case and looking around to see where we needed to go. "Or they'll have something similar."

"You can't do 'something similar' to a burger. It's a burger or it's not."

"I meant they'll have something just as heavy like mac and cheese or pizza."

"That's definitely not the same," Ilias said teasingly as we followed the green hotel carpet to our destination. His nap on the plane seemed to have left him full of energy while I felt ready to drop. I wasn't sure which of us had made the right choice. "Here we are."

Ilias had stopped in front of the nondescript black door and was pointing at the little number on the plaque next to it. He plucked the key card from my fingers and stuck it into the reader, waiting for it to beep and flash green before he opened the door and strolled inside.

"Oooh, this is nice," he said, looking over his shoulder at me. "Left or right?"

"What?" I frowned. Ilias snorted. I was clearly missing something.

"Do you want the left or right side of the bed?"

"It's a double?" It was a very naive question brought on by my stupefied state, and as soon as I'd said it, I knew I'd made a mistake. Of course there was only one bed. We were supposed to be dating.

"Actually, I think it's more like a king," Ilias said with a wide grin as I walked over to stand next to him, staring at the large bed in the middle of the room that was made up with crisp white sheets and a green runner with the hotel's name across the bottom of the duvet. "Don't worry, we can still snuggle."

"I..." I was going to tell him I was already expecting that after the plane, but instead, I just said, "I'll take the left if that's okay."

"Perfect." Ilias tossed his carry-on onto his side of the bed. "I'm just going to freshen up, then we can go and get food."

"Sounds good," I said, not bothering to watch Ilias head for the bathroom. I just stood there, staring at the bed, trying not to think about what it meant.

# CHAPTER SIX

*Ilias*

USUALLY, whenever I travelled across more than two time zones, I slept like shit for at least the first night, and getting more than four hours could be considered a major accomplishment. So it surprised me to wake up to the sound of Oscar's alarm, which had been set for six.

What surprised me even more was waking up attached to the man in question, my arms wrapped around him in some sort of death grip and my face buried in his neck.

Fuck nuggets on toast. I was never going to live this down.

This was more embarrassing than the time I'd woken up covered in garlic sauce while spooning one of my best friends at university after we'd all come back wasted from a night out and had both fallen asleep in his room while trying to eat kebabs. Apparently, I was a cuddler, and it didn't seem to matter how well I knew the person.

I lifted my head to see Oscar staring at me awkwardly like he was trying to work out how to ask me to let go.

"Sorry," I grunted, rolling away. I hoped he hadn't been awake for long.

"It's fine," Oscar said as he sat up and stretched. "I'm going to shower."

As he climbed out of bed, I tried not to watch him walk away, but it was very hard. He was wearing an oversized t-shirt that just grazed the top of his ass and a pair of loose, black shorts that weren't doing anything to disguise how gorgeous his legs were. Oscar had strong thighs that were begging to have me between them and a round butt I desperately wanted to touch. I felt like a total perv, peering over the duvet to stare at him, but in my very weak defence he was ridiculously sexy. And I'd been told I wasn't allowed to look at other men, so Oscar would have to be the object of my attentions for the week.

I felt my cock start to stir in my boxers. Shit, no, that couldn't happen. Well, it could, but it might lead to some very awkward questions.

I rolled over to the edge of the bed and sat up, hoping that moving around and doing mundane things like finding clothes to wear and repacking my bag would help. It did but only to a certain extent.

I couldn't stop thinking about waking up next to Oscar. He'd felt so warm and solid in my arms, and the smell of him seemed to cling to my senses. I wondered if I'd slept so well because he'd been there, and I both loved and hated the fact that it was probably true.

He hadn't pushed me away though.

Oscar's expression might have been less than impressed, but he hadn't shoved me off him as soon as he'd realised I was clinging to him like a limpet. Had that been because he'd only just woken up and was too dazed to move? Or was he just being polite? Or had he liked having me there?

The third option was the most unrealistic, but it was also the one that made something spark deep in my chest.

I sighed and threw some clothes onto the bed. I didn't have time for another disastrous holiday romance. My heart wouldn't be able to cope with another loss.

It didn't take us long to get showered, packed, and head down to browse the hotel's breakfast buffet. I was delighted to find they had hot, sticky cinnamon buns and stuck three on a plate to take back to the table in the corner we'd commandeered.

Oscar raised an eyebrow but didn't say anything. He was alternating between black coffee, orange juice, and a very large bowl of heavily doctored granola. Clearly, we both had our own ways of dealing with jet lag.

As we headed to the airport to catch our rebooked flight, I found myself refreshing the departures list on the website every thirty seconds because I didn't want to deal with more delays. Even though this was only a single flight, I was done with travelling now. Our destination was in sight, and I was ready to be sitting by the beach with a drink in hand, enjoying a truly beautiful part of the world.

I already felt myself getting itchy to explore the island

and to take as many beautiful photos as possible. I'd definitely be getting up early at least one day to watch the sun rise.

It was the weirdest juxtaposition because even though I loved travelling, I always hated the actual journey. I just wanted to *be* where I was going, and if I could wish for any magical powers, I'd ask for teleportation so I didn't have to deal with the queuing and the delays and the cramped legroom. It was either that or a lifetime first-class travel pass so I could at least suffer in style.

"Do you want the window this time?" I asked Oscar as we squeezed onto the packed plane.

"No, you take it. I actually prefer the aisle." He gave me a small smile, then winced as someone knocked him with their elbow while trying to shove their bag into the overhead locker.

"Sweet." I grinned and slid into the seat. "I'll let you know when I see land though because you won't want to miss that."

"As long as you don't call out 'land-ho' like some sort of pirate, we'll be fine."

"There goes that plan, then."

Oscar chuckled and dropped into the seat next to me holding his headphones and laptop. It was moments like this—with the little chuckles and sassy comments—that made it feel like Oscar's walls were starting to come down.

It had happened at dinner last night as well when we'd been having some random conversation about gaming, and he'd shared anecdotes about playing Mario Kart with his brothers and sister. The way he'd talked about them had made it clear he loved them, even if they were nosy, chaotic, and interfering.

It gave me another bit of insight into my beautiful, defensive, private travel companion, and it felt like I was assembling a puzzle from randomly dropped pieces, only I wasn't quite sure what the final picture should be.

"Marcus sent me an updated itinerary overnight," Oscar said. "Did you want to look at it? I forwarded it to you, but I wasn't sure if you were checking your emails."

"I wasn't, but I probably should." I sighed. "There's probably a bunch that need replying too if I want any work when we get back." The life of a freelancer meant I was constantly hustling, and days off were a rare thing.

I almost hated how accessible I was thanks to email and messaging, which made me sound ridiculously old and grumpy, but it meant everyone expected me to be available twenty-four seven. If I hadn't responded in a day or two, I'd pretty much have to kiss opportunities goodbye because there was always someone more eager and on the ball than me.

"They have Wi-Fi if you want to work while we're flying," Oscar said. "I could probably do with getting some stuff done too. After that we can look at the itinerary."

"Nope, itinerary first," I said as the flight attendants walked into the aisle to start the safety demonstration. "That'll give me something nice to think about while I respond to seven billion emails from people wanting me to do shit for free. Just pay me for my fucking time and experience already."

Oscar nodded. "People are assholes. I used to get that all the time. Like can you just write us an article about this city, but you'll need to fund the trip yourself and all the expenses, and we'll only pay you two hundred pounds for the finished product. And only if you're very lucky because we usually expect people to do these articles for free for *exposure*."

I laughed and several people turned to shoot me filthy looks. "Fuck exposure. I hate that word so fucking much. I have fucking bills to pay, and 'exposure' isn't going to buy me food."

"I tried to explain that to someone once," Oscar said with a wry smile. "They told me I should be grateful they were even considering me. I told them to get fucked—politely of course—but still."

"Assholes." I shook my head. "Honestly, I love my job, but that is the worst part of it. Nobody values my time or experience. They think my job is easy because I 'just take pictures all day', and they act like they're doing me a favour by giving me work, like they could do it themselves, but, you know, they'll be nice and give me something to do. But I don't need paying much because they're *just pictures*. Like, fuck off with that bullshit. Are you seriously telling me people don't pay a fortune for a Van Gogh because it's just a picture?"

"I've had the same," Oscar said. "Before I worked for *The Traveller*, people always assumed it wasn't hard to write a nice review or an article or that it didn't take me long, so they figured I should do it for free because it only took me ten minutes. I think the worst was when someone told me it wasn't like anyone was going to read it, so why should they pay for it?"

I let out a sound that was half painful groan and half derisive laughter because I'd had that too. I told Oscar that and soon we were swapping our worst freelance stories while sipping orange juice from small plastic cups, the thought of working completely forgotten. Oscar was sharp and funny, and I felt like I was being handed another puzzle piece to slot into my picture.

"Oh, shit," Oscar said when the stewardess came round with our meal. "Did you want to look at the plans?"

I thought for a second as I took my tray. "You know what, surprise me. As long as I get the opportunity to explore and the chance to get up for the sunrise one morning, I'll be good."

Oscar raised an eyebrow, his lip twitching. I wasn't sure if he thought I was being unprofessional, or careless, or something else entirely, but then he smiled, and it felt more like he was intrigued. "Okay, then. A surprise it is."

My heart skipped. And just for an instant, I wondered if I was in trouble.

When we finally stepped outside Kona International Airport several hours later, I took a deep breath and let the warm air wash over me as a gentle breeze caressed my skin.

After traipsing across airports, seemingly endless queues, an unexpected overnight stop, two flights, and nearly thirty-six hours, we were finally in Hawaii. Now it was just a thirty-minute drive to the resort, then I'd be free from the wretched journey. I could only hope the trip back was smoother.

The hotel had sent a car to collect us, driven by a cheerful man named George in dark trousers and a white shirt with the sleeves rolled over his massive forearms, who gave us a running commentary about the island and what we were seeing as we drove.

"So you here together?" he asked. It took me a second to figure out his question, and I realised he wasn't asking if we were there as friends.

"Er, yeah," I said, giving him my most charming smile and reaching across the seat to twine my fingers with Oscar's. "We're here on a press trip, seeing what the resort is like for couples."

"Ah, nice." George nodded. "They do some good stuff for couples. Got a nice spa too. Do you like hiking?"

"Yeah." I leant forward in the seat. "Got any recommendations of places we should go? Oh, and any small, local restaurants to try? I know the resort's got their own, but I'm really looking for those little places tourists wouldn't usually find—mostly because we're oblivious. Where do you like to go?"

It seemed I'd asked a good question, and soon I was taking notes on my phone while George gave me a list of places to check out for everything from pancakes to shave ice to the best sushi I'd ever eat. Oscar sat quietly beside me, gazing out the window.

"You okay?" I asked as George pulled the car into the resort. The road was lined with lush vegetation and tropical blooms that made it seem like we were stepping into another world, one far away from the dreary pavements of London.

Oscar nodded. "Yeah, just tired."

"Sure?"

"Yeah." He gave me a small smile. "I liked listening to you talk to George, and I like the sound of that sushi place."

"Me too." I grinned. "And the pancakes. I haven't had good pancakes in forever. Maybe we can go one morning? Get up early, watch the sun rise, then get a ride into Kona for breakfast?"

"I'd like that."

The car came to a stop, and George climbed out to get the door. "Aloha and welcome to St. West Hualālai." I climbed out and turned on the spot, taking in everything around me. I'd travelled to beautiful places before, but this was the first time I'd ever stayed in a resort like this.

St. West was a small, locally owned chain of hotels that had one resort on each of the four main islands of Hawaii, founded by a brother-sister duo who'd wanted to add a personal touch to their guests' stays, making local culture and produce the centre of their business. From what I'd read, they'd started small with just one tiny hotel in Honolulu that had been owned by their grandparents, and they'd grown from there.

Their brand was fast becoming synonymous with sustainable luxury that was also personal and authentic and in harmony with the natural surroundings while being respectful of local history and tradition. It sounded like just the sort of place I wanted to explore. It would be better than the enormous mega resorts owned by impersonal global chains.

"Come on," I said, reaching out to take Oscar's hand without really thinking it through. "Let's get checked in and go find our room. Then we can explore!"

"Er, yeah. Sounds good." He followed me up the steps into the hotel lobby, which was in a low, wooden building, and it was only as we reached the front desk that I realised he was still holding my hand. The realisation stunned me, and I suddenly felt light-headed. Oscar's hand was warm against mine, his skin soft and his grip firm. Despite the fact that we'd woken up cuddled together that morning, it felt like the most intimate moment I'd had with him.

It was such a simple gesture, but it felt like so much more. And I wasn't sure why. I didn't want this to be more than a fake relationship, but somewhere between my brain and my body the message seemed to be getting lost.

This was what happened when I hadn't had a romantic relationship in recent memory. A quick fuck with someone I met on Grindr or in a random bar didn't give me the romance my soul desperately craved, even if I had been trying to suppress that urge for the last ten years.

Romance would only lead to me getting hurt again, and I'd had enough of that to last a lifetime. I'd just have to content myself with soft touches and late-night cuddles from random men and hope it was enough to get by.

The clerk behind the desk didn't seem to notice my brewing internal war and was happily chatting to Oscar about the package they'd organised for us. There was one word that stood out to me though. *Suite*.

"They gave us a suite?" I hissed to Oscar ten minutes later when another member of staff had delivered us to the door of our room, which happened to be in a beautiful wooden bungalow that was practically on the shoreline. They'd offered to show us around, but I'd politely declined because I wanted to freak out in private.

"A superior suite," Oscar said as he opened the door and gestured for me to head inside. "A beachfront one. It's not their nicest, but it has the best view if you discount a couple of the speciality suites."

"Not their nicest? What the fuck?" I knew my reaction was a little overboard but still. The room was incredible.

It had dark slate floors and hardwood trim, and the walls were decorated with stunning pieces of art, all from local artists and available to purchase on request. The whole suite was bigger than some apartments I'd lived in and came complete with a luxury living space, an enormous bathroom, a walk-in wardrobe, and a terrace with plush outdoor seating which was barely separated from the beach. I stood by the open French doors and watched the waves lap against the shore and gazed at the mountains that crested the horizon.

"So, er... this is... nice?" Oscar said from behind me. I turned to see him coming out of the bedroom. It looked like the bridge of his nose was slightly pink.

"What is it?"

"Well, they're definitely treating us like a couple. There're petals all over the bed, and they've left us some champagne, a platter of sharing desserts, and fruit. And someone got the queer message because they've organised the platter in a rainbow flag. They even piped our names in chocolate onto the plate."

"Seriously? That's so cool." I'd heard about that sort of thing happening before, and I'd seen pictures of hotels going all out for honeymooning couples, but I'd never experienced it. Mostly because I'd never been on a honeymoon. "Don't touch it. I want to take a picture before you destroy it."

"I wasn't going to."

"You weren't tempted to have one tiny bite?" I teased, grabbing my camera and my 50mm lens out of my bag and slotting them together. My Canon had seen better days, but I couldn't fathom getting a new one just yet. It was an extension of myself, and I knew retiring it would be like taking away a piece of my soul.

"Maybe a tiny one," Oscar said as I followed him into the bedroom. I stopped as soon as I entered, staring at the picture in front of me.

"Wow. When you said petals I didn't think..."

"Yeah, it's a little... extra."

"Extra is right," I said, lifting my camera to take a photo. The king-sized bed had crisp white linens and a mountain of fluffy-looking pillows with an enormous heart made of pink, red, and white petals in the middle of the mattress. It had swooping, curling lines, and was more a work of art than a simple, cheesy gesture.

"Even if we were a couple here on our honeymoon, I don't think I'd want to fuck on that. I wouldn't want to damage it," I continued. Oscar chuckled. "That and I'd be worried about getting petals in my butt crack. I'm sure they're not as bad as sand, but I don't really want to be fishing florals out of my orifices for several days."

Oscar snorted. "Thanks for the visual on that."

"You're very welcome." I threw him a wink over my shoulder as I walked around the bed to the little table by the floor-to-ceiling window, which had the dessert plate set next to a champagne bucket and two glasses.

As Oscar had said, the food had been arranged in a rainbow, but it was a subtle one with sliced fruits intermingled with gold-dusted macarons and tiny bits of patisserie. There was a note next to the food welcoming us to the St. West and telling us that everything on the plate was made with locally sourced ingredients where possible and listing some of their suppliers. It was a nice touch.

I turned around, noticing Oscar hadn't said anything else. He was watching me with a curious intent, his arms folded as he leant against the doorframe. I was sure he'd seen people take pictures before, so I wasn't sure why he was staring at me. Was it something I'd done or said?

"See something you like?" I asked, giving him my most charming smile before putting my camera on the table, picking up the plate, and walking across to him. Technically, my words could be interpreted to be just about the plate, but there was a tiny part of me that wanted him to go for the alternative meaning. Oscar flushed and shook his head.

"No, I, er, I'm fine."

"Come on, they've left us this beautiful plate of food. You have to try something." I reached for a macaron and pushed it slowly into my mouth, letting the soft shell melt on my tongue. I let out a little moan because, damn, it was delicious. Oscar was staring at me again, but it wasn't the hungry look I'd expected. It was more... curiosity. And maybe frustration.

He reached out and picked up a piece of pineapple, popping it into his mouth before turning away, leaving me fixed on the spot where his lips had been.

# CHAPTER SEVEN

*Oscar*

"WHAT DO you want to do this afternoon?" Ilias asked as he followed me out of the bedroom, still holding the plate of desserts.

I gritted my teeth, not actually sure why I was frustrated. I knew Ilias was just teasing when he flirted with me, but for some reason, I couldn't brush it away.

"I'm not sure," I said. "Since we got here late, I can't remember what the plan is."

I'd memorised the original itinerary, but with the delay, everything had shifted, and I couldn't remember what we'd been scheduled to do. I pulled my phone out of my pocket and scrolled through the PDF Marcus had forwarded me. I'd meant to look at it on the plane that morning, but I'd gotten distracted by Ilias and had forgotten all about it.

As I read, I felt Ilias beside me trying to peer over my shoulder. I felt his breath against my cheek, the soft scent of peaches wafting around me. It was one thing to have him closing in on my personal space, but it was another for part of me to wish he was closer. But that wasn't the worst part.

The worst part was what was listed as the activity for that afternoon.

"We've got an hour or so to relax, then they've organised a, er, a couple's bath journey. To help us connect and recharge." That sounded like hell on earth, but I could understand where they were coming from. I was sure for most couples it would be perfect, but the idea of getting brushed down, massaged, and bathing with Ilias made me want to run far and run fast.

Not because I hated him or was totally uncomfortable around him—he'd snuggled me for one, so some boundaries had been crossed—but this felt like a whole new step. There was cuddling while clothed, and then there was watching Ilias get rubbed down while he was ninety percent naked. I really hoped the bath wasn't a shared one, but the sinking feeling in my gut told me it probably would be. At least we'd be wearing trunks.

God, I hoped we'd be wearing trunks.

"That sounds… interesting," Ilias said. "What does a *couple's bath journey* even mean?"

"An eighty-minute experience that starts with us getting brushed down, followed by a full body massage, then we get to share a relaxing salt and herbal-infused bath, which includes Hawaiian sea salt, crushed rose petals, orange peel, and a blend of herbs, which will leave us feeling rejuvenated," I said, reading the text under the heading.

Just saying it out loud made it sound worse.

"So I'm still getting petals in my butt crack. Outstanding."

"Hopefully not," I said as I turned around and raised my eyebrow. "You'll be wearing trunks."

"You mean you don't want to see me naked?" Ilias grinned. I ignored him.

"After that we've got time to explore before dinner at the restaurant. Then the rest of the week includes things like snorkelling, yoga on the beach before breakfast, a trip to see some of the island's most beautiful views, a hike, stargazing, dinner on the beach, and some time with local cultural experts." I hoped if I focused on everything else it would allow me to avoid Ilias's question.

Because it was hard to explain to someone I hardly knew that seeing him naked wasn't something I was interested in right at that second. It was a *maybe one day* kind of thing at most.

Shit. Why was I already putting Ilias in the *maybe one day* box?

"That all sounds lovely," Ilias said. "But you're avoiding my question. Am I really so unattractive that you wouldn't want to see me naked?"

"Do you really want me to answer that?" I deadpanned. Luckily, Ilias took my question for teasing because he burst out laughing.

"Ouch. Even for a fake boyfriend, you're mean."

"Sorry. I'm not good at this," I said. I knew I needed to try harder because right now Ilias was the one making the effort to keep up the ruse.

Even though we didn't have to be all over each other in

front of the staff, it would look odd if we didn't act a little bit like a couple. I didn't want someone to figure out we were faking and think we were trying to extort a free trip from them. As soon as Madelyn heard the word extortion, I'd be out on my ass before I could blink.

I'd gotten myself into this mess, and now the entire reputation of *The Traveller* was resting on my shoulders. If I still wanted a job by the end of this, I had to act like I wanted to be with Ilias. "I'll try harder."

"You're doing fine." Ilias's smile softened into something almost fond. "Not everyone is a PDA person, or touchy-feely, or a desperate romantic at heart."

"Are you?"

Ilias shrugged and reached for another macaron. "It depends."

It felt like he was avoiding answering, but since I was also avoiding telling him the complete truth, I couldn't demand he talk to me. The funny thing was, I didn't mind things like hugs or kisses or soft romantic gestures. I actually loved them. But so often they were taken the wrong way, and it meant opening myself up to people before I was ready, and ninety percent of the time, those conversations never ended well.

I'd never felt ashamed of being demisexual; it was an intrinsic part of who I was. But I was sick of people's bullshit and their offers to *fix me* with what they always promised would be the best night of my life. I didn't need fixing, and I didn't need their shit.

All I wanted was to find a man who'd let our relationship develop slowly and give me the chance to see if my sexual attraction grew once I'd gotten to know them. But most of the men I'd met didn't want that, especially when paired with my job. And after my last relationship had ended in disaster when he'd tried to make me choose between him and travelling, I'd decided it was just easier to focus on my work. At least for the time being.

One day, I hoped I'd be able to find someone who would give me the time I needed.

I just didn't expect that day to come any time soon.

Ilias held the plate out towards me. "You can't let me eat all this myself."

"I won't," I said, grateful for the change in subject. "Shall we go sit on the terrace? Then we can eat this before we go to the spa."

"I like that plan." Ilias grinned. "I'll bring the champagne."

"For what reason?"

"We're celebrating."

I frowned. "Celebrating what?"

"That we made it this fucking far. I bloody hate long journeys." He handed me the plate, and I felt myself smiling. There was something about Ilias that was starting to tug at my defences like he was unintentionally searching for a weak spot neither of us knew was there.


"Are you ready for this?" Ilias asked. "You look highly uncomfortable."

"I'll be fine," I said as I pulled on the dark blue robe I'd been given when we'd checked into the spa. "I'm just not super big on spas. I think it was because I had a bad massage in London once, and I literally couldn't get out of bed the next day. Everything hurt and not in a nice way."

It was mostly the truth, and it was an easy cover for the fact that I didn't want to explain my very complicated feelings about spending the afternoon in a bath with him.

Ilias snorted and shook his head. "Like the worst kind of deep tissue?"

"If deep tissue is supposed to make all your muscles so painful they can barely function, then yes."

"I'm sure this won't be that bad," Ilias said, tightening his own robe across his chest. "You can ask them to be gentle. I'd rather not have to do everything else by myself for the rest of the week while you lie in bed and stare at the ceiling."

"I think if I did that, Madelyn would give me the boot. I don't think she'd see it as an excuse for not doing my job. I'd be expected to drag my carcass out of bed one way or another." I headed for the door of the changing room, padding in bare feet along the dark slate floor.

The spa had a soft, wild aesthetic that made it feel like it was part of the landscape around it. There were plants everywhere, and despite the simplicity of the building's structure and décor, the place oozed sophistication. It was one of those places that was designed to make you feel at ease from the moment you stepped inside. There was luxury too, but it wasn't cloying or overstated.

"I don't think there are many things Madelyn would accept as an excuse," Ilias said as we headed for the treatment room we'd been directed to make our way to when we were ready. "I doubt she'd even accept alien invasion."

"Invasion maybe, but alien abduction would be a definite no. I'd be expected to write a review of the hotels on Mars."

"Hey, they work hard in those hotels. They deserve the recognition. And I've heard the food on the outer rings of Saturn is life changing. You'd definitely get a cover feature."

I chuckled as we entered another beautiful room that seemed to be built on a secluded plateau amongst some trees. It had a stunning view out over the bay, but the layout suggested nobody would be able to see into the space, giving us plenty of privacy. There were two massage tables in the centre waiting for us, but for the moment, there was nobody else in the room.

"As long as I survived my impromptu trip into space," I said. "It would all depend on whether the aliens had a space suit that fit me, and if they'd let me borrow it."

"Hmm." Ilias gave me a wry smile. "You'd have to negotiate. What can you offer them?"

"For my survival? They can be our new lords and masters for all I care. They can't be much worse than the British government."

"Well, I for one will welcome our new alien overlords," Ilias said. "They'd probably take one look at the state of our world and run screaming though, and then we'd be right back where we started."

I nodded and opened my mouth to say something, but a door on the other side of the room opened and two members of staff appeared. They were both powerful-looking men whose wide smiles didn't allay my fears that they'd be able to casually break my spine. Still, there was nothing I could do but remove my robe and lie down on the table with a towel across my ass.

I was still wearing a pair of swim trunks, but they were the barely there kind that clung to my skin and didn't offer much coverage beyond my dick and ass. Lewis had bought them for me last year, saying I needed at least one sexy piece of swimwear. I'd never worn them before, and the only reason they'd ended up in my case was because they'd become part of my regular travel wardrobe that went from suitcase to suitcase.

The brush down and the massage weren't as bad as I'd anticipated, and I felt myself start to relax as my masseur worked his hands in deep, slow circles across my shoulders.

"You're carrying a lot of tension here," he said softly, pressing a little harder. I exhaled deeply, staring down at the floor and trying to let the burning in my muscles bleed away. "Is that pressure okay?"

"Yeah. It's fine." It hurt, but I didn't want him to stop because it felt like he might be able to get rid of the deep ache in my shoulders and neck that had been forming over the past few days from all the travelling. Airline seats weren't exactly ergonomically designed, and it was hard to stretch out on an eleven-hour flight.

From beside me, I heard Ilias let out a deep huff and felt my spine stiffen. I'd almost forgotten he was there.

Mostly because I'd been actively trying to pretend he wasn't.

Ilias said something I didn't catch, but his masseur chuckled, and they started talking in low voices. I didn't want to be *that guy* who told them to be quiet, so I focused on my body and remembered what someone had once told me about centring myself.

I started by focusing on my toes, then my feet, then my ankles, slowly trying to work up through my body. It didn't completely work since my masseur had started on the backs of my thighs and my calves, which were apparently so tense that even the gentlest pressure had me biting my lip. When I got back to London, I was going to have to look at seeing someone on a regular basis. Otherwise, my body was going to continue punishing me for what I put it through.

"Okay," said the masseur when he'd eventually finished pressing his thumbs into the soles of my feet. "We're finished here, but I'd recommend you see someone regularly, like a sports massage therapist, because your muscles are not happy. Do you travel regularly?"

"Yeah," I said with a weak chuckle. "I noticed. And yes, I do."

"That's probably why. You need to show them a little bit of love otherwise you're going to hurt yourself," he said. I believed him. "If you want to lie here for a bit and relax, we'll get your bath ready for you. And when you're ready, come through the door on your right. The bath will be waiting and will be yours for up to forty-five minutes."

"Thanks." I heard him pad away, talking to the other masseur, and wondered if I'd ever be able to move again.

"That was nice," said Ilias from beside me. I turned my

head to the other side, resting my chin on the back of my hands. Everything was sore, but not as bad as I'd expected. "I feel very refreshed."

"I both do and don't."

Ilias grinned. "Worried you won't be able to get up tomorrow? Don't worry, I'll roll you out of bed if I have to."

"You're so charming."

"I know. It's one of my best features." He winked at me, and I tried not to focus on the way the light was playing across his skin. I'd been trying to ignore how handsome Ilias was, but it was difficult when he was stretched out on a bench, three-quarters naked.

He rolled onto his side and sat up slowly, the towel still draped across his legs. Not that it mattered because I knew what Ilias was wearing underneath since I'd seen him get changed. It was a pair of tiny white shorts that barely covered anything. I assumed when he usually wore them, men fell at his feet, and objectively, I could understand why.

Ilias was beautiful.

"Shall we go through?" he asked, standing up and walking over to fetch his robe. I tried not to look at his broad shoulders or long, toned legs. Just because I didn't want to have sex with him didn't mean I couldn't appreciate how gorgeous he was.

"Er, yeah. Sure." Ilias picked up my robe and passed it to me as I rolled myself up, groaning as I did. My muscles really weren't impressed, and for the first time, I found myself craving the heat of the bath in the hopes it would soothe all my aches and pains. I stood up and wrapped myself in the robe, following Ilias to the other door.

I knew now why I'd said what I'd said back in London and why I'd hated the idea of Ilias looking at someone else. As much as I'd tried to deny it, I was jealous.

Yes, this was just a fake relationship, but a small part of me had wanted to pretend I was enough. Just for once. And if Ilias had been throwing himself at other people, it would have burnt that idea to a crisp.

I knew nothing was ever going to happen between us, and a relationship with him wasn't something I even wanted, but that didn't change how I'd felt. Like everyone else on this planet, my emotions were messy and complicated, and they didn't always make sense.

All I could do was get through this week and hope we could be friends at the end of it.

And in the meantime, I probably needed to start acting like Ilias's boyfriend in public instead of some cold-hearted asshole who envied the way other men flocked to this beautiful man.

"Do you think it'll be one bath or two?" Ilias asked as he reached the door, throwing a teasing smile over his shoulder.

"I'm not answering that."

"You just did." He opened the door and stepped inside, letting out a delighted little laugh. The sound did something funny to my stomach, which then dropped through the floor as I followed Ilias into the second suite and saw what he was laughing at.

There was only one bath—an enormous, round pool that

was sunken into the floor so you could step straight in. It had a view out across the resort, but the focus was on the beach where I could see the waves breaking gently against the sand. There was steam curling off the water, and I saw herbs and petals floating on the surface, giving the room a heady scent that seemed to seep into my muscles.

"Well," Ilias said as he stood next to me, "the good thing is that it's as big as a swimming pool, so you don't have to sit next to me." He grinned and stripped off his robe, placing it on the nearby bench. "I wish I had my phone. My nephew Teddy would love this."

"Big fan of water?" I asked as Ilias slipped into the bath. He winced for a second, and I assumed the water was hot, then he sighed and relaxed against the side, watching me with an interested expression.

"Sharks," Ilias said. "They're his favourite thing. It's how my sister-in-law convinced him to do more swimming at school—because sharks live in water. She told him if he can swim really well, maybe one day he can go and see sharks in the wild, not just at the aquarium." He grinned. "It worked."

"That's cute." I dropped my robe, ignoring Ilias's gaze as I walked around to the other side of the pool, crouched down, and lowered myself in. The water was hotter than I'd been expecting, but it only took me a moment to adjust. It was just like being in a giant hot tub only without the jets. There was a small bench built into the side, under the water, for us to sit on. I sat opposite Ilias and stretched out my legs, letting the heat leech away my stress.

"Do you have any niblings?" Ilias asked.

I shook my head. "Not yet. I think my brother Richard will have kids in the next few years since he's marrying his girlfriend in December. The rest of them will be wait and see I think. Some of them might, some probably not."

I couldn't see Eli with children, and I got the feeling he and his partner Tristan would be the sort to just spoil everyone else's kids. They'd be the ones loading them up on sugar just before they handed them back. Jules was a maybe, but that would depend on any future partner. I couldn't see her wanting to be pregnant, but if she was with a woman who wanted that, I could see Jules being an amazing mum. Lewis was pretty fond of kids, as was his partner Jason, so they were my strongest suspects.

And Finn... it was hard for me to imagine Finn with kids, not because I didn't think he'd be a great parent but because I struggled to see him as an adult. He was still my quiet, shy baby brother who needed me to look out for him, even if that wasn't the truth anymore. Finn was a grown man with an incredible career as a voice actor and audio-book narrator, a side hustle I wished I didn't know about, and a serious boyfriend who adored him.

He didn't need me treating him like a little kid, and it was on me to see him for who he was rather than who he used to be.

"What about you? Would you want kids?" Ilias asked. I frowned. "Or is that too personal?"

"No, it's fine." I turned my head and looked out over the vista, turning the question over in my mind. "I'm not sure kids are for me. I like kids, but I'm not sure how I feel

about being a parent. It's hard, and it's complicated…"
Especially if something in the family went wrong.

I'd never blamed my mother for the loss of my dad, even if cancer had been hard to understand as a six-year-old, and I'd never blamed her for moving in with Miranda and blending our families. They'd done their best to give us all the best childhood possible, but it was always there in the back of my mind. I never wanted a child to go through what I had.

"I feel the same," Ilias said quietly. "I love my niblings to death. They're fucking awesome kids. But I couldn't be a parent." I looked over at him, noticing the pinched lines between his eyebrows, but I didn't say anything. There was a pause, then Ilias continued. "When I'm back in London, I live with my brother Dominic and his wife, Louisa. They have four boys, so I've seen the good and the bad." He chuckled wryly. "Like I said, I love them, but it's not for me. I'd rather just be that cool uncle who brings them presents from places they've never been… or something like that."

His last words had a hollow tone like there was something else going on behind his words. Every time Ilias had talked about his family, I got the feeling he was only showing me small pieces—sharing the bearable rather than the truth. He'd mentioned his family giving him grief for not being married, and I wondered if that was part of the problem.

Ilias seemed content to live life on his terms rather than someone else's, and while I could understand where he was coming from, I could also see where it might be an issue.

My family had never pressed me to be anything other than who I was. But I knew not everyone was so lucky.

We sat in silence for a while, both lost in our own thoughts while the water washed against our skin. The experience hadn't been as bad as I'd been expecting, mostly because I was able to sit across from Ilias rather than on top of him. The problem was that I hardly knew the man, and the image I had of him was distorted like I was looking at him through heavily fogged glass.

"You know," I said eventually, letting myself vocalise the nebulous thoughts swirling in my head. "I realised I don't actually know a lot about you. I know bits and pieces, but it's all random. Like that you have niblings, and you think butterflies are weird, and that you like barbecue bacon cheeseburgers as long as they don't have pickles, but those things don't relate."

Ilias laughed. "Butterflies are weird. They're the only flying insect people like. Apart from bees. And bees are far superior."

I snorted because that illustrated my point. "Okay, but that's what I mean. We're supposed to be..." I waved my hand, not wanting to say anything out loud. "So maybe we could try to get to know each other better. I think it might make things easier."

Ilias smiled, and it was the most beautiful thing I'd seen all day. "I'd like that. It sounds like fun."

# CHAPTER EIGHT

*Oscar*

WAKING up to find Ilias clinging to me wasn't as shocking the second time around. His breath was soft against my neck as he sprawled like a starfish across me and half the bed, his arm wrapped tightly around my waist like he was pinning me in place.

Gently, I tried to roll him off me by putting one hand against his shoulder and pushing, but all that did was make him grip on tighter as he burrowed his head deeper into my shoulder and let out a little snore. Unless I wanted to kick him, I was stuck until he woke up.

This wasn't what I'd envisioned when I'd told Ilias I wanted to get to know him better. I was thinking more like twenty questions or deep conversations about things that were important to us, not being hugged to death.

"I like burritos but not avocado," Ilias muttered, and I chuckled. That was something new. I felt him stir, then stiffen, and I assumed he'd come to and realised he was once again doing his best limpet impression.

"Good morning," I said.

"Morning," said Ilias as he detached himself and rolled away looking sheepish. "Sorry, I, er, I didn't mean to do that. Again."

"It's fine."

"Are you sure? I can always sleep on the sofa next door."

"I'm sure." The sofas in the suite's sitting room were fairly comfortable to sit on, but I wasn't sure they'd be great for sleeping. Plus, the idea of Ilias spending the night next door made me uncomfortable because I didn't have any more right to the bed than he did. "You're not that bad, and it doesn't wake me up."

Ilias grinned, and I realised that probably said more about me than I'd intended. "You like me snuggling you?"

"Is that snuggling? It felt like I was being smothered."

"If I was going to smother you, you'd know."

"Kinky," I said in the most deadpan voice I could manage. Ilias laughed, throwing his head back into the crisp pillows. He really was beautiful when he smiled, and his joy radiated out of him like sunshine.

"Only if you ask nicely." He turned onto his side and propped his head up on his hand. "So, what are our plans for today?"

"What am I, your butler?"

"Do butlers keep diaries? I think that would make you my secretary." He smirked. "You'd be a cute secretary."

"I'd quit on day one," I said. "You could sort out your own shit."

"No, you'd stay forever because I'm charming and witty and you'd take pity on me."

"How do you manage to have a job if you're disorganised?"

"I'm not," Ilias said. "I just like hearing you saying what we're doing."

"Oh..." I felt my face burning, then I swallowed. "I, er... Well, this morning we can get breakfast, then go to the beach for a bit. We're too late for pre-breakfast yoga."

"That's okay. I'm not feeling yoga anyway," Ilias said. "I think I'm still too sore from yesterday."

I nodded because my muscles were definitely complaining, and I hadn't even moved. "After breakfast, we can go to the beach for a bit and explore. This afternoon we've got snorkelling with the hotel's marine biologist, then a few hours of downtime and then tonight we're going stargazing at Mauna Kea."

"Stargazing?" Ilias had a dreamy smile on his face. It was so soft and natural it caught me off guard.

"Yes, apparently the sky around here is perfect for it. We should be able to see a lot as long as it's not cloudy."

"Have you been before?"

"Not here," I said. "But I went once when I was in South Africa a couple of years ago. It was..." I tried to think of a way to describe what I'd seen that night, lying on blankets on the top of the Jeep and looking up into the vastness of the universe. It had altered my perspective in a way I couldn't explain in that it had given me a sense of how small I was. How inconsequential my existence was to the rest of the galaxy. It had been beautiful and devastating all at once. "Incredible," I said finally. "There's nothing like it. I can't really describe it without spoiling it, and I think if I tried, I wouldn't do it justice."

"When I was little," Ilias said, "I always wanted to be an astronaut. I thought I could go to the moon and see all the stars up close." He shook his head, looking almost embarrassed by his statement.

"That's sweet. What stopped you?"

Ilias shrugged, and I wondered if the question was too personal. "Dreams change, and it didn't help that I really suck at maths. Numbers and I are not friends, and I think that's a pretty crucial part of being fired into space. What about you? What did you want to be when you grew up?"

"Indiana Jones," I said. Ilias chuckled.

"You'd look good in a fedora."

"I don't. I've got the wrong-shaped head." I smiled, remembering the time Finn and Lewis had bought me one when I was seventeen. I thought I'd looked very cool, but nobody else did. "But I did want to be an explorer, to find new places and ancient ruins. Maybe teach history on the side. Then GCSE history put me off the subject for life because it was all the economics of the Second World War and the teacher sucked the life out of it. I also realised how much stuff Indy took from Indigenous peoples that belonged with them rather than in a museum. After that, I realised I'd rather see things where they were meant to be instead of in a place that was convenient."

"Honestly, shit teachers are the worst. My physics

teacher was like that. He could make the sun going super-nova sound about as interesting as wet paint. And he had this really nasal voice, which I know he couldn't help, but oh my God, it just made him sound like some sort of fly as he droned on and on." Ilias shook his head. "I'm surprised I actually passed."

"Same here. Although that might have been because my stepdad, Terry, is a history nut, and he managed to explain everything in a way that was actually interesting. He used props and everything—mostly leftover chocolate coins from Christmas—but I got to eat them afterwards."

"What? You lucky fucker. I just had one of my brothers trying to help, then getting cross with me because I wasn't as smart as him." Ilias rolled his eyes. "I love him, but he's a knob sometimes. He works in insurance now, and honest to fucking God, one conversation with him is enough to put you to sleep."

"Is that the one you live with?"

"No. Dominic works in finance or something. Jerome is the insurance guy."

"And you have three brothers?"

"Yeah," Ilias said. "There's also Lucas, who teaches economics. I'm the baby." He sighed, and again, it felt like I'd nudged against a sore spot like a bruise that wouldn't quite heal. It made me want to know more but also to take a step back. I didn't want to hurt him, and pressing on something he didn't want to share wouldn't be fair. "You still got to travel though. Not quite Indy, but you've seen more places than most people."

"Yeah," I said, glad for the change of subject. "When I

discovered that travel writing was a thing, that people would pay me to go to places and write about them, it was a no-brainer really. Everyone always said it was tough to break into, but it was what I wanted, so I just kept muddling through. Sometimes I think my mum expected me to give up and come home, but all I ever wanted was to be somewhere else. And now I get to be."

Ilias was quiet for a moment, then he sat up and stretched, giving me a smile. "Come on. We should really get up. Madam Rossi would kill us if she caught us lazing around. I really need to take some photos this morning."

"Yeah, I should probably make some notes."

"Who knew this holiday would be work?" Ilias grinned, and I laughed as I watched him slide out of bed.

We spent the morning together but apart, taking up two beautiful loungers on the beach as we worked.

Ilias pottered back and forth, disappearing off to take photos, reappearing to swap lenses, and practically bouncing with happiness as he showed me what he'd captured so far. It was mostly pretty shots of the suite, the shoreline, and the resort, but there were also more vibrant, artistic ones of the local fauna and the waves playing across the beach.

"I can give Marcus options," he said before raising his camera to take a photo of me tapping away on my laptop. He caught me totally by surprise, and when he looked at the picture, he laughed. "You didn't have to pull a face."

"I didn't."

"Yeah, you did." He grinned and held the camera out for me to look at. I had a half-shocked, half-irritated look on my face, and I rolled my eyes as I handed the camera back.

"Delete it, please."

"Nope. I'm keeping it." He took a sip from the large glass of fresh mango and pineapple juice one of the staff had brought each of us. "I'm going exploring again. Man the fort while I'm gone. And don't steal my juice."

I laughed as he wandered away, his bare feet pattering against the sand and leaving a trail of footprints behind him. I was almost tempted to follow.

The snorkelling was fun, and I enjoyed listening to the hotel's resident marine biologist, Kailani, talk about the local coastal environment, the lives and journeys of various species of fish, and ongoing conservation projects.

I made as many notes as I could in the old, battered notebook I always carried, and we had a long, in-depth conversation about tourism and its environmental effects because it was something I found myself thinking about more and more as I travelled.

I knew my career as a travel writer meant I focused on getting people to explore the world, and I was happy to play tourist if it meant I got to see the places of my dreams. But more and more, I wanted to look at ways to do that sustainably, if at all possible, and make sure I was contributing to the local economy, rather than just putting money into the pockets of billionaire resort owners.

I knew the situation was nuanced, and that I was probably a hypocrite at times, but I was trying, and I hoped that would be enough.

While we talked, Ilias slipped in and out of the water with his camera, his face a picture of delight every time he surfaced with new photos to show us. Kailani pointed out various features he'd managed to capture and gave us some great recommendations for some local places to visit for dinner, adding to Ilias's ever-growing list of restaurants we needed to find time to visit. At this rate, we could probably spend the week going from restaurant to restaurant without doing anything else.

"Do they give us food tonight?" Ilias asked as we sat out on the suite's terrace a couple of hours later. He sat cross-legged on one of the large, plush outdoor sofas, uploading photos to the laptop balanced across his knees. "Or do we need to get something beforehand?"

"They feed us," I said. "I think it's something like a vegetable lasagne."

"Awesome."

"Is there any food you don't like?" I asked, sitting down on the sofa opposite him. "Apart from burger pickles, avocados, and your grandmother's pot roast."

"I don't hate burger pickles. They just have to be on the *right* burger. They don't go with barbecue sauce, bacon, and cheese."

"But you do hate the pot roast." I grinned, and Ilias scowled.

"I told you that in confidence."

"Your grandma isn't here."

"True." He tapped something on the keyboard, then frowned as if he was trying to remember something. "How did you know about the avocados?"

"Er… you talk in your sleep."

"Motherfucker," Ilias hissed, and I laughed. "What else have I said?"

"Nothing else that I've heard. Just that you like burritos but not avocado."

"That's because avocado is slimy and disgusting." Ilias shuddered dramatically.

"You're a terrible millennial. How else are you going to continue destroying the housing market and the economy if you don't eat your fair share of avocado toast?"

Ilias snorted, his eyes dancing with amusement as he looked up at me. The sight caught me off guard, stealing my breath from my lungs.

"Don't worry. I'll do that by not having kids, travelling the world, never settling down, and adopting… I don't know, twenty cats. And I'll make sure you eat all my avocado toast."

"Deal," I said. "So you're a cat person?"

"Actually, I don't have a preference, but I feel like I could be one of those weird old cat gays. I could make them all wear hand-knitted jumpers."

"Doesn't that work better on dogs?"

"Yes, but it's weirder if you do it to cats," Ilias said with a sparkling grin. "And to answer your original question, I also don't like aubergine or butternut squash. They're too mushy and gross. And squash is just tasteless."

"It's not that bad."

"Ah, ah, ah," Ilias said as he wiggled his finger at me. "These are my food preferences, not yours."

"Sorry." I felt my face heat, and something in my

stomach twitched. "I think I do that a lot... tell you how you should feel."

"Not really." Ilias shrugged. "And it's not something unique to you. Besides, you're not telling me *bad* things." I frowned, and Ilias continued. "It's your turn by the way."

"To?"

"Tell me what food you don't like. Aren't we doing this whole turn-taking thing?"

"Oh..." I didn't know why I felt suddenly flustered. It was just a question, a simple one at that, but the fact Ilias wanted to know things about me made me feel like I was under a spotlight. "I'm not that picky really, but I'm not a fan of offal or blue cheese."

"Those are understandable," Ilias said with another smile. "Internal organs and mouldy cheese aren't high on a lot of people's lists."

"Do you like them?"

"Not really. If I *had* to eat them, I would, but they're not my first choice. Except for my grandma's blue cheese cookies. I'm not sure if they actually have blue cheese in them— I've never asked—but they're this perfect balance of salty and sweet and just a little sharp. They're not overpowering at all."

"That actually sounds good," I said. "But you can't beat peanut butter and chocolate."

"Yes, you can," Ilias said. "Easily."

"Really? Those are fighting words."

"Peanut butter and chocolate is such a basic choice," Ilias said as he shut his laptop and slid it onto the low table between us. "I can give you a whole list of cookies that are better."

"Such as…" I grinned and gestured for him to continue.

And that was how I found myself arguing about cookie flavours with Ilias for the rest of the afternoon.

# CHAPTER NINE

*Ilias*

I WAS glad we'd been offered Arctic-style hooded coats and gloves before we left the visitor centre on Mauna Kea because I hadn't packed anything nearly warm enough for a night-time excursion up the side of a dormant volcano. The sun was just starting to set as we drove up the steep side of the mountain to the summit area where we'd get to watch the sky transform into a beautiful blaze of colours.

Oscar sat next to me in the back of the 4x4, gazing out of the window as our guide, Jeff, talked us through some of what we were going to see. Behind us, a second 4x4, driven by Jeff's husband, Ki, held the other three guests on the evening's trip. My camera bag sat on my lap, packed full of as much gear as I'd been able to fit inside. I really needed a Mary Poppins-style bag that would let me pull out enormous lenses with ease. It would make travelling so much easier.

"Are you excited?" I asked as we crested the summit and pulled onto a flat area that would allow us a perfect view of the sunset as well as let us watch the enormous telescopes located on the volcano to rotate into position. It felt like I was on the best school science trip imaginable, and I knew I'd easily be able to fill several memory cards with photos before the night was out.

"Yeah," said Oscar, giving me a small smile as the car came to a stop. "Are you?"

"I thought that was obvious?" I grinned and reached for the door. I wasn't sure how Oscar had put up with me for the past few hours as we'd toured the visitor centre and eaten dinner because I'd peppered everyone we'd come across with a million questions. This was the closest I'd ever come to living out my childhood dream of being an astronaut, and I was going to savour every moment of it.

"It is, but it's polite to ask." He climbed out his side and glanced around us at the snow-covered rock. The sky was starting to set itself ablaze as clouds played around the mountain. We were higher than I'd anticipated, and it had taken me a while to acclimatise to the altitude. It was why, Ki had told us over dinner, we'd stopped at the visitor centre first.

"When you're ready," said Jeff as he beckoned to us with a gloved hand, "we can go over to the rest of the group, and Ki can talk about the observatories. You'll be able to set up your camera too."

My steps felt full of springs as I followed him, a new giddiness forming in my chest. Oscar walked in step beside me, his face framed by the hood of his coat. Parkas weren't sexy on anyone, but somehow Oscar looked good in one, and the light of the setting sun played across his face, casting shadows across his jaw.

I'd always thought Oscar was handsome, but there was something different about him in that moment. Maybe it was because I'd started to get to know him better, or maybe it was because the high altitude was impairing my cognitive function, but I had the ridiculous urge to slip my gloved hand into his.

I shook my head, reaching for the zip on my camera bag and fumbling it open as Ki began to talk about each observatory in turn. Across the horizon, the sun turned the sky into an unearthly spectacle of colour and fire. I'd watched sunsets before, hundreds of them, but this one took my breath away in a whole new way.

I slotted my camera together at speed, lifting its bulk to my eye as I attempted to capture the majesty before me. I knew any photo I took would never do the sight justice, but I had to try.

Beside me, Oscar let out a slow breath. I lowered the camera for a moment, turning my head to see his dark eyes fixed on the flaming clouds that danced across the sky.

"Wow," he said softly. "It's beautiful."

"Yeah," I said, never taking my eyes off him. "It is."

He turned his head, and I felt my face heat as I suddenly pretended to be very interested in my camera, praying he hadn't noticed me staring at him. Our relationship was supposed to be fake. I wasn't supposed to be developing *any* kind of feelings for Oscar. Especially not since my last holiday relationship had ended in heart-breaking disaster.

They were memories I could barely bring myself to relive, even ten years later. I'd worked so hard to pack them all away in a neat little box, but one look at Oscar gazing at the sunset was threatening to bring them crashing down around me.

"You okay?" Oscar asked, and I realised I was staring off into space without focusing on anything, my camera held limply in my hand.

"Yeah," I said. "Just thinking."

Oscar hummed but didn't say anything, for which I was eternally grateful. I lifted my camera again and tried to focus on my job, pushing down the memories that were forcing their way to the surface. Now was not the time to get lost in them, I told myself. It was time to focus on the here and now.

I took a deep breath and let it out slowly, wiggling my toes in my trainers to ground myself.

The sun sank lower, and above us the sky began to darken, promising a glittering blanket of stars waiting to be unveiled.

When most of the colour had faded, Jeff guided us back to the car to take us a little way down the mountain. "The climate and air density is more comfortable there," he explained as he drove, the car bumping over the rough path. "Makes it easier to stand around for hours stargazing. It's going to be a good night for it."

"I can't wait," I said, but I knew I didn't sound as enthusiastic as I had earlier. I pursed my lips, wishing my past would stay buried. Next time, I was going to weight the box and throw it deep into the ocean of my memory, hoping it would get swallowed up and stay there.

Something brushed against my hand, and I jumped. Beside me, Oscar pulled his hand away like he'd been stung. Bollocks, I hadn't meant to frighten him.

"Sorry," he said quietly. "I didn't mean to make you jump."

"It's not you." I shook my head and felt my lips form a wry smile. "I've just been thinking about something, and it… threw me."

There was a pause, then Oscar reached out again and squeezed my hand. It sent a warm wave of comfort flooding through me. "I'm sorry. If you ever want someone to talk to, you can talk to me."

"Thanks. I'll be fine though."

"I know, but the offer still stands." I looked across at him in time to see something flicker across his face. If I hadn't known any better, I'd have said it was fondness.

"Sometimes it helps, especially if it's painful."

"Who said it was painful?" I asked more sharply than I'd intended, and I winced.

"Nobody," he said even softer than before, and there was an echo of pain in his tone like the ghost of a memory dancing across his words. "But you just looked… sad. And I…" he trailed off, then shook his head. "Anyway, I'm here if you want me."

I suddenly felt a pang of guilt because Oscar hadn't done anything but offer kindness. "Thanks."

The car bumped farther down the mountain until we eventually came to a plateaued area. It was more sheltered than the summit but offered a perfect view of the night sky. We climbed out of the cars, and Jeff and Ki began setting up some enormous portable telescopes so we could look for various constellations. Above us, the last veils of sunset had pulled aside, leaving a glittering blanket of a billion stars. Cutting straight through the middle was a hazy band of light, which almost looked like a wisp of cloud amongst the stars: the Milky Way.

I tilted my head back and tried to take it all in, marvelling at the untold beauty before me. I'd seen pictures of the Milky Way before, but I'd never seen it with my own eyes. It was vast and ancient and pulled at something deep within my soul. I felt smaller than before like some mythical giant had fixed its eye upon me. I knew I needed to take some photos, but I couldn't tear my eyes away.

"It's beautiful, isn't it?" Oscar said from beside me. "Makes you realise how small and singular you are."

"Yeah." I glanced across at him and realised he was looking at me. And he didn't turn away when his eyes met mine. It felt like I was being pulled into a black hole, powerless to resist the warmth in his gaze.

"Do you want to look through one of the telescopes? Ki said he can point out some of the constellations, and he can talk us through some of the Hawaiian star lines. I think we can see Jupiter as well."

"Maybe… in a minute."

"Do you want to just stand here instead?"

"Yeah," I said quietly, looking back at the sky. "I think I do."

"Do you… do you mind if I stand next to you?"

"No, of course not." I shot him a smile and watched his face relax. Had he been worried I wouldn't want him around? The thought made something snarl up inside me so quickly it was painful. We stood in silence for a while, not quite touching but close enough that I heard Oscar's breathing. It was one of those perfect, quiet moments where everything else just fell away.

"Earlier," I said eventually, "I was thinking about someone I knew... He, er, he died."

"Shit," Oscar said. "I'm sorry."

"It's fine." I shrugged, trying to pretend it wasn't a big deal. But it was. Oscar was the first person I'd told, even vaguely, in years. "I haven't thought about him in a while, but something about tonight brought the memories back. I thought I'd dealt with it, but maybe..."

"You can deal with death," Oscar said, "and your feelings about that person, that situation, but it never really goes away. You can't get rid of it. There's no magic wand you can wave to erase them from your memories. There's just time."

"Your dad?" I asked, thinking back to our conversation over lunch in London.

"Yeah." He nodded. "I was only five when he was diagnosed with lung cancer and six when he died. It was hard because it didn't really make a lot of sense. And my mum was so busy and tired, and Jules was only four, and Finn was maybe a year..." He thought for a second.

"He wasn't quite two when Dad died. Anyway, I guess I still have a lot of emotions around that, even though it's been twenty-six years. My mum did her best and so did the school, but it was still hard. Especially because I was the oldest, and I know she never meant to put pressure on me, but I felt so much responsibility to be good and helpful and to look after the others. And then a year later everything changed when mum and Miranda got together. But that's a different issue."

"I'm sorry." I wished there was something more I could say.

"Thanks." He tilted his head back, gazing up at the sky. "I guess what I mean is that I get it. I do. Time makes it hurt less, and therapy can help you close up the wounds, but that still leaves scars. And although scars fade over time, they're still there, and sometimes they pull. I think all you can do is accept that and find ways to carry on. We can't let grief rule our lives or let it shape our fate. It's part of who we are, but it's not everything."

Something in his words resonated, soothing the ache deep inside my chest that had threatened to tear itself open. I'd never imagined a whirlwind summer romance could change the course of my life, but ever since that final night, I'd closed part of myself off because I hadn't thought love was worth the pain.

I wondered what would happen if I told Oscar everything. He'd probably understand.

But I couldn't bring myself to say the words aloud. Not yet.

I'd bared my soul more openly tonight than I had in a long time, and I couldn't face doing any more. But maybe one day. Soon.

Because it was becoming apparent to me that Oscar

might be the one man who could make me do what I'd refused for the last ten years: fall in love.

# CHAPTER TEN

*Oscar*

"SHIT, do you have a plaster? I think my trainers have rubbed." We were halfway down a steep, narrow trail under the shade of thick trees as we explored the native forest of Kalōpā State Park, and every step I took was already agony.

I'd stopped walking once I realised going any further wasn't going to work, and I wiped a bead of sweat from my forehead as I bent down to rummage through my bag. I'd thought this was one activity I was fully prepared for, but apparently not. My travel first aid kit was still sitting on the suite's bathroom counter from where I'd emptied my bag to repack it, and I'd forgotten to put it back.

"Maybe," Ilias said. He'd been walking ahead of me and was farther down the trail, but at my question he turned and walked back towards me. "Didn't you bring any?"

"No." I pulled off my trainer and noticed blood was

already seeping into my sock. Bastard trainers. They'd never done this before, and now it was like they were trying to eat through the back of my feet. "I left them in the suite by mistake. But I've never had any problems with these trainers before."

"Yeah, but they're not exactly hiking boots," Ilias said. "You had the itinerary before we left London. You could have bought some."

"You're not one to talk." I gestured to his expensive-looking black trainers and raised my eyebrow. "Do you have a plaster or not?"

Ilias opened the small bag he was carrying, which seemed to be ninety percent camera equipment, a small bag of dried mango, and a tiny bottle of sunscreen, and peered inside.

"You're in luck," he said. "I have two."

"Can I have both of them?" I asked. Ilias shot me a look. "Please."

"Here you go."

"Thanks," I said as I took the plasters.

"Next time, remember to check everything before we leave," Ilias said with a teasing smile. "You owe me two plasters."

"I'm sure I can make it up to you." I carefully pulled the backing off the plaster and stuck it over the raw skin.

"Do you need anything else?"

"Do you have anything else?" I asked as I pulled a second pair of socks out of my bag so I could double them up and protect my ankles. "Are you suddenly Mary Poppins with an unlimited bag?"

"No, but I'd love that. It would make life so much easier." He grinned and took a swig from the bottle of water he was holding in his other hand. "You know, I was just thinking about that yesterday. Have you suddenly developed mind-reading powers?"

"If I had, do you think I'd be reading your mind?" I relaced my trainer and reached for my other foot. That ankle wasn't nearly as bad, but I put a plaster on it as a precaution before doubling up my sock.

"How rude, and after I just saved your underprepared ass!"

"You can't call yourself prepared," I said as I zipped up my bag. "You're just lucky. Do you actually have anything else useful in there? Or is it just snacks, sun cream, and lenses?"

"Your pasty ass will be thanking me when you start to burn."

"I have my own. And you'll burn too."

Ilias shrugged. "Mediterranean complexion. I'll be gorgeously bronzed while you look like a fucking lobster."

"Don't be a twat."

"Just because you know I'm right doesn't make me a twat." He shot me another of his smirks and turned to head back down the trail. I pretended not to notice the way his shorts wrapped around his thighs.

Instead, I focused on putting one foot in front of the other and on the lush rainforest around me. This was the first of two hikes we were doing this week—the second would be on Friday when we'd head to Papakōlea's green sand beach—although the hotel had promised us there were other trails that were easy to explore if we wanted to do more.

I'd been excited to get off the beaten track and explore the native forest where most of the plant species were on the island before it was discovered and settled by the first Polynesians. But something about spending the day with Ilias, without any guides or scheduled activities, had made me nervous. It felt like something had changed between us last night under the stars on Mauna Kea.

Maybe it was because I'd been more open with him than I had been with anyone in years. Maybe it was because he'd shared something deeply personal with me. Maybe it was because we'd both opened up about painful parts of our pasts. Or maybe it was a combination of all that and more.

Whatever the reason, the night had left me feeling emotionally drained and completely buzzing, and I'd lain awake for hours staring at the ceiling with Ilias wrapped around me while I tried to figure out what I was feeling.

But all I'd done was go round and round in circles.

"Come on!" Ilias called from farther down the path. "You're so slow." He was balanced on the root of a tree, looking perfectly poised as a breeze rippled through his hair and fragments of sunlight played across his face.

"I'm not slow. I'm setting a leisurely pace."

Ilias snorted. "I don't think there's a difference."

"Do you always just go rushing off?" I asked, trying to keep a note of irritation out of my voice.

"Again, not rushing. I'm just enjoying myself. Aren't you?"

"I am, but I get the feeling we hike differently. I bet

you're one of those people who just wants to reach the top as fast as possible like it's some sort of competition." I'd been hiking with a few people like that, and I'd hated every second of it. What was the point of spending the day somewhere picturesque if you didn't stop to enjoy the view?

"There you go with the judging again," Ilias said. "Just because I'm faster than you, doesn't mean I want to get to the end as fast as possible. Although... when we head to Papakōlea I might rush a little just because I've never seen a green sand beach before."

"That's..." I thought for a second, ducking under a low-hanging branch and brushing away some insects. "Okay, that's fair enough."

"Ha! See? You'll rush too."

"I didn't say that."

"You did in context," Ilias said gleefully, skipping over some roots. He paused, gazing up at the canopy of trees shifting above us. Beyond them, the sky had started to turn grey as thick clouds began to roll in. "I think we're about to get wet."

"Looks like it." I stopped and opened my bag, pulling out the lightweight, waterproof jacket I'd stashed inside. It was one of those that folded up inside its own little bag, and while it wasn't the most fashionable thing on earth, it was light and practical. We'd been told the forest got a lot of rain due to its location, so it had made sense to shove it in my bag.

"I can't believe you brought that but not plasters," Ilias said as he watched me unfold the coat and sling it on.

"Did you bring one?" I asked.

"A coat?" Ilias shook his head and grinned. "No, I'm not afraid of a little rain."

"You're going to get soaked."

"And? Does that matter? I can shower back at the hotel."

"You'll get cold," I said as I began to walk again, plucking the map out of Ilias's hand as I passed. "And I'm not going back early just because you forgot a coat."

"Am I five or something? Seriously! Stop treating me like a fucking child. I'm a grown-ass man."

"A grown-ass man throwing a temper tantrum." I knew I was poking him and being an asshole, but I couldn't stop myself. There was so much difference between carefree, snarky Ilias and the quiet, contemplative man from last night. The change had almost given me whiplash.

Then again, I was a different person today too, so I had no idea why I was making such a fuss. Was this some sort of ridiculous defence mechanism my brain had concocted to detach me from Ilias? Had it seen me starting to fall for him and decided it was time to put an end to that train of thought before it went anywhere?

"Fuck you!" Ilias snapped. "I—" But he didn't get a chance to finish that sentence because, with a deep rumble of thunder the heavens opened, and water cascaded onto us. "Fuck, that's cold!"

I hummed and nodded, not quite as smug as I'd been two minutes ago because although my jacket was water-proof, it only protected parts of me and there was now water running down the back of my neck and soaking into my shoes. Ilias looked at me and laughed, throwing his head back to the sky and twirling around, arms outstretched, on the narrow path. The rain dripped down his face and plastered his hair flat, but all I could see was the joy radiating from him.

"You were one of those kids that jumped in puddles, weren't you?" I asked, unable to stop myself from smiling.

"And you weren't?"

"Not really."

"You haven't lived until your wellies are full of water and squelching with every step," Ilias said. "Come on, we still have a trail to finish!" He marched past me, the trail already starting to turn to mud under his feet. He took the map back and disappeared through the trees.

"Come on, slowpoke."

I sighed and walked after him, knowing that no matter what I said or what I thought, I wasn't going to win because Ilias's joy was too powerful.

When we arrived back at our suite several hours later, we were still soaked to the skin.

The rain had eased off quickly, but by the time the sun had returned, the damage had been done, and Ilias and I squelched around the rest of the park, mud caking our feet and legs. The taxi driver who'd collected us had muttered something under his breath about tourists, and both Ilias and I had tipped him generously in an attempt to make up for the trouble.

Ilias kicked off his shoes as soon as he stepped through the door and began walking through the suite peeling off layers as he went until he was just in a pair of tight, black boxers that clung to his skin. I ignored the way my heart raced and bent down to unlace my shoes.

"You were wrong by the way," Ilias said as he put his camera bag on the coffee table, lovingly checking over his equipment. "I didn't get cold."

He looked up at me from where he now sat on the floor.

"I'm sorry," I said. "I didn't mean to be an ass."

"You're forgiven." Ilias grinned at me. "You know, if we were actually dating, this would be where we'd have extravagant make-up sex to cancel out our fight."

"Were we fighting?" I asked as I tried to ignore the rest of his statement. Ilias might have been utterly gorgeous and full of sunshine and wry charm, but that didn't mean I wanted to have sex with him.

At least… I didn't think I did.

Acid rose in my throat as a feeling of panic started to set in. I was *not* going to be attracted to Ilias. Except I'd already admitted to myself that I wouldn't mind if I was.

Everything I found out about Ilias drew me closer to him, and I was starting to want something I was so afraid I wasn't allowed to have. Sure, Ilias flirted with me, but would he keep doing that if he knew a quick suck and fuck wasn't in the cards? At least not for now.

"A minor disagreement still counts as a fight," Ilias said. "At least it would if we wanted to have make-up sex."

"If you're that hard up, you can go and jerk off in the shower."

"And you wouldn't want to join me?" He winked as he spoke, and his tone was over-the-top flirtatious, so I knew he was joking. But there was a flash of seriousness behind his eyes that made me hesitate. And for a split second, I almost considered saying yes.

"No thanks," I said, swallowing the rest of my words. "You go ahead."

"Sure?" Ilias climbed off the floor and sauntered over to me. He waggled his eyebrows. "It's big enough. And we've already shared a bath."

"I'm sure."

"Your loss." He walked away from me towards the suite's enormous bathroom, pausing in the doorway to look over his shoulder. "I had fun today. Just don't forget your plasters next time."

He grinned and kept on walking, leaving me standing in the middle of the suite caught in a hurricane of my own emotions.

# CHAPTER ELEVEN

*Ilias*

"WHAT DO you want to do now?" Oscar asked as we paused in the shade of some overhanging trees.

We'd been walking along the wide footpath next to the waterfront after spending the morning exploring Kona. So far, we'd done a couple of local museums and historic landmarks and walked all the way along the pier to look out over Kailua Bay.

It had been very low key, and I'd enjoyed the change of pace.

"I don't know," I said. "Are you hungry? Want to grab some late lunch?" We'd gorged ourselves on the hotel's incredible breakfast buffet first thing this morning, but now I was starting to feel a bit peckish.

"Sure." Oscar gave me a warm smile that made heat kindle in my gut. "Why don't we make a start on that list of yours? We've barely touched it yet."

"Yes!" I grabbed my phone out of my pocket and pulled up the extensive list of restaurant recommendations I'd been collecting.

We'd only managed one so far, and that was a bar and restaurant not too far from the hotel that we'd made it to last night. The food had been pretty good, and Oscar and I had spent the evening trading movie recommendations over freshly caught and grilled mahi mahi.

"What sort of thing do you fancy? Sushi? Mexican? Oooh! How about Nakoa's? I've had like four people recommend it to me," I said as I scrolled down the list and noticed the little number four in brackets next to the restaurant name.

"What sort of food is it?" Oscar asked. "I'm going to say yes. I'm just curious."

"Well, the restaurant's full name is Nakoa's Fish Market Bar and Grill, so I'm assuming it'll be fish," I said with a grin. "And George said they do awesome poke, and we should try their lau lau too."

"Let's go there then. Do you know where we're going?"

"No, but I have the power of Google Maps so the internet can do it for me." I tapped the address into my phone and discovered it was about a ten-minute walk back along the bay and tucked away down a couple of side streets. "Ta-da, let's go."

A soft breeze brushed across my skin as we walked, dispelling some of the heat. I couldn't believe we were already halfway through our week, and in another couple of days we'd be on the long journey back to reality. I knew it would be impossible to stay here, but it had been nice to escape the constant chaos of my family and the continued hustle of my day-to-day life and just be.

Despite my reservations, Oscar had turned out to be a lot of fun to spend time with, even if he could be a little grumpy at times. But I'd decided that was all part of his charm. He laughed at my terrible jokes, rolled his eyes at my ridiculous flirting, snarked at me when he was stressed and apologised later, listened to me when I talked about my family and my past, and never seemed to dismiss my experiences as something I just needed to deal with.

He was everything I'd been avoiding for the last ten years wrapped up in an incredibly handsome package.

The fact that he hadn't fallen for my subtle attempts to see if he would come to bed with me, if I felt so inclined, was almost making me want him more. I'd never had anyone resist me like that before, even when I wasn't trying.

Maybe it was because I felt like I could be myself around Oscar that I'd accidentally decided to show him all of who I was. I thought nothing was going to happen, so there was no point in pretending to be someone I wasn't. I'd been myself all week, and nothing I'd done seemed to have fazed him. It was... refreshing, terrifying, and a little bit of a turn-on.

Nakoa's looked deceptively simple from the outside with a hand-painted wooden sign over the door. It was located at the front of an old warehouse, which made sense if it was also part of a fish market. Oscar pulled open the door and gestured me through.

As soon as I entered, I was hit by a wall of chatter and

delicious smells. The restaurant had high ceilings and bright blue walls with the lower half decorated in wood panelling, and the room was filled with wooden tables, plenty of them already occupied. Staff bustled around, and at the other end of the room I saw a counter that divided the restaurant from the kitchen, behind which a variety of chefs moved around all chatting and laughing.

It didn't take us long to get seated, and soon I was staring at the menu, trying to work out what the fuck I wanted to eat.

"Any thoughts?" Oscar asked, giving me a wry smile from over the top of his menu.

"How about all of it? Seriously, how am I supposed to decide?" I glanced down the list of food again then over to a large blackboard on the wall that had the day's fish and their prices listed in large, colourful lettering. "I definitely haven't eaten enough poke, so I want some of that, but that ahi katsu sounds so good and so does the lau lau and the boneless short ribs... oh, and they have fish tacos and slow-roasted pork." I looked up at Oscar. "Do we have dinner plans?"

He shook his head. "Not tonight. Tomorrow we've got the dinner on the beach."

"Oh, right." I tried to ignore the way my heart raced at that idea. I'd never wanted to do anything that romantic before, but suddenly it sounded like the perfect way to spend the evening. "I can gorge myself now, then you can roll me back to the suite."

Oscar laughed. "Does that mean I'll be spending the evening by myself?"

"You could keep me company." I smiled at him sweetly. "We could watch a film or something."

"That would be nice… We could go for a walk along the beach too. Watch the sunset."

"I'd like that," I said, trying to keep myself from blushing furiously like some sort of preteen on his first date. I was saved from further awkwardness because our waiter arrived, and we realised we hadn't made any sort of decision. We ordered a couple of local beers and promised to be ready to order by the time he returned.

"Okay, serious decision time," I said.

"Why don't we both get different things and share?" Oscar asked. "If you're okay with that. They do a mixed plate with two items and a side. We could both get one of those and try four different dishes."

"That is a good plan, but it still means I have to narrow it down to two… What are you getting?"

Oscar frowned and pulled at his bottom lip, high-lighting the deep bow at the top of his mouth. I quickly turned to look around the restaurant so he didn't catch me staring.

"I'm going to get the spicy house poke with ahi because I don't get much fresh tuna at home and the boneless short ribs with… seaweed salad. Does that help?"

"No." I laughed. "Fuck it. I'm getting the sweet house poke, some lau lau, and spicy crab on the side, and I'm going to order some tacos too. Just because I can."

The waiter returned with our beers, and we ordered. I took a sip of my drink and nodded. It was a shame I wouldn't be able to take any back with me because Dominic would have loved it.

"What are your plans when we get back?" Oscar asked. I sighed. I knew he was just making conversation, but I'd been trying very hard not to think about London.

"Not sure. I'll try to edit these photos as soon as I can," I said, making a mental note to take a snap of our food when it arrived. "Then I'm not sure. I've got a couple of potential things lined up... but I'm thinking I might need to find a regular photography job as well."

It was the first time I'd said that out loud, and I was surprised I'd admitted it.

"Really? How come?"

"Honestly, I love taking travel photos—it's my dream—but despite my best efforts, it's not paying all my bills." I sighed. "It doesn't mean I'm going to give it up. I'm just thinking about taking some more commercial jobs in between or setting up a little studio to do portraits and family photos so I have a regular income. My Instagram does a lot for me, and I've got plenty of photos in the bank to keep it going for a while, but I really want to be able to live by myself and have a little bit of freedom."

Oscar nodded. "A little studio sounds like it could work. I'm sure there are lots of small places you could rent, and you wouldn't have a lot of overhead, just equipment and running costs. And you could take your own bookings so it would make it easy to work around travel projects. Plus, you sound like you're pretty good with kids."

"Yeah, it's just actually getting it started," I said. "I know I should probably do something, but it's finding the motivation. I know it's not giving up, just diversifying my portfolio, but still."

"Hey, it's okay. You'll get there." Oscar reached his hand across the table to where mine was resting. His fingers interlaced with mine, and he squeezed gently, sending a bolt of electricity up my arm. I swallowed, looking across at him.

His dark eyes met mine, warm and full of kindness, and for a moment it felt like nothing else existed in the universe except the two of us. Time slowed to a crawl, and I heard every beat of my heart. I took a breath and gripped his hand, holding it in mine. I hadn't realised how much a simple gesture could change everything.

"Thanks," I said eventually, still not letting go.

Oscar opened his mouth, then closed it again and shot me a smile.

We were still sitting like that two minutes later when our food started to arrive, but it didn't feel like the bubble around us had burst. The moment just continued to stretch out around us like it was curious to see where it went.

The food was delicious, and Oscar and I swapped fork-fuls of the different dishes like it was something we'd done a thousand times before. It felt *right* in a way I couldn't explain.

"What do you think?" Oscar asked as he watched me eat one of the short ribs he'd slipped onto my plate.

"It's... amazing." The beef was tender and delicious and almost melted in my mouth, but that wasn't what made it special. It was the fact I was sharing it with Oscar. I knew this wasn't a date, not really, but if it was, I'd have counted it as the best one I'd ever been on.

We spent the rest of the meal talking about everything and nothing, sharing the food and trying to work out what we liked best. There was no clear winner, and I understood why so many people had recommended the restaurant. If we had time, I would definitely suggest coming back before we went home.

"I'll get the bill," Oscar said. "I can expense it."

"All of it?"

He shrugged. "Most of it at least. It's all part of the job."

"Suggesting we get all the food and then paying for it? You're the perfect lunch date," I said, hoping my tone was light enough that I could pass it off as joking.

"I try." He gave me another one of those smiles that melted me from the inside out. I knew I was going to have to sit down and figure out what the fuck I was feeling because I couldn't continue like this.

While Oscar sorted the bill, I reached for my phone to make a note on my restaurant list and frowned. There was a message from Dominic. He never messaged me unless it was something important.

DOMINIC *Sorry to bother you. Hope you're enjoying your trip. Just a heads-up that Sophia just announced she's getting married, Anna is having another baby, and apparently there was some sort of big blowout about Zoë not being married. Rumour is she and Auntie Tonia had a screaming match at lunch the other week. I'm guessing it was mostly Tonia doing the screaming. Also, you got brought up as an example of someone who is single and successful*

*and happy? Idk what happened, but just wanted to warn you before you came home. I think it's going to get messy.*
Dominic *Also Teddy says hi and wants to know if you've seen any sharks?*

I sighed, wishing for just five minutes my family could not try to set a world record for drama. I knew the reason Zoë wasn't married because she'd told me at one of the numerous weddings we'd been to over the past few years. But my aunt Tonia seemed to be stuck in God knows what time period and seemed to think her eldest daughter was defective for not wanting to get married and pop out children like her other two daughters.

And it looked like I'd have to suck up all my opinions for yet another wedding in the next couple of years. Maybe I could make a bet with Zoë about which one of us would get asked first when it was going to be our turn.

"You okay?" Oscar asked. I looked up from my phone, knowing exasperation was written all over my face.

"Just my family being... my family." I chuckled wryly. "They can't go ten minutes without starting something."

"Want to talk about it?" He stood and offered me his hand. "We can get some shave ice, and you can bitch to your heart's content."

*You might just be the perfect man* I thought as I slipped my hand into his. We headed out into the mid-afternoon sun, and not even my family's desperation for drama could create any clouds.

# CHAPTER TWELVE

*Ilias*

THE SUN WAS JUST SETTING over the horizon, splashing colour across the sky and setting the ocean ablaze as Oscar and I made our way down to the beach for dinner.

A path of lanterns had been laid out for us, leading to a small table on the sand with two chairs at right angles to each other, facing the water so we could watch the last of the sunset. The table was surrounded by torches that hadn't been lit yet.

It was a beautiful sight, and I almost tripped over my feet because I couldn't stop staring. Oscar caught me by the elbow and chuckled as I righted myself with a grunt.

"I don't think it would be the best start to the evening if you face-planted on the beach," Oscar said dryly.

"How do you know that wasn't my aim?"

"If that's what you really want, next time I won't stop you."

I grinned as we were seated at the table, the soft, ocean breeze fluttering across my face. "Have you ever done anything like this before?"

"Dinner on a beach?"

"Yeah."

Oscar shook his head. "No. It always seemed like one of those things people do on their honeymoons or anniversary trips. I suppose that's why they've organised it for us since this article is supposed to encourage couples to come and stay here."

"Shit," I said suddenly. "I should take a picture of the set-up." I had my camera with me since it had been pretty much glued to my hand for the past week, but I'd been so drawn in by the idea that this was for me that I'd totally forgotten to do my job.

"Quick, put everything back. Straighten the table. Then go and stand over there"—I pointed to a part of the shoreline where I knew he'd be out of the shot—"so you'll be out of the way." I waved my hands at Oscar like he was a stray pigeon I was trying to shoo away.

"Seriously? You could just ask them for a press shot. I'm sure they've got one."

"Nope, my job is to give Marcus *options*, and if I don't do that, Madelyn will have me blacklisted from *The Traveller* forever, and I'll be forced to follow you around and annoy you... like a ghost but one who's still alive. Now shoo!"

Oscar stood and shook his head, laughing as I nudged him away. He took his glass of wine and wandered along the shore as I straightened the table with the help of a lovely member of staff, who I made a mental note to tip very generously later. I'd make Oscar do it for laughing at me.

I darted up the beach, towards the path we'd come down, and snapped a few pictures. I was quickly starting to run out of light, and I hoped the pictures would look more atmospheric than shit. I cursed myself internally for forgetting about my job, but I'd been drawn in by the idea of such a romantic evening.

It made me sound like a sucker, and I'd have to come up with a more convincing excuse if Marcus asked me why there weren't any good pictures of the set-up. I'd just blame the weather, that usually worked.

"Can I come back now?" Oscar called. He was sipping his glass of wine near the water's edge, and I could have sworn there was a mischievous smile on his mouth as he watched me.

"Fine," I said as I put the lens cap back in place and walked back to the table.

"You know," he said as he settled himself back at the table, "there are more tables set up along the beach. You could have just taken a photo of one of them."

I turned my head and noticed another couple of dining areas dotted along the sand, just far enough away from each other to give the diners privacy. Which was why I hadn't noticed them. The one at the far end looked occupied, but the middle one was still empty. I sighed and raised an eyebrow at Oscar who was trying not to laugh.

"Really? You couldn't have pointed that out earlier?"

"I thought you'd seen them!"

I snorted and shook my head. "Asshole."

Oscar shrugged. "I've been called worse."

"Me too. But I'm not sure that's appropriate dinner conversation," I said, reaching for my glass and gazing out across the water. The sun was barely visible now, and a soft, purple darkness was starting to set in. Around us, golden light began to flicker into being as the staff lit the torches.

"You mean your family dinners don't usually end in people insulting each other?" Oscar asked with a laugh.

"If they didn't, I'd be worried. I'd assume someone had been abducted by aliens." I sipped my wine. "It was why I wanted to avoid it for a change."

"Fair enough." There was a pause, then Oscar said, "You okay after yesterday?"

"Yeah. I'm fine." I'd spent part of the afternoon bitching to him as we walked around Kona, lost ourselves in local art galleries, and paddled on the beach. By the time we'd gotten back to the hotel, I'd felt a lot better.

Today had also proved to be a wonderful distraction, as we'd spent it with a local cultural ambassador, John Kamakaonaona, who'd talked a lot about the history of the island and Hawaiian traditions and culture. He'd been incredibly interesting to listen to, adding warmth and weight to his words. It had given me an extra appreciation for this beautiful island and the people whose land it was. I felt humbled by their history and annoyed at myself for never really considering the history of colonisation in this part of the world.

Then again, the UK government had always been good at carefully erasing British colonisation from the history curriculum—at least while I was at school.

"Honestly," I continued, "I'd have been surprised if there *wasn't* any drama this week. There's always something."

"That sounds exhausting."

"It is, but they're my family, so what can I do?" Oscar frowned but didn't say anything. I sipped my wine and chuckled. "Okay, new topic. I feel like all I've done this week is bitch about my family."

"It's fine. I kind of understand, even if mine isn't as dramatic as yours, although..." He grinned. "We've had our fair share. Like the time I dumped pasta salad over the head of one of Richard's girlfriends."

I stared at him, wide-eyed in shock and glee. "Excuse me. How have you not mentioned this before? I need details!"

"It's not that exciting," Oscar said. "Basically, he brought this woman to dinner, and bear in mind that before he met his fiancé, Richard had the shittiest taste in women. Anyway, turns out she was really into this aloe vera shit, and she kept trying to recruit us into her fucking pyramid scheme."

"Ah, one of those."

"Yeah." Oscar chuckled, sitting back in his seat as our starters arrived: charcoal barbecued octopus with cucumber namasu. We thanked the staff before Oscar continued.

"Anyway, she soon realised none of us were interested so she tried to corner my brother Finn. He's my youngest bio brother, and I just... I fucking hate people messing with him. He's really quiet and shy, especially around new people, and I always get really fucking angry when people don't leave him alone when they can see he's uncomfortable. I mean, he's an adult now, but I still think of him as that toddler who used to hold my t-shirt and suck his thumb and follow me around like a little duckling."

He shook his head and reached for his cutlery. "Long story short, the woman wouldn't leave him alone, wouldn't let Finn get a word in edgeways, and ignored me when I told her to back off. So I picked up the bowl of pasta salad from the middle of the table and tipped it over her head. Not really sure why, but it seemed like a good idea at the time."

Unable to keep a straight face any longer, I burst out laughing. "Fucking hell! That's amazing. I wish I'd thought of something like that before when my cousins were being dickheads. What sort of pasta salad was it? What did everyone say?"

"Er... I think it was a pesto one?" Oscar thought for a second. "Yeah, it was definitely green. And it had cherry tomatoes in. I felt really bad afterwards because I should have tried something else and what I'd done was such a dick move. I offered to pay for her dry cleaning, and I apologised a lot, but it didn't really do much good. I think Richard was this close to punching me, but he didn't. He punched Eli last year though."

"Why?"

"Because Eli is dating Richard's best friend. They're actually really cute together. But Richard and Eli have always butted heads. They're the right age gap for it. Richard and I were never close, but we never fought because we were too evenly matched. Jules is a girl and would *definitely* kick all our asses, and Finn and Lewis were the babies. Eli can be a proper shithead sometimes, and he and Richard are total opposites, so it was bound to happen."

"See? Your family is just like mine. Just smaller," I said.

Oscar laughed. "Is that a good or bad thing?"

"Not sure, but it's nice to meet someone who gets it."

Oscar nodded, and our conversation turned to the food, which was incredible as always. The octopus was followed by an ocean grill with ahi tuna, mahi mahi, shutome, and uku plus a variety of vegetable sides and a couple of delicious sauces including a yuzu kosho butter than I'd kill to be able to take home in a bucket.

"Can I ask you something?" I asked randomly as I picked up some tuna with my fork. There was a question floating around in my mind that had been nagging at me for weeks, but I'd never considered giving it a voice before now.

"Sure."

"Why did you offer to write an article aimed at couples if you're not actually in one? I mean this is lovely," I said, gesturing around at the setting, "but wouldn't you have rather spent it with someone you were actually dating?"

Oscar frowned, and in the glow of the torchlight, I could swear he was blushing. "It's a good question," he said slowly.

"You don't have to answer if you don't want. I realise it might be really personal." Perhaps Oscar had skeletons in his cupboard the way I did. Although considering what had happened to me, that was probably a poor metaphor.

"No, it's fine. Mostly it was a miscommunication. I told Madelyn how my brothers were starting to settle down and how I could only recommend a few places for them to go on holiday and that I wanted a series that really focused on safe places for queer couples since the magazine never really considers that when it recommends destinations. And I think something I said must have given her the wrong idea because she told me she'd send me and my partner..." He shook his head and reached for a piece of mahi mahi. "That and the fact her niece got engaged to her girlfriend and gently pointed out the same problem to Madelyn when she began recommending places for their honeymoon. So it had a personal connection for her, and I think Madelyn just put two and two together and made five, and I'm definitely not the person to tell her she was wrong."

"Yeah," I said, raising my eyebrows. "I wouldn't either." I'd known some of what Oscar had said, but the Madelyn information was new. It made perfect sense though, and I was glad he hadn't told me about it earlier or the weight of expectation might have crushed me.

"As for the boyfriend thing... well, you know how hard this job is on relationships, and for me..." He pursed his lips like he was thinking about saying something. I didn't interrupt his thoughts. "For me things can be harder because I'm demisexual."

He was looking at me with fierce eyes and a clenched jaw like he was daring me to say something. But all it did was give me another piece of my Oscar puzzle, one that was bright and shining and seemed to magically connect so many of the other pieces.

"It means I don't experience sexual attraction without feeling a strong emotional connection to someone. I can't just do quick hook-ups, and with my job, people don't usually want to give me a chance. I'm gone too much to make a relationship worth the effort."

I nodded, choosing my next words carefully.

"Thank you for telling me," I said as I gave Oscar my warmest smile. "Your reasoning makes a lot of sense, and I can imagine that some people are quite... shitty about it." Oscar raised an eyebrow, so I continued.

"My cousin Zoë is aro ace, and we've talked about it several times. She's very happy, but people are still dicks about it. They don't believe her. They tell her she hasn't met the right man and that everyone *wants* to fall in love." I toyed with a piece of shutome.

"I can believe people must say similar things to you. And I can imagine it hurts." I bit my lip. "I'm really sorry if I've made you uncomfortable with all my flirting."

"Actually," said Oscar, "it's been... nice." He huffed out a laugh and shook his head. "I don't think that's the right word, but you don't need to apologise, Ilias."

He reached out across the table and brushed his fingers against my wrist.

# CHAPTER THIRTEEN

*Oscar*

SPARKS SHOT down my arm as my fingers brushed against the warm skin of Ilias's arm. I let out a slow breath, trying to work out what the hell I was doing.

"I think the reason I was such a dick about the idea of you going off with other guys was because I was jealous." The words came out slowly, and I almost regretted saying them out loud.

"I know this relationship is fake, but I think you're funny and interesting and really fucking handsome," I continued. "And I guess I just wanted to pretend that, for once, someone might actually want me. Sorry."

Ilias was looking at me with an expression I couldn't place as golden torchlight played across his face. He looked even more beautiful if that was even possible. Then he smiled, and I felt some of the tension in my chest begin to ease like someone had loosened the vice around my ribcage.

"You were jealous?" There was a gentle, teasing lilt to his tone, but it wasn't malicious. Instead, it just made my skin prickle.

"Yeah. No need to make a big deal out of it."

"Hmm, no promises there," he said. "But that can come later."

I raised an eyebrow. "Later? What comes now?"

"Now, we're going to act like the grown-ass adults we're supposed to be and talk."

"That sounds horrifying. Can't we go back ten minutes and pretend this conversation never happened?" I asked, only half joking. This was the price of opening my mouth, but at least Ilias hadn't dismissed me yet. There was still time though.

"No, definitely not. I'm too interested now." His smile widened, and he twisted his hand around to catch mine, interlacing our fingers on the table. "So... you wanted to pretend this was real. Does that mean you actually want it to be real?"

"Shit. Straight into the deep end. I was hoping we'd start with something simple."

"I think it's a little late for that," Ilias said. "Would you like me to throw you a life raft?"

"Is there one?" I didn't know conversations about this sort of thing usually came with emergency provisions.

"Yes. If it helps, I think you're gorgeous and charming, even with your grumpy shell."

"I'm not grumpy," I said, knowing my defensive tone wasn't going to help my case. Ilias chuckled.

"Yes, you are. You're like a little sea urchin. All prickly on the outside and squishy in the middle."

"Aren't the squishy bits my internal organs?"

"Don't nitpick," Ilias said. "That wasn't my point."

"I know. I'm trying not to think about your point because... because if that's how you feel, then I'm not sure what happens next." I reached for my wine and took a sip, wishing I didn't feel so off-kilter. This conversation wasn't rocket science—we weren't trying to calculate how to fly to Mars—all we were trying to do was work out how we felt about each other.

"Why not?" Ilias asked, giving my hand a squeeze then releasing me. He began to pick at his food again, and I realised we hadn't finished dinner. The whole set-up had melted away as soon as I'd told him about being demi. "It doesn't have to be complicated."

"Doesn't it?"

"No. Not if we don't want it to be."

"But how... Why..." I stabbed a piece of tuna and tried to shake out my thoughts. "I don't know if I can give you what you want."

"How do you know what I want?" Ilias raised an eyebrow. "You haven't asked me."

"But don't you want..."

"To have sex with you?" Ilias asked. "Do you really think that's all I want?"

"No, I don't. But it's a reasonable question from my perspective. Virtually all my relationships have ended because I don't feel anything for the other person, or if I do, it's not soon enough for them. I like you, Ilias, but I can't put a timetable on anything."

"Okay," he said like it was somehow no big deal to him. My head was spinning. "I understand that. But I like you, Oscar, and I can wait." He reached for his own glass, looking at me over the rim. "I need to know where your line is though. Does that include all kinds of physical touch and romantic gestures? I know you said you were fine with me holding your hand, but I don't want to cross any boundaries. I won't make you uncomfortable."

I shook my head, feeling my face heat. Damn him for being so sweet and considerate. I suddenly felt like a teenager all over again. Or at least a teenager in one of those indie movies I'd been obsessed with.

"I... I quite like romantic things, hand holding, cuddling, kissing... It doesn't even have to be chaste kissing."

"Oooh, spicy kissing. I'm down for that."

"I'm not sure if you're mocking me," I said with a wry smile.

"I never joke about spicy kissing."

I snorted, the pressure around my chest easing again only to be replaced with a kaleidoscope of butterflies. I hadn't felt like this around anyone for a very long time. Ilias sipped his wine again, then glanced out over the water like he was pondering something.

"Since we're sharing secrets," he said slowly, "there's something I should tell you."

"What sort of something?"

Ilias took a deep breath and turned to face me, pain etched into his features. "Do you remember when I told you about my… friend. The one who died?"

"Yes…" I said, suddenly wondering where this was going.

"He wasn't just my friend," Ilias said quietly. "He was my fiancé."

I stared at him as all the fragments I'd collected over the last week suddenly assembled themselves into a beautiful, tragic photo. And everything I knew about Ilias suddenly inverted itself. I thought about all the times he'd talked about the digs his family had made and how much each of them had hurt. Perhaps that was why Ilias didn't seem to do relationships. Except he wanted one with me…

"What happened?" I asked.

"Car accident. We were only nineteen. Kind of one of those whirlwind summer romances with someone I'd grown up with. I'd seen him every summer at my nonna's in Italy for as long as I could remember, and that year we just… clicked. We were young and stupid, but we decided to get married. Only there was a storm…" He trailed off and took another breath. "We'd decided to drive to Turin so we could fly to Paris to get married. We hadn't really thought it all through. It was all just a spur of the moment thing. Then it started raining, and we couldn't see, and there was this tree."

"Shit. I'm so sorry."

"Thanks. The worst part was that nobody knew Daniele and I were together, so I couldn't do anything. I just had to pretend I'd lost a friend rather than the man I'd actively been planning a life with. I think everyone just thought my grief was survivor's guilt rather than anything more," he said. "I don't know if it would have lasted, and maybe it wouldn't have, but ever since, I've just closed myself off. It's been easier than getting hurt. Until... Fuck." He shook his head. "Until you and your bloody, stupid, beautiful face and your grumpy charm, and the fact that you were honest with me. That you told me that it never goes away like you'd never expect me to forget or pretend it didn't happen. Like... like you understood a little of what I felt."

I didn't know what to do or what to say. So I did the first thing that felt natural. I reached across the table to retake his hand and squeezed it so tightly I was worried I might break it. "I would never ask you to forget something like that. And I'm so sorry for everything you went through."

"Thanks." Ilias smiled at me, but I noticed his eyes were shining with unshed tears. "It's kind of nice actually. To tell someone about it, someone who isn't being paid to listen to me."

I knew he was trying to make light of it, but it was hard to let the comment pass. "Does anybody in your family know?"

"Zoë does because she found me drunk and crying at a family wedding about a year after it happened. She was the one who encouraged me to get therapy rather than just trying to bottle it up. But apart from that, no, they don't."

"Do you think..."

"I'd ever tell them?" He shook his head. "Probably not. And anyway, it's not something I want to revisit with them. It's been ten years. I don't want to go dragging Daniele's memory up. Besides they'd just go on and on about it, and someone else would inevitably make it all about them. It would be too painful, and I'd rather just leave it to rest."

I nodded, silently thinking a large proportion of Ilias's family could go do one from everything I'd heard about them. But now wasn't the time to say that.

"Thank you for telling me," I said. "You didn't have to."

"Yeah, I did. Because you shared a piece of yourself with me, and I needed to do the same. It's why I've only gone for hook-ups, even though I crave more." He let out a hollow chuckle. "And now I sound desperate and needy. You must think I'm ridiculous."

"No, I don't." And I didn't. All I thought was that Ilias was a man desperate to be loved. How hard must it have been for him to close himself off to what he really wanted because he was scared he might lose something important. "I think you're being honest with me, and that's really fucking hard. But I'm grateful for it."

"Really?"

"Yes, I am."

"I guess," Ilias said, "I'm the same as you but in a different way. You say you can't put a timetable on our relationship, and you can't promise you'll want anything more. I can't promise you I won't freak the fuck out about whatever this is tomorrow. It's been ten years, and I've worked so hard to let go, but brains and hearts are funny things, and I can't guarantee trying this won't hit some magical switch I don't know about and make me want to run away."

"If that happens, tell me," I said, reaching across the

table to cup his face in my hand. "And I'll throw you a life raft."

"You will?"

"Yes. I won't let you drown, Ilias. I know this will be scary for both of us. All I'm asking is that you don't shut me out."

"I'll try," he said, and I knew that was as good as I'd get. But I didn't mind. We were wading through uncharted water, and the only way to go was slow.

I'd never considered the idea that Ilias's issues might be bigger than mine, but maybe this was something we both needed—a person who saw us, a person who could empathise with where we were coming from, even if we couldn't totally understand.

"Thank you."

Ilias leant into my hand, his cheek warm against my skin. The green flecks in his eyes danced in the light and his mouth looked soft and plush. I had the overwhelming urge to kiss him, but I wanted to wait. I didn't want Ilias to think I was kissing him out of some kind of pity.

"So what do we do now?" Ilias asked.

"I don't know. We could finish our dinner. Maybe go for a walk along the beach? It'll be dark, but we'll be able to see enough."

"I'd like that." He sat back, and my palm tingled at the absence of his touch.

We finished our fish, which luckily hadn't gotten too cold, and after that came dessert in the form of the most elevated shave ice I'd ever seen with coconut sorbet, pineapple granite, strawberry pearls, and some tiny, crispy passion fruit meringues. It was delicious though—cool and sharp and fresh and perfectly balanced to finish off the meal. I knew I'd been utterly spoilt by the food on this trip, and I wasn't looking forward to trying to conjure up things in my tiny kitchen every night when I got home. Maybe I needed to look at taking a cooking class.

Ilias and I kept talking throughout dessert, but the conversation turned more to work and our trip and working out if there was anything we still needed to do before we left.

"Tomorrow," Ilias said, "we have to get up and watch the sun rise. I still haven't seen it yet. Then I can also take some photos on the beach while it's quiet."

"What unholy hour will you be turfing me out of bed at then?"

"Half five." Ilias grinned. "Sunrise is at just after six, and I want to make sure I get a good spot." He thought for a second. "Actually, maybe closer to quarter past would work better. I don't want us to miss it."

I groaned but conceded, simply because Ilias had said *us*, and that word carried a lot more weight than it had a couple of hours ago. "Fine. I'll set an alarm."

"Perfect. And afterwards, we can go get pancakes at this gorgeous local place Rachel at reception recommended. I think it's run by a family friend of hers. Anyway, apparently they do the best breakfasts on the island, so we have to go and check it out."

"I suppose breakfast will make up for being thrown out of bed so early," I said with a grin, watching as Ilias rolled his eyes.

"Don't make me go without you."

"You wouldn't. You'd miss me too much."

Ilias snorted. "Would I?"

"Fine, but you wouldn't leave your boyfriend behind. That would be rude." I'd meant it in a teasing way—an offhanded joke about the situation—except it felt different now. Ilias stared at me, his mouth slightly open in surprise.

"No," he said. "I guess I wouldn't."

# CHAPTER FOURTEEN

*Ilias*

I ALMOST REGRETTED my decision to get up so early when the alarm first went off, but as I stood on some rocks, watching the sun come up from behind the mountains and splashing a riot of colour across the sky, I knew any missed sleep had been worth it.

The resort was still quiet, the only sounds a harmony of bird calls, the soft brush of the sea on the sand, and the occasional member of staff making a start to their day. It was peaceful and perfect.

I took a deep breath, letting the calm wash over me as I lifted my camera. I'd made sure I had enough time to adjust the settings and find the best shot, and I was sure the photos would be perfect.

Beside me, Oscar stood on another rock in bare feet and loose shorts, his hair still fluffy from sleep. He looked gorgeous, and I kept having to ignore the temptation to focus solely on him.

After I'd poured out my soul to him last night, I hadn't been sure how he'd respond. I'd never told anyone apart from Zoë and my therapist, Jon, about Daniele, so I didn't exactly have a bar for expectations. But Oscar's response had still surprised me. He'd been supportive, but he hadn't pushed. All he'd asked was that I was open with him, and that if I started to struggle, I'd talk to him. Neither of those things had been on my expected response list, and I wasn't sure if they were things most guys would have done or if it was just an Oscar thing.

My gut told me it was the latter, and that made my insides squirm.

We hadn't really finished having the whole *are we dating* conversation, and although it seemed like we'd decided to take our fake relationship in the direction of a real one, the actual words hadn't been said. I wasn't sure *why* I needed to hear them, but I did, and it frustrated me.

Was that a conversation only teenagers had or was it something everyone in a relationship did? Was this part of the healthy discussion of boundaries and parameters that my therapist had talked about in terms of relationships? Jon had said clear, open communication should be the basis for any relationship—romantic, professional, or familial. I'd tried to explain that most of my family didn't work like that, but he'd encouraged me to take the first steps anyway.

"Can I ask you something?" I asked finally, not looking away from my camera as the sun bathed the tops of a distant forest in deep pink.

"Sure."

"Are we dating now? Like real dating, not fake."

"Yes?" Oscar sounded confused. "I thought so anyway. Are we not? Did I misunderstand what you meant?"

"No," I said. "I mean, yes, I want us to be together. I just… wanted to double-check." I looked down at him and found Oscar smiling at me. "Sorry. Am I being weird? I'm kind of new at this."

"Not weird," Oscar said, offering his hand to help me climb down. I glanced at the sky again, but the sun had fully risen now, and it would be difficult to get any more photos. I took his hand and let him guide me down to the sand, which was cool beneath my feet. "If it wasn't clear, it was probably good to ask. Didn't we say we were going to talk to each other?"

"Yeah, but that was in terms of big emotional stuff." I waved my hand. "Not whether this was actually a thing or not."

"Okay, well, I vote to make communication a thing we do all the time."

"If you insist," I said with a grin, slinging my camera bag over my shoulder. "You're one of those people who reads all the details in a contract, aren't you?"

"Don't you?"

"Depends on the contract. A work one, definitely. Made that mistake before."

Oscar snorted. "I can believe that."

"I'm going to pretend you're being nice to me." I stuck my tongue out at him and began to walk down the beach towards a cluster of rocks near the shoreline that had excellent rock pools.

"I am being nice," Oscar retorted. "I just said I can believe you didn't read something through."

"It was only once. And luckily I wasn't out much money. The only reason I noticed was because Dominic asked me something about the job, and I checked the details. He might have been horrified to find out I hadn't actually read it all, and the lecture I got bored me to tears. It was enough reason to read everything through in the future. Well, that and the money."

"I'm not sure if I should feel sorry for you or not," Oscar said as he walked next to me, leaving a trail of footprints in the wet sand.

It was still quiet, and there was nobody else around. I reached out and interlaced our fingers. Oscar said nothing, but he squeezed my hand and let me lead him towards the shore.

We spent nearly an hour exploring the beach, enjoying the stillness. Today was our last full day in Hawaii, and I wanted to remember every moment of it because it was inevitable that things would be different when we got back to London.

We both had jobs and lives to return to, and while we'd both said we wanted to try this, there was a small part of me that worried any form of relationship would get lost in the shuffle. I didn't even know where Oscar lived.

"What are you thinking about?" Oscar asked. We were sitting on some rocks, watching the sea play around the base of them. The sun was already starting to feel warm on the back of my neck.

"Home," I said. "How it's going to be so different from this. We've been in this perfect bubble all week, and as soon as we get back, everything is going to change. Sorry, that sounds really pessimistic."

"It does. Uncharacteristically so." He put his arm around my waist and pulled me against him, and I let my head drop until it was resting on his shoulder. "I'm supposed to be the grumpy one here."

I chuckled. "You said it, not me."

"You're going to hold that over me, aren't you?"

"I guarantee nothing." I tilted my head up to look at him and grinned. "But yes, I am."

"Oh, joy." Oscar's voice was deadpan, and it made the butterflies lodged in my chest take flight. "I know what you mean about things being different though. Real life seems distant here, even though we're *technically* working. But I guess we both just have to do our best to see each other as often as possible, do dinner, movies... things like that."

"Okay." I lifted my head so I could look at him better. Oscar really was fucking gorgeous inside and out. A soft breeze tousled his hair. I reached out and traced my hand along his jaw. "Did I tell you how handsome you are? I'm not sure I did."

The bridge of Oscar's nose began to tint, which somehow made him even sexier. There was something about the fact that he didn't seem to appreciate how fucking hot he was—maybe it was because I'd met so many men who knew they were hot and tended to act like twats.

"Thanks. You're very handsome too."

I ran my thumb along his bottom lip, tracing the soft fullness. One day, I hoped he'd let me kiss him. I couldn't think of anything I wanted to do more than kiss Oscar.

"You should kiss me," Oscar said, pulling me closer. We were virtually nose to nose, and I felt his breath ghosting over my skin.

"Are you sure?"

"Yes." He leant closer, his other hand coming up to cup my jaw. "I want you to kiss me. Please."

I closed the gap between us and let my mouth brush against his. His lips were soft and tasted like salt. Oscar's hand tightened around my waist, holding me there as his lips moved against mine.

What had started as something sweet and barely there melted into a deep kiss that shook me to my core. It was the sort of first kiss that only seemed to exist in films. But maybe that was because there were feelings I couldn't describe attached to the kiss, feelings I didn't even want to consider.

The kiss seemed to stretch out into eternity and beyond, but eventually we broke apart, our foreheads resting together as the sea splashed against the rocks around us.

Oscar sat back, his expression full of warmth. "I wanted to do that last night," he said finally.

"Why didn't you?"

He shrugged. "It didn't feel like the right moment with both of us baring our souls. I wanted a moment that was just us, no baggage attached."

That was so sweet I didn't quite know how to deal with it. "You really are a romantic at heart, aren't you?"

"I suppose." His nose tinted again, and he looked down at the rocks like he was suddenly very interested in the way the sea had worn them away. "I don't get many chances to be romantic. So many people seem to associate romance with sex, or they think it's only for long-term relationships."

"Well, you can be romantic with me," I said. "And I'll never expect anything more. Dinner can just be dinner. Flowers can just be flowers."

"You like flowers?" Oscar asked, looking up at me as if the statement had surprised him.

"Yes. Is that bad?"

"No." He was smiling suddenly. "I love flowers."

He leant over and kissed me again like he was so delighted by my declaration that he couldn't resist, and it made me melt inside. God, this man was so adorable it hurt. He was so prickly and defensive, but underneath there was a soft, lonely man desperate to be loved.

We were like two halves of a whole but presented differently. I hid my worries under carefully constructed extroverted enthusiasm, and his hid behind a thick castle wall surrounded by an alligator-filled moat. The mental image made me giggle, and Oscar pulled away and raised his eyebrows.

"Something wrong?"

"No, nothing is wrong." I wondered if I should tell him, then I realised I'd have to. Otherwise Oscar would probably think I was laughing at him rather than my ridiculous imagination. "I was just thinking how similar we are but also different. And I was thinking about how you hide your worries behind a wall... and that it was probably a castle wall surrounded by a moat filled with alligators."

"Why alligators?"

"I don't know. They seemed like the logical choice."

Oscar grinned and shook his head. "No, if I had to have amphibious guard animals, I'm choosing hippos. You don't fuck with hippos."

"Very true." I nodded sagely. "Hippos are scary as fuck. I keep thinking I'd like to see them in the wild but also not because I don't want to die."

Oscar laughed. "If you ever change your mind, let me know. I have a friend who runs a safari lodge in Botswana, and he's always saying I'm welcome to visit. He opened the place with his dad about ten years ago. It's small, local, and really embedded within the community."

"Really? That would be awesome."

"Shaun would look after us, and Botswana is not too bad for LGBTQ+ travellers. Besides, I don't think you'd be interested in spending time with anything other than your camera."

"I'd say that's not true, but it is. I've always wanted to do a safari."

"Maybe I'll have to see if I can get Marcus to swing us a trip." He grinned. "If not, we'd have to save up and pay for it like regular tourists."

"How awful!" I said, pretending to gasp. "I'd be up for that though. Most of the places I stay as a freelancer are pretty cheap. This is the nicest place I've ever been sent on a press trip."

"I'll try to get you on more. I'll tell Marcus you're the only photographer I want to work with."

"Are you going to throw a diva tantrum?" I laughed. "If so, please let me know so I can come and watch."

"More like begging and pleading and promising to do whatever it takes to get him to consider it," Oscar said with a wry smile. "But since we've done such an excellent job with this one, I'm sure he'll say yes."

There was something about the way Oscar said he wanted me with him. Like it was meant to be teasing, but it had ended up sounding sincere. And the thought that he wanted me was enough to make my heart soar.

# CHAPTER FIFTEEN

*Oscar*

UNSURPRISINGLY, it was raining when we got back to London.

It poured it down for a week, which made me want to do nothing except hole up in my tiny studio under a mountain of blankets and watch the rain out my window. Sadly, I had an article to write, and Hawaii had never felt farther away. All I could do was spend every day dreaming about the past week and hoping to capture it in prose. The only issue was that every memory, every thought, was tied to Ilias.

Ilias on the beach, peering into rock pools and lying on his stomach with his camera in hand and sand on the soles of his feet. Ilias emerging from the sea like fucking Daniel Craig only a million times more attractive with water running over his chest and plastering down his hair.

Ilias getting excited over an enormous cone of shave ice

from a street vendor in Kona or chatting to the owner of the restaurant we'd had breakfast at on our last day, the pair of them laughing together about pancake toppings and spam fritters. Ilias on the slopes of Mauna Kea in his oversized, Arctic Parka, gazing up at the stars, lost in thought.

Ilias waking up in my arms, his body pressed against mine with his face buried in my neck, smelling of peaches and vanilla and salt.

In truth, I didn't know whether these thoughts were a help or a hindrance. The article was supposed to be aimed at couples, so perhaps it wouldn't matter that every word seemed connected to Ilias. Or perhaps it would be so dreamy and nonsensical that Marcus would send the entire thing back covered in comments and tracked changes.

Or, even worse, just send a note back telling me to redo the entire thing. Usually, I was confident in my abilities as a writer, but this one had me spinning in circles.

There was a fine line between basically writing a love letter to my no-longer-fake boyfriend and writing an article people wanted to read.

Two days after I turned it in, I headed into *The Traveller*'s offices for a couple of meetings about future issues, my next project, and the draft of my article. Normally, I loved the fact that I mostly got to work from home, but it made it worse on the days when I had to go in and the weather was shit. The rain seemed to have doubled down, and it inevitably meant I arrived at the office looking like a drowned rat with wet feet.

Vanessa took pity on me when I delivered her a small bag of fridge magnets and a box of cupcakes and offered me a cup of tea and a promotional towel from an old event. Marcus was less sympathetic and asked me if I knew what an umbrella was.

"I had one," I said as I found a space at one of the hot desks in the open-plan office. "It's just pissing it down."

"I'm nearly done with your article by the way," Marcus added, disappearing back into his office. "Give me ten minutes, and I'll send it over to you."

"Is that a good sign?" I asked. "Or a bad one?"

Marcus turned in the door of his office and shot me a wry smile. I held my breath. "It's good. We'll catch up in a bit."

I flopped into the chair, feeling myself instantly relax. I opened my laptop, then pulled my phone out of my pocket. Ilias and I had spoken on and off over the past week, but it had been more sporadic than I'd intended. I'd been busy with the article, and he'd been busy editing the photos and dealing with his family.

Half our messages had been about work, and the rest had been anecdotes about our days. I missed the conversation and the casual intimacy we'd had in Hawaii—like falling asleep with him next to me or joking about whatever we happened to be doing.

I knew I should've suggested we meet up and work together, but it hadn't crossed my mind, and I hated how quickly I'd slipped back into work mode without considering anything else.

OSCAR *Good news. I don't think I totally fucked up the article.*
ILIAS *Success! Did you get it back then?*

OSCAR *Not yet, but Marcus said it's good, and he'd tell me if it was shit.*

ILIAS *Does this mean we're going on another trip? I'm sick of this fucking rain already.*

OSCAR *I'll ask!*

I stared at the screen, my thumbs hovering over the keyboard as I debated asking my next question. It shouldn't have been a big deal because we were *supposed* to be doing this dating thing for real, but my heart was thundering in my chest so loudly I was surprised nobody had noticed. Why had coming home made everything different?

Then another message popped up, and Ilias asked the question for me.

ILIAS *We should celebrate you not fucking up. What are you doing tonight? Want to get dinner?*

OSCAR *Sure. That sounds great. Where do you want to go?*

ILIAS *I don't mind. Surprise me!*

I thought for a second before the perfect place suddenly popped into my head. We quickly made some arrangements until I noticed an email from Marcus had arrived in my inbox with the draft of my article attached. I steeled myself and clicked it open.

Marcus had just left a brief note in the email saying I'd done a good job and there were only some minor corrections for me to deal with.

I let out a sigh of relief and quickly opened the document to work through the edits. It was mostly just spelling and grammar because my comma usage was horrible and a couple of corrections to my language where my phrasing was clunky or something wasn't quite clear.

"Oscar, are you free?" Marcus asked from the door of his office as I finished correcting my final paragraph.

"Sure." I hit Save and headed for his office, my shoes squeaking on the polished floor. I felt better than I had that morning, a new lightness in my chest knowing I'd done a good job. Marcus waved at the chair opposite his desk for me to sit down, taking his own seat and picking up his enormous mug of coffee. He grinned at me over the rim.

"So, how was the trip?"

"It was great. Hotel was lovely, the location was perfect, the food was amazing, and they put a great itinerary together for us."

"I guessed," Marcus said. "The article made it sound ideal." I nodded, a little confused about why he'd asked. Then it clicked into place when he asked his next question. "Did Ilias like it? Did you enjoy getting to spend some time together?"

"Are you asking me to spill details about my relationship?" I raised an eyebrow but grinned. Marcus was my boss, but I considered us friends too. "He did enjoy it. He got super excited about everything. I think he filled about three memory cards with photos. And he's great at finding all these local places tourists don't usually find. He just asks everyone where they'd recommend, what things we needed to do, things like that... but he asks in this way that's not demanding? More like he just wants to know what they think and what they love most about where they live. He wants real experiences, not ones curated for tourists. He doesn't judge what a bar or a restaurant looks like from the outside, and he finds all these hidden gems you'd never have known existed if you didn't ask."

Marcus smiled at me and nodded. "The perfect person to travel with."

"Yeah," I said. "He is. We… we get on really well, even though we're different."

"I'd hope you would if you're together."

"I mean…" I tried to think and cover my tracks, wondering if I'd suddenly exposed myself. "Some couples get on really well at home but hate travelling together. They have different ideas about what they want, they like different things, they fight all the time. I think travelling together can be a big test."

"It is. No question about it," Marcus said. "The first time Annie and I went abroad together, we went to Rome on a city break, and our luggage didn't arrive with us, so we had to spend the first day trying to buy clothes. Then I got us totally lost on the way to the Colosseum, and we ended up having a screaming match in the middle of the street where she called me a fucking asshole. Which had a grain of truth to it at the time."

"And now you've been married what, six years?"

"Yeah." He grinned. "It was the worst fucking trip of my life, and I genuinely thought she was going to dump me as soon as we got back. But we made it through. Turned out getting lost worked out well for us. We found this tiny gelato shop and ended up sitting outside eating mountains of the stuff and talking everything through. We found the

Colosseum eventually and ended up joining a tour we hadn't paid for. The guide didn't even notice." He chuckled. "I learnt a lot though, and afterwards, we got pizza squares and ended up walking back through Rome at midnight. It was one of those perfect moments you never see coming."

"That sounds amazing." I thought about Ilias and I sitting on our little patio after we'd gotten back from Manua Kea, drinking hot chocolate and eating cookies, not really talking about much but not wanting to be anywhere else.

Like Marcus had said, it was one of those perfect moments I'd never seen coming.

"It was, and it wasn't. But I'm glad you had better luck than I did with your first trip," he said before taking a long swig of his coffee, then frowning when he realised it was empty. I knew in five minutes he'd have another one because caffeine didn't seem to affect Marcus the way it did most people. "So, would you be happy to do another trip together?"

"Already?" I knew I sounded stunned, and Marcus laughed.

"I thought you said you liked travelling with him."

"I do, I just didn't think you'd be up for sending us together again so soon," I said. "I thought I might have to... I don't know, beg or something."

Marcus snorted. "Nah, no begging required. We're doing a feature for the July issue on ten of Britain's best seaside hotels. The list has already been narrowed down, but they need reviewing. We've got a load of PR photos, but

I'm happy for you to take Ilias and get some realistic ones we can use for padding. It'll be quite intense. Three weeks and fifteen hotels all over the place. We've tried to organise them in a rough order so you don't have to backtrack too much, but it depended on the dates places had available. Do you have a car, or do we need to get you a hire?"

"I'd need a car," I said. "I don't have much use for one of my own."

"Makes sense." Marcus scribbled something down in a notebook while I tried not to let my head spin. I didn't mind taking on another assignment so quickly—it was all part of the job—but taking Ilias with me was an unexpected twist.

We'd managed to make it to Hawaii and back intact, but being trapped in a car together for long periods would be totally different.

"That all sounds good though?" Marcus asked. "Happy with that?"

"Of course," I said because I couldn't exactly turn him down. "Sounds like fun."

"Weather might be a bit rubbish." Marcus glanced out the window at the pouring rain. "But I'm sure you'll manage."

"We'll be fine."

"Great. I'll get Vanessa to send you the details, but I believe the first one is down in Cornwall next Thursday. We'll catch up before you go. In the meantime, can you make sure you get the Hawaii article finished and submit your pitches for the next locations. We want another three if possible—at least one European, one in Asia, and one of your choice." Marcus continued to rattle off details about things he needed me to do in the next few days, but I was only half listening.

I was thinking about the fact that I was going to be spending the next three weeks with Ilias while my stomach squirmed.

# CHAPTER SIXTEEN

*Ilias*

"ILIAS! CAN YOU GIVE ME A HAND?" Dominic's voice blasted through the house, and I wondered whether my brother had ever considered a career as a drill sergeant. He certainly had the attitude of one.

"Ilias!"

"I'm coming," I said as I pulled open the bedroom door, still buttoning my shirt with one hand. I was supposed to be having dinner with Oscar that evening, and if my brother put a spanner in those plans, I was not going to be impressed.

He'd be coming home to a shark in his fucking bathtub, then he could explain to Teddy why he couldn't keep it as a pet. I wasn't sure where I'd get a shark, but I could improvise. I stuck my head around the living room door, trying to keep my irritability in check.

"What?"

"Here," Dominic said, handing me one of the twins, Sam. "Can you just hold him for a second while I sort Matti. We've had an explosion. And keep an eye on Nico."

I wrinkled my nose, grateful I didn't have to deal with that. Sam tugged at the collar of my shirt and tried to stick a wet, sticky finger in my ear, which I ignored. Nico was lying on the floor in a pair of Star Wars pyjamas, playing with a wooden set of trains, not unlike the kind I'd had as a kid.

"You okay, buddy?" I asked, walking over to him and bouncing Sam on my hip, who was now sucking on his own hand. Presumably so he could stick it back in my ear.

"Yeah," Nico said, not looking up from his collection of trains. I noticed he'd connected several of them together using the magnets on the ends of each piece.

"You making a giant train?"

"Yeah." Nico looked up at me and grinned. "Wanna see if it falls off."

I raised an eyebrow at my nephew's attempts to facilitate a train crash, then decided I wasn't getting involved. Mostly because I had vague memories of doing something similar. Something wet and slightly slimy brushed against my cheek.

"Really, mate? Come on, I just had a shower," I said, looking at Sam who burbled happily and grinned.

"You look nice," Louisa said, appearing through the living room door. "Big evening plans?"

"Just meeting a friend for dinner."

"That sounds fun." She held out her hands and scooped Sam out of my arms. "Let me take him before he drools all over you. Nico, it's nearly bedtime. You can have fifteen more minutes, then it will be time to brush your teeth." Nico whined, and I wondered how easily he'd be torn away from his apocalyptic train visions.

"Where are you going?" Louisa continued, pivoting back to me. "Anywhere nice?"

"Er, this place Oscar recommended. Raphael's. It's a Mexican place."

"Oooh, sounds amazing. If it's good, you'll have to let me know, and I'll drag Dom. It's been ages since we went out for dinner."

"And leave me here with the hellions for the evening?" I grinned, listening to Nico make explosion sounds from behind me.

"I can ask Astrid to stay," Louisa said.

"I'd be fine. And if you come back and I've been tied to a chair and your kitchen has been ransacked, you'll know never to leave me unsupervised again."

Louisa laughed. "So this friend…"

"He's just a friend," I said, feeling a twinge of guilt about lying to her. Louisa wasn't as bad as everyone else, but if I told her, she'd probably tell Dominic, then all sorts of very unfun shenanigans would occur. What Oscar and I had was so new and fragile that I didn't want to do anything that might damage it, so I'd keep up the little white lies to my family for as long as necessary. "Someone I know from work."

Louisa hummed but didn't say anything. "Okay, well, have fun. I'll see you later."

I took the permission to escape, planted a kiss on Sam's

cheek, said goodnight to everyone, and hurried up to my room to grab the last of my stuff.

Luckily, I wasn't running too late, and it didn't take me long to grab an Uber and head towards the centre of London. When the car pulled up outside a bar, I frowned because this definitely didn't look right.

"Hey," said a familiar voice from behind me. I turned to see Oscar waiting for me, looking all sorts of handsome in a pale blue shirt and dark jacket, an umbrella tucked under his arm.

My chest lurched, the sensation catching me by surprise. It hadn't been that long since I'd last seen him, but suddenly it felt like I was a man dying of thirst who'd finally seen water for the first time in days.

"Hey," I said, swallowing hard.

"You made it okay?"

"Yeah." I glanced up at the building. There was music pouring out the door, and even from out here the lighting looked dim. "Is this really a restaurant?"

"Sort of." Oscar gave me a wry smile. "I thought it was my turn to take you somewhere secret for once."

He reached for my hand, and a bolt of lightning shot through me as our fingers connected. It sent me reeling, but there was no time for me to adjust before I found myself being led into the bar and through a maze of tables and bodies to the far side where a giant man in a dark suit was leaning against the wall.

"Oscar Moore, party of two. I booked in earlier," Oscar said. The man muttered something into an earpiece, then nodded at him, gesturing for us to go through a door I'd only just noticed.

"Oh my God," I muttered as we descended some stairs, trying to take in all the details. The decoration was currently very sparse, but in the distance, I saw more light, and there was the very faint sound of a guitar. "Are you taking me to a secret restaurant? How did I not know about this place?"

"Do you know about everywhere in London?"

"No, I guess not." I grinned at him, still holding his hand. "How do you know about it? You're not that cool."

Oscar laughed. "My brother Lewis told me. His partner Jason brought him here when they started dating, and apparently, it's something of a favourite. I'm surprised I managed to get in."

"Have you been before?"

"Only a couple of times when Lewis has been staying in London," Oscar said as the décor slowly shifted into something bright and vibrant, and the corridor began to fill with the delicious scents of cooking meats and spices. I took a deep breath and felt my stomach rumble.

"I thought it might be nice for us to come together... so we can catch up... and just, er, just enjoy ourselves."

He looked almost nervous, and I wondered why. It wasn't like this was anything different from what we'd done in Hawaii.

Except we were at home, in the real world, and that made everything we did real too. Okay, now I understood why he was nervous.

Oscar pushed the door open, unleashing the music and

the clattering of plates, and the chatter of patrons, and the sizzle of food. The restaurant wasn't large, but it had an instantly warm and welcoming vibe, and I already knew I was going to love it.

"Welcome to Raphael's," said a charming man with a lightly accented voice and salt-and-pepper hair and silver rings on his fingers. "I am Raphael, and you must be Oscar Moore and guest. Please follow me, and I'll take you to your table."

We followed him across the small room, my head constantly turning as I tried to take in all the details. But my thoughts were thrown by an unfamiliar voice calling, "Oscar?"

Oscar stopped and turned, and because I was still holding his hand, I turned too. Sitting at a nearby table, tucked into a corner just out of the way, was a slight man with bright pink hair and a beaming smile who was waving at my date frantically. Next to him were two other men, and my jaw dropped when I realised who the fuck they were.

One of them was Henry fucking Lu, superstar actor and Hollywood darling, and the other was his brother Jason, TV star turned theatre actor. What the fuck was going on?

The man with the pink hair beckoned us over, and I followed Oscar in bemusement.

"I thought it was you!" the man exclaimed excitedly. "I didn't know you were coming here tonight."

"It was a last-minute thing," Oscar said, then he glanced at me and realised I was doing my very best not to stare. "Oh, fuck. Ilias, this is my brother Lewis"—he pointed to the pink-haired man—"his partner Jason, and Jason's

brother, Henry. Everyone this is Ilias Verrati, my...
boyfriend."

Oscar looked at me with a worried expression like he
was wondering whether he'd said the right thing.

I nodded and swallowed, dialling my charm up to
eleven. I'd always found it was the best thing to do when I
was nervous.

"Boyfriend makes me sound like I'm about twelve." I
grinned. "It's lovely to meet you all."

"Fuck, are you here on a date?" Lewis asked.

Beside him Jason chuckled. "I told you not to bother
him."

"I know, but I couldn't help it," Lewis said. "Sorry, I'll
let you go."

"You can join us if you want," Henry said, giving us
both an easy smile. "I'm sure Raphael won't mind."

"Hen, they're on a date. They don't want to spend their
evening stroking your ego," Jason said as he rolled his eyes
at his brother. "Don't mind him, he's just being needy
because he got a bad review."

"Don't tell them that," Henry said. "I'll lose all my
charm and mystery."

"You never had any of that to begin with," said Jason.

I held back a nervous laugh, still slightly stunned by the
situation. Raphael appeared behind us, swooping in to
distract the party at the table to give Oscar and me a
moment to talk.

"We can get our own table," Oscar said quietly. "I'll take
the fall. This was supposed to be dinner for us, and I don't

want you to feel uncomfortable or forced into a situation you didn't want."

"Thanks." I smiled at him softly, squeezing his hand tightly. "I am tempted to say no, but on the other hand... how many chances am I going to get to have dinner with Henry Lu? Also, why the fuck didn't you tell me your brother is dating Jason Lu?" I grinned at him playfully, hoping he'd know I was teasing.

Oscar chuckled. "Honestly? Because it kind of doesn't feel like a big deal anymore. It was a bit weird at first, but now Jason is just Jason. He's a really nice guy."

"Again, that is weird as fuck, but I'll forgive you... as long as I get some food because I'm starving!"

"Okay, we'll join them. But maybe tomorrow we can have lunch? Just us. I want to see you again. And I've got a work thing to talk to you about."

"Oh?" My interest was suddenly piqued. "Where are we going now? Somewhere glamorous I hope."

"Sort of. Marcus wants us to review a load of British seaside hotels. The hotels will be nice but the weather less so."

I shrugged. "It counts."

I leant over and pressed a kiss to his cheek, breathing in the scent of Oscar that I'd missed so much over the past few days. Over his shoulder, I saw Lewis smiling as he pretended to be very interested in his drink.

Raphael was very happy to put a table together for us, summoning some black-clad waitstaff to help pull some chairs over and bring some extra glassware. The other three seemed to know him quite well and were joking and chatting with him about football, food, and Raphael's partner, Tomas, who apparently ran the bar upstairs.

I understood why they liked the restaurant because after only five minutes Raphael had made Oscar and me feel like we were at home. The restaurant had that small, vibrant feel—like it was run with love and passion and care—I craved.

I found myself seated between Oscar and Henry, listening while Raphael talked through the menu, asking the others what they'd ordered, and making recommendations. When I'd told him I was happy for him to choose what he thought was best, Raphael's face lit up like my niblings at Christmas, and he bounced off towards the kitchen like I'd just made his day.

"So, Ilias," Lewis said. He was sitting opposite me and giving me the biggest smile I'd ever seen. "What do you do?"

"I'm a freelance travel photographer and occasional writer, mostly for magazines and websites, but I sometimes do things for travel companies and hotels."

"He's amazing," Oscar said from beside me. "You should see some of the shots he took when we were in Hawaii."

"Oh my God, you have to tell me about that," Lewis said. "I'm so jealous! You go to all the best places."

"We could go if you want," Jason said, giving Lewis a fond smile that made something funny pull in my chest. It was how I felt when I looked at Oscar. "When my run comes to an end."

"Maybe... I'll need to check the diary."

"Edward won't burn Lincoln down if you take a couple weeks off," Jason said, and Lewis chewed his lip. I got the feeling I'd just walked into an ongoing conversation and was the only person at the table who didn't really understand the context.

"A holiday would do you good, Lew, and you'd love Hawaii," Oscar said. He turned to me. "Have you got any photos from Manua Kea with you? Or from Kona?"

"Just a few," I said with a wry smile. I had everything uploaded to my Dropbox, which was connected to my phone. I pulled up a folder of photos I'd edited and showed them some of my favourites like the Milky Way cutting through the dark sky, the amazing food from Nakoa's in Kona, an underwater shot of a shoal of glittering fish, and the sunrise over the trees from our last morning... the one where Oscar had kissed me.

I glanced over at Oscar while Henry and Lewis were talking to each other about one of the photos. There was a soft expression on his face that reminded me of the one Jason had given Lewis, and it made my stomach clench. I'd barely seen him that week, but it felt like no time had passed.

I reached my hand under the table and brushed my fingers against his thigh. To his credit, he didn't jump. He just looked down, and when he saw my hand, he smiled, then reached down to squeeze it.

Our food appeared a few minutes later, an epic spread of pork belly carnitas tacos, baja fish tacos, mole fries, and a big plate of carne asada with drunken black beans, blue corn tortillas, and a bright, sharp chimichurri that hummed on my tongue. Raphael had said it wasn't quite authentic, but it was something one of their chefs had made one night with some leftovers and he couldn't resist sharing it with everyone because it was so good. I had to agree and made a mental note to come back here as many times as possible.

The conversation eased into subjects like work and life and travel, including an in-depth discussion of bucket-list destinations. It surprised me how easy Henry and Jason were to talk to because there was always that myth of the superstar.

Jason was funny and down to earth, and I could see why Oscar had said he was just another guy. Henry seemed to have boundless energy and a touch of ego, but it was tempered by good humour and an endless ability to laugh at himself. It felt very different than dinner with my family.

"So, where are you off to next?" Lewis asked as we finished off the last of the food. I wondered if I'd still have room for pudding. "Are you off to review somewhere else for your queer couples feature?"

"Not yet," Oscar said. "I need to pitch the rest of the destinations by Friday. Then next week, we're off to Cornwall." He gave me a slightly sheepish smile. "Sorry, you don't know many of these details yet. It was only finalised this afternoon."

"You don't have to tell us then," Jason said. "Wait until you get back."

"When are you back?" Lewis asked, frowning.

"Why?"

"Because it's Mimbles's sixtieth at the start of May, remember? I know she said she didn't want a fuss, but we thought we'd do a small family party or something. Leo's brother co-owns a restaurant near Nottingham, and they have a separate dining room for functions and parties. I already spoke to someone there and booked it for Sunday lunch. They're going to do us a cake as well. I put the details in the group chat a couple of weeks ago."

Beside me Oscar froze, and I got the feeling he'd totally forgotten it.

"Er, yeah. I remember," he said quickly, reaching for his drink.

"Liar," Lewis said with a grin. "You forgot all about it. Don't worry, I won't tell your own mother you forgot her sixtieth birthday. Seriously, it's fine. I'll send you all the details. Just come for lunch, and all will be forgiven. Oh, and bring Ilias. Everyone would love to meet him."

I stared as four pairs of eyes turned on me. Bollocks. Oscar and I had only just started this thing, and now I was expected to meet his family. I felt panic welling up inside my chest, and I looked at Oscar, hoping he'd see the fear in my eyes. I knew it wasn't rational, but I wasn't ready for this. I'd never done a family event with a boyfriend before, and it felt like there was a crushing weight on my chest.

"We'll come," Oscar said. "On one condition—you don't tell anyone we're dating. This is all very new, and we're not even sure where this is going. I don't want anyone to put pressure on us."

Lewis opened his mouth, then closed it and shrugged. "That's fair." Then he chuckled. "Nobody in our family is ever open about their relationships, are they?"

I got the feeling there was a story there, and it was a nice distraction. "What do you mean?"

"Well," Oscar said, seizing on the new topic and running with it. "Lewis hid Jason from us for what, six months?"

"I didn't hide him! I just... didn't want you to know..." Lewis flushed the same pink as his hair, and Jason leant over and kissed his temple. "At least I wasn't Eli... I didn't get punched in the face when I brought my boyfriend home."

I snorted. "Was that the one you told me about? No, wait I think that was the pasta salad lady."

"Oh my God! He told you about pasta salad lady?" Lewis asked. "He really does like you."

"Wait a minute. We were talking about you, not me," Oscar said, and the two of them descended into friendly bickering. A new warmth flickered inside my heart as I watched Oscar.

I couldn't believe how quickly he'd stepped in to change the subject, to make sure I was comfortable. Heat pooled in my gut, and I reached out to rest my hand on Oscar's thigh.

He placed his hand on top of mine, letting it rest there.

# CHAPTER SEVENTEEN

*Oscar*

RAIN SPLATTERED the bedroom window as thick, grey storm clouds gathered across the sea, the wind whipping the waves into stiff peaks. Marcus had been right that the weather wouldn't be the best, and it seemed as if the cliché about April showers was going to hold out for the rest of the week.

Not that a little rain was going to stop me from enjoying our brief sojourn along the south coast.

"I'm guessing we won't be taking that walk into town this afternoon, then?" asked Ilias. He was lounging on the beautiful four-poster bed in the sea-view room we'd been offered at August House, the hotel in Fowey that was our stopping point for the night.

He looked so effortlessly handsome like that—propped up on some pillows, flicking through something on his phone, his jeans hugging his thighs. I wasn't sure when I'd started to truly appreciate how physically gorgeous Ilias was, but now that I had I could hardly tear my eyes away.

"Probably not. Unless you want to get wet," I said, glancing back out the window in the hope of seeing a strip of clear sky on the horizon, but nothing had changed. "They have offered us afternoon tea if you feel like dragging yourself downstairs."

"Done." Ilias grinned at me and wiggled off the bed. "Do I need to change?"

"No... I think you look great." He was still wearing the hoodie he'd travelled down in, but I didn't think the hotel had a dress code for the lounge.

"You're sweet, but on second thought, I probably need to put on something clean." He glanced down at himself, pulling out the hem of the hoodie to examine something. "I think I dropped cream cheese on myself earlier."

"I can't see anything."

"There's a little white stain here," Ilias said, pointing at a mark on the large, pouch-style pocket on the front. "It's okay. I've got a clean shirt in my suitcase."

He tugged the hoodie over his head, taking his t-shirt with it, leaving him standing half-naked in the middle of the room. I swallowed, suddenly tempted to reach out and run my fingers across his bronzed skin. I'd seen Ilias shirtless in Hawaii—in fact it was how he'd spent half his time —so I wasn't sure why this was so different. It just was.

A new heat blossomed inside me, a pang of desire echoing through my body. New but not unwelcome.

"You okay?" Ilias asked, and I realised I'd been staring off into space. I blinked. Ilias was crouched on the floor, rummaging around in his suitcase.

"Yeah. Fine."

He raised an eyebrow and hummed but didn't say anything. He'd started to be able to read me, and that surprised me because I'd never had anyone get that close before. Not even people I thought I might have been in love with.

The only other person who knew me as well was Finn, and that was because I'd never been able to hide anything from him. He'd always had this uncanny ability to read me like a book. It was something Finn could do with our whole family.

Ilias pulled a white shirt out of his suitcase and slung it on, buttoning it part of the way up. It had a deep collar anyway, and with Ilias leaving a button or two undone, I could see more of his perfect chest.

He caught me watching and winked. "Like what you see?"

"Yes..." I said quietly, throwing Ilias off guard for a second because I'd never responded like that to his ridiculous flirting.

"That's new." He grinned and walked over to me, putting his hand around my waist. "I like it. Do you?"

"Yeah. I do." I tilted my head and kissed him, reacquainting myself with the curves of his mouth. Fuck, I loved kissing him. I hadn't gotten to do it nearly enough in Hawaii and definitely not enough since we got back.

I'd stolen some brief kisses after dinner last week and when we'd met for lunch, but I wished I'd invited Ilias over so we could have spent hours on my bed just doing this.

Ilias still smelt like peaches and vanilla, and it was starting to get addictive.

We broke apart slowly, and Ilias's other hand reached out to cup my jaw. "I missed kissing you," he said. "You have the best mouth."

"And you've only seen a fraction of what it can do," I teased.

Ilias's smile widened, and there was a hungry look in his eye. His touch was still gentle though.

"Now I'm even more intrigued." He leant forward to kiss me again, drawing me to him with his fingers. "We should go downstairs," he said as he pulled away. "I don't want to waste our afternoon tea or get us put on the naughty list for missing a reservation."

I sighed, knowing he was right. Whatever I wanted had to come second to my job, at least for the moment.

Ilias grabbed the key card off the desk where he'd left it and reached for my hand. "Come on, I feel like we need to have a conversation, and what better way to have it than over copious amounts of food."

I chuckled but followed him out of the room and down the corridor, taking everything in as I did.

The hotel had originally been built as a family mansion in the late nineteenth century by a local resident who'd made his fortune in Canada via the lumber trade, and after changing hands a couple of times in the fifties and sixties, it had eventually been bought and converted into a luxury hotel about twenty years ago.

According to the information we'd been sent, the current owners had done a lot of restoration work and returned a lot of their rooms to their original usages. And although I could see the odd bit of wear and tear—mostly because I was looking for it—it seemed to have been beautifully maintained.

When we got downstairs and finally managed to navigate to the right place, we found ourselves sitting in a corner of the library next to a window that overlooked the gardens and down to the estuary. It was still pouring with rain, but the room was warm and cosily lit with squishy armchairs. I sank straight into mine and wondered if I'd ever be able to get up.

A smiling member of staff brought over a tea menu and poured us a couple of glasses of champagne while we made our decisions, then disappeared once we'd chosen, promising that our drinks and food would be over shortly.

"A tea menu?" Ilias said, raising an eyebrow accompanied by a wry smile. "I've definitely not been to fancy enough afternoon teas if I get a whole menu of teas to choose from. Mind you, that might be because I'm more of a coffee person."

I chuckled and reached for my glass. "And here I thought the fanciest thing about this afternoon was the champagne."

"It's definitely more my style." Ilias winked, and my heart skipped. He picked up his own glass and took a sip, settling back in his chair and looking at me with interested eyes.

"So… when you said you liked what you saw—and I mean who can blame you—" I snorted, and Ilias ignored me. "What did you mean by that?"

"I've always thought you were attractive," I said. "You know that."

He shrugged. "I know, but you've never said it like that. And you've certainly never responded to me with anything other than an eye roll or snark."

I opened my mouth to disagree, then realised he had a point. I took another sip of my champagne and glanced out the window at the rain. This was a world away from our first conversation about what I wanted, but it made me smile as I realised how many of our most heartfelt and intimate discussions seemed to take place over food: our first lunch in London, lunch at Nakoa's, dinner on the beach…

Maybe food somehow made it easier to be open with him because the meal provided some form of distraction.

The waitress appeared with a large tray laden with two tea sets and some plates, carefully unloading everything onto the table while another member of staff appeared beside her carrying an enormous, three-tiered cake stand.

It was laden with neat finger sandwiches, little pastries in sweet and savoury, delicate choux buns with chocolate curls balanced delicately on the top, perfect miniature cakes, and several enormous, fluffy scones that were perfectly golden and studded with fruit. There were little dishes filled with thick clotted cream and three varieties of jam.

I really hoped we weren't going to be expected to have dinner any time soon because there was only a five percent chance I was going to want anything more than some toast.

I reached for a couple of sandwiches, trying to think about where my train of thought was supposed to have been going.

"Like I said before, I've always thought you were attractive. But I guess it was more objective? Like I was looking at a picture or a painting or a model? I don't know if that's really the best analogy." I took a bite of one of the sandwiches and chewed. Across from me, Ilias was pouring himself some tea but not saying anything like he was happy to wait for me to continue on my own time.

"But recently, or I guess today... something felt different. I like you, Ilias. I really do... You make me feel like I can be myself around you, even when I'm stressed and grumpy because you just take it all in stride and tell me to calm down. I missed you so much during the week, and I kept thinking I should invite you over, but I was so scared that what I'd felt... what we'd said in Hawaii was just a fluke but, now... now I know it's not, and I'm starting to feel like I want more."

"I missed you too," Ilias said, piling his plate with sandwiches. "You could have just messaged me or called. But I know what you mean. This is different for both of us, I guess, and that takes some getting used to. And I'm just as guilty. I could have said something too."

"We're a right pair." I snorted. "Was your week that bad?"

"No, mostly just being piled on by niblings." He smiled

at me. The smile had a hungry edge that seemed to have nothing to do with the sandwiches. "So, what does more look like to you?"

"I'm not sure that's a conversation we should have in public," I said, my voice low and teasing, and Ilias's eyes widened almost comically.

"Now we definitely have to have this conversation. You'll just have to whisper."

"Fine. I want to lay you out and kiss you until you can't remember your own name. I want to explore every inch of your body with my fingers and my mouth, find every little spot that makes you moan, every spot that makes you desperate, every spot that makes you beg." I spoke quietly, barely above a whisper, but I knew Ilias had heard every word from the way he was staring at me.

"I want to go so slowly that it almost feels like torture, but you never want me to stop. I want to know what it feels like to have your hands all over me, your mouth wrapped around my cock. I want to lose myself in your kisses, your touch, and every breath you take. I don't know if I want to fuck tonight—I'm not sure I'm ready for penetrative sex yet —but I'm sure I can think of enough other things for us to do."

Ilias's mouth was hanging slightly open, his food forgotten. He blinked at me, and I wasn't sure if I'd stunned him into silence or scared him.

"Motherfucker," Ilias hissed. "I take it back. We shouldn't have been having this conversation in public! Now we're going to talk about something really fucking boring until I can get up again."

It took me a second to process what he'd said, then I burst out laughing, the sound bouncing around the walls of the library and drawing a couple of disgruntled looks from our fellow guests.

"Are you that desperate?" I asked.

"For you? Yes."

# CHAPTER EIGHTEEN

*Ilias*

OSCAR WAS DEFINITELY TRYING to kill me in cold blood. Or maybe it was hot blood, considering the subject. But either way, he was ruthlessly mean and teasing, and I loved every second of it.

Trying to focus on afternoon tea was really fucking hard when I was… really fucking hard. I was half tempted to ask the staff to box the food up so we could take it upstairs and enjoy it after I'd stripped Oscar down and spent the rest of the afternoon dissolving him into a puddle of goo.

But unfortunately, this was a work thing, and while Oscar could easily write a short review of the hotel without experiencing every single aspect, we were still representing *The Traveller*, and the weight attached to that name was so heavy it could easily drown us.

"I have a question," I said as I reached for one of the

enormous, fluffy scones on the top of the cake stand. I was hoping a change of subject would help divert my train of thought. "Do you have particular ratings standards you have to stick to when you review places? Certain things you have to look for? Is there a secret list of *Traveller* dos and don'ts?"

Oscar nodded as he took a tiny patisserie piece made of meringue and cream off the stand. I tried not to watch him lick cream off his fingers.

"We do have things we look for, and we're supposed to try to stay impartial and not let our own feelings get in the way of things. Like if a hotel has a great restaurant but it mostly serves fish and seafood, and that's not your sort of thing, you have to try to review it from the point of view of a guest... and obviously, Marcus, or whoever, isn't going to expect someone to review a seafood restaurant if you're allergic, but you get the idea.

"We're looking at the whole package and how it feels as a guest. We don't have a tick-box list or anything, and we're slightly less rigid than something like an international hotel review guide, but there are standards places have to meet—mostly borne out of the fact that *The Traveller* is a luxury travel magazine, so places have to meet certain requirements for our readers."

"Couldn't suggest anyone stay somewhere less than four stars," I said with a wry smile. "How would they cope?"

Oscar snorted. "Perish the thought! Although, we have actually recommended hostels and small budget hotels. Things don't have to cost a fortune to be nice."

"Then how come I always end up staying in the really shit ones?"

"That's all on you." Oscar laughed. "Don't you research places?"

"Mostly." I shrugged and pulled my scone apart before reaching for the dish of clotted cream. "But sometimes it's fun to say fuck it and just book somewhere random. I wouldn't always recommend it, but I've stayed in some interesting places."

"Like?"

I thought for a second. "The love hotel in Tokyo was an interesting one. I mean it was very clean and pretty comfortable, but I hadn't anticipated the amount of porn on offer. Or the amount of neon."

"Seriously? I feel like it had to have been a lot of porn to surprise you," Oscar said with a raised eyebrow and a mischievous grin. It was the sort of grin that did funny things to my insides.

"Rude! But accurate." I reached for the raspberry jam and began to pile mountains of cream and jam onto my scone. "Another interesting one was this little hotel I stayed at in Berlin. It was down a slightly dodgy-looking alley, and I had no fucking clue where I was—turned out I'd used completely the wrong entrance. The place was a little run-down and there were some weird stains in the shower, but the interesting part was realising the bar was full of a group of German leather daddies on tour. Really funny guys and pretty cool to talk to. They taught me how to talk dirty in German."

Oscar was staring at me, then he burst out laughing.

"You know, I'm really not surprised. Do you remember any of it?"

"No, sadly not." I shook my head. "I got quite drunk to be honest. But I do follow a couple of them on Instagram, and one of them still sends me a Christmas card from him and his husband every year. They keep trying to get me to visit them in Frankfurt for the Christmas market. I should really try to go."

I shoved half my scone into my mouth, realising too late that it was too big and now I had cream and jam all over my face. If I'd been going for sexy, I'd failed miserably. Oscar handed me a napkin, giving me an amused look.

"That isn't the sort of white stuff I'd envisioned seeing on your face," he said. I'd have snorted with laughter if I wasn't suddenly staring at him while trying to chew frantically. "But it is good to know that if we fill your mouth enough, you're quiet."

"You know," I said, finally swallowing, "I'm not sure whether to be impressed or horrified or turned on at that utter cheese. Gotta be honest, I think it's a little of all three."

Oscar laughed. "I'm glad I amuse you."

"You are actually quite funny when you're not grumpy or acting like you have a stick up your butt." I wiped the cream and jam off my face.

"I'd argue with you, but even I know it's true."

"I like your grumpy side though," I said, reaching my hand across the low table to brush against his. "It's cute."

"Not sure I like being cute."

"Shut up and take the compliment." I threw the napkin

at him, and Oscar caught it, giving me one of his rare, warm smiles I'd come to crave.

The ones that felt like they were just for me.

Later, after we'd finished afternoon tea and pottered around the grounds under an enormous golf umbrella we'd borrowed from reception, Oscar and I found ourselves back in our room.

The rain that had slowly eased off over the course of the afternoon had suddenly returned with a vengeance, accompanied by a wild wind that rattled the windows and whipped the late-spring blossoms off the trees.

Our bedroom didn't have a fireplace, which I was grateful for because the last thing I wanted was the wind howling down the chimney while I was trying to seduce my man.

Not that I really had to do much seducing.

Ever since our earlier conversation, there had been a palpable tension between us. Both of us had tried to divert it with conversations about work, or food, or the merits of David Bowie, but none of them had worked. I had already decided that unless he asked for something different, I was going to let Oscar take charge.

He knew his body, his desires, and his limits better than anyone, and it would be better for him to communicate what he wanted rather than me trying to guess.

Oscar was lying on the bed next to me, looking perfectly relaxed and oh-so gorgeous. My heart was racing, and I was trying to pretend I didn't want to jump his bones more and more with every passing second. I'd been with guys who had wanted to take it slow before but not for a while.

Recently, my romantic trysts had amounted to nothing more than a couple of gratuitous fucks with whoever was interested, and although they'd been satisfying and fun, they were a world away from what I was doing with Oscar. And that wasn't a bad thing. It was just different.

But deep down, the part of me that craved soft touches and romantic gestures… the part of me that wanted to feel loved again… was rapidly escaping any and all chains I'd weighted it down with and was rising to the surface of my consciousness.

"What are you thinking?" Oscar asked.

"Not much," I said because now wasn't the best time to tell him about my past flings. He knew enough about them already. "Just about how handsome you are… and how much I want to kiss you again."

"I'm sure I can help with that." Oscar reached out with one hand and cupped my jaw, drawing me towards him. My body moved instinctively until we were pressed together, my hand gripping the front of his shirt as our lips met in a deep kiss.

This time there was no initial softness; there was just heat and want. Oscar's tongue caressed the seam of my lips, and I moaned as they parted to allow him access. There was a natural power in his touch that sent shivers down my spine. Oscar's hand trailed down my neck to my chest, gently rolling me onto my back. I pulled him on top of me, spreading my legs around him and silently cursing the tightness of my jeans.

Oscar nipped at my lip, and I gasped, need bubbling under my skin. He followed it up with another kiss that had me melting into the bed. My cock throbbed in my jeans, pressing against the stiff material. I shifted my hips, trying to find some relief and moaned as my erection brushed against Oscar's.

"Fuck," I said, pulling back. My heart was already racing, my chest rising and falling faster than it should. I didn't know how Oscar had managed to undo me so quickly, but it was both delicious and unnerving.

Maybe it was because I'd wanted this for so long, or maybe it was because there were other feelings involved, not just my desire to get off as fast and filthily as possible.

"You okay?" Oscar asked as he looked down at me, his eyes searching my face like he was looking for something to be concerned about.

"Yeah." I grinned and tugged his mouth back to mine. "Don't ask ridiculous questions."

"It's not ridiculous. I want to know that you're enjoying yourself."

"Yes. The answer is yes," I said. "Less talking, more kissing."

The sound of Oscar's laughter vibrated through his touch as he kissed me. Fuck, we were wearing too many clothes. I wanted to be naked. Now. Or at least released from the confines of my fucking jeans!

Oscar had said he wasn't ready for penetrative sex, and that was absolutely fine with me, but I was really, *really* hoping our epic make-out session ended in orgasms because I was a greedy, needy man who wanted to know exactly what Oscar looked like when he came.

I groaned as Oscar moved his mouth down my neck, pressing hot, open-mouthed kisses to the sensitive skin.

"You should unbutton your shirt," he said when he reached my collar, looking up at me with eyes full of heat.

"You could do it," I said teasingly.

Oscar tilted his head in acknowledgement, his lips curling into a wry smile. "Okay. I will." He knelt up and leant over me, running his fingers slowly down my body until he reached the bottom of my shirt. He popped the buttons open easily and flicked the sides of the shirt wide. "Much better."

"Do I get to see you do the same?"

"I suppose." He smirked and reached for the buttons on his own shirt. "It's only fair." As he slowly stripped off his shirt, I wiggled out of mine and tossed it onto the floor, not taking my eyes off the miles of golden-brown skin that were being exposed. I wanted to run my tongue down his chest and see what happened when I sucked on the dark nubs of his nipples.

"What about my jeans?" I asked, pointing casually to my bulge in the hope that Oscar would take pity on me and give me an excuse to get naked. "Can I take those off too?"

"No. Not yet." He stretched out over me, his lips millimetres from mine. "I want to explore first."

"But—but… that's not fair!"

"Don't pout, baby," he said. "I promise to make you feel good."

I opened my mouth to fire off some witty rejoinder, but

nothing came out except another moan as Oscar trailed his lips across my chest and flicked my nipple with his tongue, his eyes locked on mine.

There was something about the way Oscar was lavishing me with attention that unleashed a hurricane of fiery butterflies in my stomach. Usually, my partners and I had an unspoken agreement motivated by selfishness that we'd make the other person feel good under the understanding that they'd reciprocate. It was all about getting ourselves off and our own pleasure.

But with Oscar... I got the feeling he wanted to make me feel good purely for the enjoyment of it. And that was weird. Because I hadn't experienced anything so selfless in a long time.

"You okay?" Oscar asked, pulling back and frowning at me.

"Yeah, I'm good."

"Are you sure? You seemed to drift off on me."

I shook my head. "It's not you. It's me actually. I, er, I can't remember the last time someone wanted to take care of me the way you do."

I felt my skin heat and knew the blush must be spreading down my chest. I hated being so open and vulnerable, but Oscar had made me promise I'd talk to him whenever I was freaking out. And I would. Even if I wouldn't go so far as to say I was freaking out... yet.

"It's laughable really," I said, trying to resist the urge to bury my face in the pillow beside me. "I mean, we've barely done more than kiss, but... but everything feels different to me."

"Different good or different bad?"

"Different good. Just... strange. Like you don't expect anything from me. Like you're doing this"—I gestured to my chest—"because you want to, not because you think you have to if you want me to do the same."

Oscar's frown deepened. "I'd never expect you to do that. Do most men?"

I shrugged. "I don't know. Maybe? But I mean, when I have sex with guys, I want them to enjoy it too. I'd be an ass if I didn't."

"Okay. But do you want them to enjoy it for selfless reasons or because you don't want them to think you're shit in bed? Or a selfish dick?" There was a smile playing at the corners of his mouth now. "Or because you don't want them to leave you hanging because you didn't get them off?"

"Probably the second—the selfish dick left hanging," I said, then sighed. "Sorry, I'm fucking this up. God, I'm so in my fucking head."

Oscar leant forward and pressed a kiss to my temple. "It's okay, I promise. You're not fucking this up."

"Feels like it," I muttered. I usually used sex to get out of my head, not to get further in it. Oscar kissed my nose, then my mouth.

"You're not. Do you want to stop?"

"Fuck no. I think I might explode if you do."

"Okay," Oscar said. "No stopping. Do you want me to keep going? Or do you want to do something different?"

I thought for a second, wondering what something different might mean. I was tempted. But I also wanted to see what Oscar would do if he kept going. "You can keep going."

"Good." He kissed me again, sliding his tongue into my mouth. He began to work his way down my body again, worshipping every inch of skin. It was a heady experience.

I'd never been worshipped before.

I groaned as he flicked and sucked my nipples, pulling them between his teeth until I gasped before moving farther down my chest. His fingers teased the waistband of my jeans, and I bucked up into his touch. Oscar didn't say anything. He just smirked as he flicked open the top button.

"Fuck yes," I said. "Whatever you're thinking of doing, please do it. Unless you're thinking about stopping, then don't."

"I wasn't planning to," Oscar said, his voice as soft as silk. He popped open all the buttons on my fly, then sat back so he could tug my jeans over my hips, leaving me in nothing but my skin-tight boxers that clung to my cock.

Oscar had seen me in a similar amount of clothing in Hawaii, but this felt so much more intimate. He threw my jeans onto the floor and traced his finger over my engorged dick. I let out a little whine, desperate for more.

Oscar slid down the bed so he could stretch out in front of me, his mouth inches away from my cock.

"I'm not above begging," I said, half in jest and half deadly serious. "Just so you're aware."

"If I wanted you to beg, you'd be doing it by now."

I moaned, and my cock jumped. "You can't say shit like that."

"Why not?"

I couldn't give him a reason.

Oscar grinned and pressed wet, open-mouthed kisses along my cock, soaking my boxers and making them cling even tighter. My dick was practically visible through the dark material. I spread my legs wider. I knew I wouldn't get more than Oscar offered, but the movement allowed me to get my feet flat on the bed, which meant I could casually push my hips upward, silently begging for more.

"Do you want something?" Oscar asked, raising an eyebrow.

"Yes. I thought that was obvious," I said. I'd tried to go for teasing, but my voice came out shaking and desperate.

"I promised to make you feel good. Do you trust me to do that?"

The question caught me off guard. I nodded. "Yes... I do."

"Good. Then let me take care of you. In my own time. I promise it will be worth it."

I wanted to argue that promises weren't really worth that much, all things considered, but that felt pointless. Especially when Oscar pressed another kiss to my aching cock, then reached for the waistband of my boxers.

I lifted my hips so he could pull them off, letting my cock spring free. Oscar hummed appreciatively, his eyes roaming over my body like he was trying to commit the sight to memory.

"You're gorgeous," he said quietly. "Did you know that? I could look at you for hours and never be bored." He smiled and looked away for a second. "That probably sounds creepy. Sorry."

"No… it's not." I sat up, scooting closer to him so I could draw him in for a kiss. I didn't know how to tell him that his words made me feel cherished in a way I'd never experienced. "You're very welcome to stare as much as you want. I can take some pictures too if you'd like." I winked, and Oscar chuckled.

"Don't tempt me." Oh, I was one hundred percent going to take some very sexy pictures next time I had a free hour and the house to myself. If only to make Oscar blush. He put his hand on my chest and pushed me back onto the bed. "Now, stop distracting me. I want to suck your cock."

I groaned, flopping back onto the pillows and grinning up at him. "Got it. No more distractions."

Oscar rolled his eyes, but he was smiling fondly at me. While I watched, he unbuckled his belt and unbuttoned his jeans, discarding them and leaving him in only a pair of olive-green boxer briefs that perfectly highlighted his cock.

After he was finished playing with me, I needed to get my greedy hands on him because I wasn't leaving here without making him feel good, and this time it would be for purely altruistic reasons. Mostly.

I still needed to know what Oscar looked like when he came.

But any more thoughts I had were driven from my mind when Oscar wrapped his fingers around my shaft and slowly flicked his tongue over the sensitive, wet head.

"Fuck!" I gasped as Oscar began to use his tongue to explore my cock like he was trying to map the damn thing out.

I moaned and bucked my hips as Oscar's fingers

caressed my balls, then swore again as he wrapped his lips around the head and sucked me slowly into his mouth. Jesus fucking Christ, he was going to ruin me. And I was happy to let him.

Another moan slipped from my lips as Oscar sucked me deeper into his mouth, and I gripped the sheets to stop myself from thrusting my cock into his throat. His other hand wrapped around my slick shaft as he worked my cock faster and faster, wet, sloppy, sucking sounds filling the room.

Heat simmered under my skin like my blood had turned to liquid fire. I already felt the familiar pressure building in the base of my spine, tightening my balls as my orgasm threatened to overwhelm me.

"O-Oscar," I said, reaching for his head. He looked up at me, his slick, swollen lips wrapped around my cock and his eyes shining with desire. "I'm... I'm getting close."

Oscar just winked at me and hummed his approval, sliding his tongue up the underside of my dick and pumping me hard. I came with a broken curse as I emptied myself down his throat, my pulse thundering so loudly I heard it in my ears. Oscar pulled off with a wet pop, licking his lips as a crease appeared between his eyebrows.

"Something wrong?" I asked, trying not to sound like I hadn't just run the London Marathon.

"No," Oscar said. "I'd just forgotten how weird cum tastes. It's actually kind of disgusting."

I stared at him for a second, then laughed so loudly I surprised myself. "I'm going to pretend I'm not hideously insulted."

"It's not just yours if it helps. All cum is disgusting."

"Then why did you swallow it? You didn't have to."

Oscar shrugged. "I don't know. I thought maybe that whole absence makes the heart grow fonder shit might be real." He grinned. "But mostly it was that I'd forgotten how much I don't like it. It's… been a while."

I shook my head and sat up, pulling him into my arms for a kiss. "You never, ever have to swallow if you don't like it. Just pull off, and I'll come on myself, or in your hand, or on your body, or wherever you want."

"Okay," Oscar said. "But sometimes, I'd like it if I came inside you. And maybe the other way around."

"Done." I sealed the deal with a kiss. "Just let me know when and where."

"I feel like I'm ordering something." He snorted.

"You are. A very sexy package," I said with a wink, making Oscar laugh again. It was the most beautiful sound in the world.

"Stop. That was awful."

"You still laughed."

"It was a pity laugh," Oscar said as I kissed him again, tasting myself on his tongue. I didn't think it was *that* bad, but my opinion wasn't important. I was never going to force Oscar to do something he didn't like.

I slid my hand down his chest, slowly sliding my fingers over his half-hard cock. Oscar groaned, and I felt his dick jump inside his boxers. "You still want me though."

"Of course," he said. His hands were resting on my chest, his skin hot against mine.

"Good. Because I want you too." I pushed Oscar gently

onto the bed, settling myself between his legs. "If you want me to stop, all you have to do is say."

"Okay." He nodded, and I trailed kisses down his neck and onto his chest, spending as much time on him as he had on me. It still didn't feel like enough though. I wanted to spend hours, days, weeks even, exploring his body and unlocking all Oscar's secrets.

Oscar made such sweet sounds that my dick was considering a second round of its own, but I ignored it in favour of stripping him naked and pressing soft kisses along his inner thighs.

Oscar groaned and spread his legs wider, giving me the briefest glimpse of his puckered, furry hole. It made me want to pull his cheeks apart and dive between them, working the sensitive skin with my tongue until Oscar was nothing but a puddle in the middle of the bed.

I pressed a kiss to his taint, loving the way he moaned. I spat into my hand and wrapped it around his cock, jacking it slowly as I teased his balls with my tongue. Oscar moaned and cursed, making something spark in my chest. There was something delicious about the fact that I was bringing him pleasure.

"M-more," he said. "I need more."

I dutifully obliged, sinking his cock deep into my mouth and tightening my lips around him. The scent and taste of him filled my senses, and I moaned, desperate to make him come.

Oscar's hips jerked, and I let him thrust into my throat. My eyes watered, but it made another zip of delight thrum through me.

"Ilias, I'm... fuck, I'm getting close," Oscar said, his hand finding my hair and tilting my head up to look at him. "Fuck! Wow... you look..."

I returned his earlier wink and teased his shaft with my tongue before pulling off with a pop. "You can come in my mouth. Or my hand. Wherever you want."

"Can I..." Oscar's expression faltered for a second, and he bit his lip, his eyes closing as another wave of pleasure washed over him. "Can I come on your face?"

"Mmm, yes," I said. "You can definitely do that." I jacked his cock faster and faster, not willing to tell Oscar that he'd accidentally—or maybe deliberately—stumbled onto something I absolutely loved.

The idea of being marked up by him ticked so many boxes that I could easily get hard again. I sucked the head of his cock, sending him closer and closer to the edge until Oscar grabbed my hair and pulled me off.

"I'm going to come," he gasped, a fraction of a second before his cock pulsed in my hand and painted my face with ropes of hot cum.

I closed my eyes as it splattered on my skin, feeling it dripping off my nose and catching on the edge of my eyelashes. Some of it landed on my lips, and I stuck my tongue out to lick it up. I didn't mind the taste as much, but I'd always preferred salty to sweet.

"Shit," I heard Oscar say. "Let me get you a tissue." I felt him move and bit my lip to suppress a laugh when I heard a crash.

"You okay?"

"Yeah. I'm fine. Here." He shoved a towel into my hand,

and I lifted it to my face, carefully wiping my eyes. "I probably need to aim better next time."

I snorted. "Can you aim cum?"

"I don't know, but I can try," he said as he leant down to kiss me.

# CHAPTER NINETEEN

*Oscar*

"WHERE THE FUCK ARE WE GOING?" Ilias asked, looking at the road around us, then down at his phone.

"You told me to go left at the last turning, so I went left."

"I think you've gone wrong."

"Then who's fault is that?" I asked. Ilias might have had a point though. The overgrown lane covered in potholes barely counted as a road in my opinion, and I somehow doubted there was a hotel at the end of the godforsaken track.

The car clunked as I navigated it over yet another pothole that looked more like a lunar crater.

"I swear to God, if we fuck up this car—"

"Then we'll call the fucking AA," Ilias said exasperatedly. "They can come and find us."

"If they can." I sighed. "Look at the map again. Where am I meant to be going? Does this even lead anywhere?"

There didn't seem to be anything around except stone walls and huge hedges. Every now and then I spied a field full of sheep or cows through a gate.

"I don't know. I haven't got any signal," Ilias said. "I can't load the map."

"Brilliant. Just fucking brilliant. I'll have to find somewhere to turn round."

"Don't blame me."

"I'm not," I snapped as I looked for somewhere big enough to turn the car around. I knew Marcus had hired us an SUV for a reason, but the bloody thing was too fucking big. Not that there was room to manoeuvre anything bigger than a golf cart on this road.

"Yes, you are. You didn't have to come down here."

"Where else was I meant to go? You said this was the way?" I gestured pointedly at the road as if it would somehow illustrate my point.

"According to fucking Google!" Ilias threw his hands up in the air. "This is how you get those stories of drivers stuck in bloody rivers or some shit because they refused to use common sense."

"So you're saying I should have ignored you?"

"Yes! But only up to a point."

"And what point is that?" I asked as we rounded a bend, and I felt a pang of relief as I spied a lonely-looking farmhouse and a yard. The open gateway would be big enough for me to pull into.

"I don't know, but I'm not always wrong." He sighed in frustration. "Fine, let's say we were both wrong and leave it at that. I should have noticed the road looked weird, and you shouldn't have gone down somewhere with grass in the middle."

"Fine." The car crunched on the loose stones in the driveway as it came to a stop, and a thought popped into my head. "Do you think there'll be someone here we can ask for directions?"

"Maybe," Ilias said, then laughed. "God, it's so nice to go somewhere with someone who'll ask for directions."

"Your family won't? That's so fucking weird."

"I know. Heteronormative toxic masculinity for the win. My grandpa once spent an hour driving round Exeter because he refused to believe he was lost. My mum eventually lost her temper and got out to ask for help, and my grandpa just pretended he'd known where he was going the whole time."

"Yeah, we're not doing that." I switched off the engine, unbuckled my seatbelt, and opened the car door. The air smelt like manure and salt, so I guessed we weren't very far from the sea.

It was only supposed to have been a two-hour drive between August House in Fowey, and our next stop near Torquay, but we'd already been in the car for over three hours. First, it had been road works, then an accident, and now at least one wrong turn.

My muscles ached from sitting for so long, and I groaned as something pulled in my calf. I really needed to find a sports massage therapist when I got back to London.

I heard the soft lowing of cows from somewhere nearby —a field or a barn maybe. The other car door thumped closed, and I realised Ilias had gotten out too, stretching his arms over his head and rolling his neck.

"Shall I knock on the door?" he asked, pointing towards the low farmhouse to the left. "Or do you think I'll have more luck in one of the barns?"

"I don't know." It was mid-afternoon, but that meant nothing in terms of farming. It wasn't as if it was a regular desk job with set hours. "I don't think we should go poking around though."

"I'm not going to," Ilias said. "I'm just going to see if anyone's around so we don't spend another three hours driving in circles."

"You can drive next time."

"Fine. You can be the map man, and then I can get huffy at you when you send me down shitty grass tracks." He shot me a grin and headed through the gate before I could respond. A dog barked and made me jump, and suddenly I wondered if we should have even stopped.

I shook my head. This was not a horror movie.

At least, I hoped it wasn't.

A man appeared from one of the barns. He was younger than I'd expected with dirty blond hair and a confused expression. He was wearing green overalls that didn't disguise his broad shoulders or firm thighs. Ilias waved cheerfully and called out a hello.

I swallowed, suddenly feeling a weird pang of jealousy as the man's expression relaxed into an easy smile. He was close enough that I could see him giving Ilias a casual once-over.

Ilias was chatting away, and I heard fragments of their

conversation from where I stood—something about "lost", and "his fault", and the name of our hotel. It seemed like Ilias was laying on the charm, and I wasn't sure whether it bothered me or not.

I'd always known Ilias was charismatic, and he'd admitted he'd perfected the skill of charming people, but there was something about watching other people fawn over him that made my gut tighten possessively.

It was a new feeling for me, and not a particularly pleasant one.

That was my issue though, not his, and I wasn't going to act like some jealous dickhead because someone else could see how amazing my boyfriend was.

I heard my name and looked over at Ilias, who was pointing at me, a bright smile on his face. The other man looked momentarily crestfallen, and I almost wished I'd been able to hear what they'd said. I probably shouldn't have felt smug.

"What did he say?" I asked when Ilias returned to the car a couple of minutes later.

"We're not far away. About ten minutes." He grinned and opened the car door, sliding onto the seat. I climbed in. "Apparently, we should have taken the turn *after* this one. So we just need to head back along the lane, onto the main road, then take the next left, and that'll lead us down towards Torquay. Then we just follow the signs."

"Okay, at least we're in roughly the right place," I said as I pulled the car back onto the track. "Nice of him to help us."

"Yeah. Seemed like a nice guy. Kinda cute too."

"Seriously?"

"What? I have eyes!" Ilias scoffed. "But nobody is as cute as you." He put his hand on my thigh and squeezed.

"It's not... I'm not..."

"Oh my God, you're jealous!" Ilias laughed, the sound filling the car with sunshine.

"I'm not jealous," I said, keeping my eyes on the road. "You're just very charming and gorgeous, and I have to accept that other men will notice that too."

"Uh-huh, and you're not going to get jealous at all?"

"Nope, because we are adults, and I trust you. Plus," I said, a teasing smile crossing my lips, "we're together, which means I won."

"You are jealous, and it's so fucking adorable," Ilias said, and I heard a note of satisfaction in his voice.

"But I just said—"

"Yeah, but what you really mean is that, although you trust me and you think I'm cute as fuck—which I am—you'd rather other people didn't acknowledge that I am, indeed, cute as fuck."

"It's not that," I said. "Seriously. It's just... I've never really thought of myself as... I don't know, relationship material? I mean, I've had relationships, but they've never ended well, mostly because of work. And I think I'm still struggling to get my head around the idea that you want to be with me. That you *want* me. And when I see other guys looking at you, I start wondering whether they'd be better for you than me."

"That's ridiculous."

"Is it?"

"It is to me," Ilias said, his tone softening as he continued. "But I can see why you'd feel that way. Just remember that I want you for you. I don't want anyone else."

"Okay." And I believed him.

Mostly.

The Orange Pig in Babbacombe Bay, just outside of Torquay, wasn't what I'd expected at all.

From the name, I'd been thinking more of a rustic seaside pub that was slightly kitsch, but instead, it was a whitewashed stone building with blue windows and a red roof, a terrace that looked right out over the bay, and steps that led down to the sea. It was more of a boutique hotel and spa than a pub, and Ilias and I soon found ourselves being shown into an airy bedroom, lit by the afternoon sun.

"Wow," Ilias said as he wandered over to the large windows that curved across the far wall. "This is beautiful."

"It really is." I looked around the room, making a note of the details I saw. The bed was large and made up with crisp white sheets and orange cushions scattered across the duvet. "Do you like it more than the last one?"

"The view is better." He turned and looked at the bed, grinning mischievously. "Bed's not a four-poster though, so I have to take points off for that." He walked over to it, kicking off his shoes as he went, and launched himself onto the mattress landing with a thump and a happy sigh.

"Oooh, it's comfy though, and it doesn't squeak," he said, rolling over so he wasn't face down in the pillows. "They get bonus points for a non-squeaky bed. Nothing worse than having a hot man in your bed and realising the mattress is going to tell the entire hotel you're fucking."

"Are we going to fuck, then?" I slid onto the bed next to him and smirked. I leant down to kiss Ilias because it had been far too long since I had kissed him. The desire I felt when I was around him was almost overwhelming. I couldn't remember ever feeling like this before.

"We don't have to if you're not up for it."

"I don't have any lube, so the penetration part is out," I said, rolling on top of him. I loved the way Ilias felt underneath me, and I loved the way he looked up at me from under his long, dark eyelashes. "But I want something."

"We can definitely do that."

I kissed him again, sliding my tongue into his mouth as an idea strolled leisurely through my head. "You know, we technically had a fight today."

"We did." Ilias grinned and hooked his arms around my neck to draw me closer. "We should make up. Thoroughly."

"Very thoroughly," I said as I started to trail kisses down his neck.

# CHAPTER TWENTY

*Ilias*

"ARE YOU NERVOUS?"

"No," I said, checking my hair in the car window before flashing Oscar a smile. "Why would I be nervous?"

"Because you're about to meet the entirety of my family, and their partners, all at once. It's the sort of thing that would make most people run away screaming." Oscar looked like he was still trying to wrap his head around the idea that I wanted to be there. Like he'd never expected me to even consider saying yes.

"Relax. People love me. I'm charming." I pressed a kiss to his cheek and reached for his hand.

In truth, I was absolutely fucking terrified of what was about to happen, but I wasn't going to tell Oscar that. Mostly because he looked about ready to throw up. He'd spent the past few days nervously dumping information on me about his siblings, some of which

I'd heard before and some of which didn't seem necessary.

But I wasn't going to tell him that because getting it out seemed to help him, and that was the most important thing.

"Did you get your mum's present?"

"Oh shit. Yeah, hang on." Oscar dived into the car to grab a gift bag, which he thrust into my hand, and a large potted rose, which we'd attempted to tie a bow around. It looked rather lopsided but in a charming way.

We'd made a pit-stop at a garden centre recommended by our last hotel, and I'd spent half the time in the little coffee shop while Oscar paced up and down and studied every plant with military precision.

"I hope she likes it. I know she was redoing some of the rose beds at the house last time we spoke. I hope she hasn't filled all the spaces."

"I'm sure she'll love it," I said, giving him my brightest smile. "You spent three hours at that garden centre yesterday. I think if we'd been there any longer, you'd have morphed into a bush yourself."

"Thanks… I think." He shifted the rose in his hand so it was leaning against the crook of his arm. His free hand reached for mine. "Come on. Let's get this over with."

I chuckled as we headed for some stone steps that seemed to lead towards the pub. "We're not going into battle. This isn't the first day of the Somme."

Oscar muttered something I couldn't hear, and I shook my head and smiled.

The path led us towards a honey-coloured stone building that surrounded a small courtyard. There was a large terrace out front, which had a few tables laid out across it, each occupied by diners enjoying the early-May sunshine. I could see how much of a sun trap it would be in the summer.

Ahead of us were some wide, double doors that were already open. There were a few people milling about, but they looked mostly like staff. Oscar had looked at the rows of cars when we arrived and said he thought most of his family were already here, and it made sense that they'd already have gone through to the private dining room Lewis had mentioned rather than taking up space in the lobby.

"Hello," said a warm voice as we stepped inside. It belonged to a tall, broad-shouldered man in a well-tailored suit, who had an easy smile and radiated calm and experience. "Welcome to The Pear Tree."

"Hi," said Oscar. "We're with the Baker-Moore party. I know we're a little late. The traffic was a nightmare."

"No worries. They're all through here. If you'd like to follow me, I'll take you through." He gestured for us to follow him into a warm, brightly lit dining room that was already packed with people. The whole place smelled absolutely divine, and it was making my stomach rumble. We'd grabbed an early breakfast at our last hotel in Norfolk, but it had been a long time since then.

"You're just in here," the man added as he opened another door. I heard the buzz of chatter from the other side, which died down the moment Oscar stepped through the door ahead of me, letting go of my hand as he did.

I got a glimpse of a sea of faces. Some of his family stood

and some sat around a long table that ran the length of the room. I spotted Lewis, with his bright pink hair, at the far end next to Jason, chatting to a tall, blond man who seemed to radiate Disney Prince energy and a man with dark curls that seemed to have been forced into some sort of pompadour who I thought was Eli.

Oscar had shown me photos of everyone, but most of their faces and names had started to blur into one.

"Surprise," Oscar said, breaking the silence. The room exploded into chatter again as an older woman with short grey hair and glasses approached us, a beaming smile on her face.

"Hello, darling. I didn't know if you were going to be able to make it. Lewis said he wasn't sure."

"You didn't think I'd miss your birthday, did you?" Oscar asked wryly, then adjusted the rose so he could hand it over. "This is for you. I hope it's okay. And there's a gift bag too."

"Here," I said, extending my hand. "And since your son is just going to leave me standing here like an awkward goldfish, I'm Ilias. It's so lovely to meet you."

"I was getting there," Oscar said.

"Sure you were."

"I was. Mum, this is Ilias Verrati. He's a travel photographer. He came to Hawaii with me, and he's helping me with the seaside hotels. Ilias, this is my mum, Eleanor."

Eleanor looked between us and raised an eyebrow before shaking my hand. "It's lovely to meet you, Ilias. Call me Mimbles. Everyone else does." She looked over her shoulder and beckoned to another woman with long lavender hair and a soft smile. "Miranda, this is Ilias."

"Hello, darling," Miranda said, giving me a beaming smile and pressing a kiss to my cheek before doing the same with Oscar. "It's so nice of you both to come."

"We wouldn't have missed it," Oscar said.

"I'm assuming Lewis knew," Eleanor said. "Since there are the correct number of seats."

"Er... yes? We bumped into him in London a couple of weeks ago." Oscar's ears went slightly pink, and I was ninety-nine percent sure both Eleanor and Miranda saw straight through our "we're not together" ruse. Which, if we were honest, wasn't that great to begin with.

We'd told Lewis we didn't want him telling everyone we were dating, and Oscar and I had decided on the drive over to keep up that pretence. Only now that we were there it seemed ridiculous.

"I see," Eleanor said. There was a beat of silence, then Oscar broke.

"Fine, Ilias and I were out to dinner, and Lewis, Jason, and Henry were there. And we weren't going to tell anyone that we're dating because it's still new, but apparently, I'm shit at hiding things, so..."

Miranda and Eleanor exchanged looks, and Eleanor smiled. "I wasn't going to say anything, you know."

"But... the look..."

"Age-old parenting technique. It's so much better to wait for someone to admit something rather than force it. I've always thought silence worked wonders," she said.

"I can't believe I fell for it," Oscar muttered. "Again."

"I'm sure there are stories there," I said.

"Yeah, but nothing exciting." He sighed, then reached for my hand, sliding his fingers into mine. "Sorry. I didn't mean to tell."

"It's fine. I thought it was a little ridiculous anyway."

"You could have said so earlier."

"I know, but you were stressed, and I didn't want to add to that," I said, squeezing his hand and resisting the temptation to lean over and kiss him. Out of the corner of my eye, I saw Eleanor and Miranda watching us.

"Thanks. That's sweet of you." Oscar hesitated for a second, then pressed a kiss to my cheek. I felt my face heat and my heart race. I hoped I didn't end up with sweaty palms too.

Oscar turned back to his mums. "I'm sorry. I hope you don't mind me bringing Ilias, even though this is new. We're between hotels, and I felt bad dumping him somewhere for the day."

I chuckled. "I could have stayed in the car. Or gotten lunch somewhere else."

"Nonsense," Eleanor said. "You're very welcome. Oscar, you should introduce him to everyone before the food arrives. Apologies, Ilias, it's going to feel like being thrown to a pack of wolves. If they misbehave, just remind them it's my birthday, and I've told them to be good."

"Don't worry, they can't be any worse than my family," I said.

"I wouldn't count on it," Oscar added quietly, looking around the room. "Let's get the worst of them out of the way first."

"You're making it sound like they're all horrible."

"They're not. They're just... Well, you'll see." He led me down the room, briefly pausing to introduce me to Miranda's ex-husband, Terry, and his husband, Paul. At the far end, Lewis's gaggle had grown, and they were all pretending they weren't looking at us.

"Honestly," Oscar muttered, "it's like a group of bloody mother hens."

"Hi!" Lewis said brightly as we approached. He was fizzing with energy like a Coke bottle waiting to explode. "You came."

"I promised we would."

"I know but still."

Everyone stared at us in polite but expectant silence. Oscar sighed. "Family, meet Ilias. Ilias meet family. Specifically, Eli and his partner, Tristan"—he pointed to the two I'd seen earlier, and Eli shot me a sly grin—"my sister Jules, my brother Finn, and his partner, Gem"—he pointed to a woman in a sharp suit with freshly faded dirty blonde hair, a tall, slim man who just gave me a small smile, and a shorter man with reddish-brown hair and a tweed jacket —"and you've already met Lewis and Jason. And over there are Richard and Ruby"—he pointed at a man and a woman who were now chatting with Miranda and Eleanor.

"So, this is what Lewis has been so secretive about?" Eli said. "He told me he bumped into you a couple of weeks ago but was suspiciously light on details."

"I didn't say anything though," Lewis said.

"You could have," Eli said. "I wouldn't have told anyone."

"That's a lie," Jules said with a snort.

"No, I'm not in the habit of outing relationships to the family chat after *someone* sent drunken photos of my boyfriend to you lot."

"Okay," Lewis said. "First of all, you're making it sound way worse than it was." He looked at me and waved his hands as he explained. "My friends and I took Tristan under our wings at a Halloween party where Eli was DJing, and we all took drunk selfies at McDonalds."

"And then you sent them to Finn and Jules."

"But I wanted them to see how cute Tristan was."

"And then you ambushed us," Eli continued, raising an eyebrow. He was smiling though, and I got the feeling the whole situation amused rather than frustrated him.

"You needed it," Jules said. "Otherwise, you'd still be trying to avoid Richard."

"Nope. We'd have told him eventually."

"I'm sorry," said Finn quietly but not so quietly that he was spoken over. "We're not making a good impression."

"You're fine," I said. "Trust me, you're a hell of a lot better than my family. They're… dramatic but not in a good way."

"Sounds like there are stories there," Eli said. "But I'm much more interested in you. So, tell us, how did you meet our beautiful big brother? Did you make him swoon?"

Oscar snorted. "Definitely no swooning."

"Aww, not even a little?" I asked, nudging his elbow. "I can't actually remember where we first met. I think it was… Rome?"

"Yes… No, wait." Oscar chuckled and shook his head. "It was Madrid. Do you remember? In that shitty bar."

"Oh shit. Yes, it was." I laughed as the memory rushed into my brain. "The night of the Champion's League final when Real Madrid were playing, and neither of us had realised."

The place had been packed to the rafters with rowdy football fans, and I'd barely been able to hear anything. I'd ended up standing at the bar and found this gorgeous man standing next to me. We were both there on the same group press trip, so I'd vaguely recognised him. I'd offered to buy him a drink.

"You bought me a drink," Oscar said quietly. "Lots of drinks actually."

"I did. And then you walked me back to the hotel when they were setting off flares in the street. I threw up on your shoes."

"You did." Oscar was looking at me now, a smile playing across his lips. There was something warm in his expression, and for the first time, it felt like I was being seen, but I didn't know why.

There was something about the moment that made my heart race faster than I'd ever felt.

Even with Daniele.

# CHAPTER TWENTY-ONE

*Oscar*

THE EMOTION that rushed over me as I looked at Ilias should have scared me in its intensity.

It was a swirling vortex of warmth and want and a deep connection I'd never experienced. I wanted to let go and give into it, to let the feelings pull me under and overwhelm me, but there was a glint of apprehension in Ilias's eyes that made me hesitate. Was this too much for him? Did he not feel the way I did?

Or was there something else? Something related to Daniele and everything that had happened between them.

I knew Ilias had said it had happened ten years ago, but I also knew scars like that never truly healed. It was evident from our conversations in Hawaii that Ilias was still dealing with the remnants of his emotions, even if he thought he'd processed them.

But now wasn't the time or place to ask him about it.

I wasn't going to bring up something like that in front of my family, and we weren't able to escape outside because Richard and Ruby had strolled over to introduce themselves.

Then, as soon as they'd finished, the dining room door opened, and some black-clad members of staff appeared bearing trays.

"Let's sit here," I said, indicating some seats near the end of the table. That way Ilias and I wouldn't be hemmed in on all sides and spend the entire meal fending off questions.

I knew Ilias could hold his own, but I didn't want him to feel like he was being interrogated. I knew none of my family had malicious intentions; they were just nosy as fuck.

It was like giving something shiny to a flock of magpies and then expecting them not to want to play with it.

Plus, I didn't want to detract from my mum's birthday by making this all about me. Which, in hindsight, I'd already done by bringing my new boyfriend without any sort of warning. I'd really fucked that one up.

"You okay?" Ilias asked in a low voice as he slid into a seat next to Tristan. "You seem a little distracted."

"Yeah, just thinking that I might have fucked up a little by not giving everyone some warning. Feels kinda like a dick move to just surprise people with a new relationship. Not that I don't want you here. I don't regret bringing you. I should probably have just given everyone a heads-up."

"You're fine," said Finn, who was sitting on my other side at the end of the table. He gave me an encouraging smile. "Hindsight is a wonderful thing, and it's never easy to introduce a new relationship, especially to a family like ours."

Across the table, Jules nodded. "Yeah, we get it. It's... difficult."

Finn's eyebrow twitched, and I looked at him, then at Jules, who was focusing on her beer. I was pretty sure I was missing something there. Something Finn clearly knew and thought Jules should share.

The answer was obvious, and I was surprised it had taken me that long to figure it out.

"Jules," I said, "have you got a girlfriend?"

Her eyes widened for a second, suggesting I'd hit the nail on the head. "Er... maybe? We're working some stuff out." She licked her lips and tapped her finger on the table, which had always been Jules's nervous tell. "It's complicated because she's got a daughter, who I fucking adore by the way. That's not the issue. It's just, y'know, distance and work and things get more difficult when there's another person to think about. Especially when they're small."

"I get that," Ilias said from beside me. "Sorry. I hope you don't mind me listening. I don't have kids, but I have a ton of niblings, and I live with my brother, his wife, and their four boys, so I get to see the good, the bad, and the really fucking ugly sides of parenting."

"Nah, go ahead." Jules gestured. "This is my problem. I know fuck all about kids."

"I've found that the best thing to do, especially if they're older than four or five and are more like small people, is to just treat them like that. Like, sure, you need boundaries and rules and a fuck ton of patience because they're kids, but if you don't talk to them like they're babies and don't dismiss them, then you'll be off to a good start," Ilias said. "You're not trying to be another parent, so stick to what her mum has established, but get to know her as a person, and you'll do fine. And if you're not sure where to start, just find something she's interested in and take it from there."

"Thanks," Jules said, giving him a smile. "I'll give it a try."

"No worries. And you'll probably learn loads of random shit. My nephew Teddy loves sharks, like, to an almost obsessive level. And as a result, I've learnt more about sharks in the past six months than I have in my entire life." Ilias chuckled. "I can even tell you all the names of the sharks at the London Aquarium since I've virtually lived there every weekend since I first took him."

"My nephew is the same," Gem said. He sat opposite Finn, next to Jules. "He's just turned eight, and he's a pretty cool person. Right now, he loves all things ice hockey because my brother-in-law took him to see a game in Edinburgh last November. Last I heard, he was trying to teach himself to rollerblade in the hopes it'd teach him how to skate. My sister said she'd had to move everything breakable out of the downstairs because he kept crashing into things."

Ilias and Jules laughed, and the conversation moved on to something else as the starters were served. We'd all chosen our food from a limited menu Lewis had sent around a couple of weeks ago.

I saw him checking something on his phone as the staff

slid plates carefully onto the table, and I assumed he'd made a list in case anyone had forgotten what they'd ordered.

The food was utterly delicious, but what made the meal so memorable was watching the way Ilias had slid so easily into my family. He talked about his niblings and his job, and he asked Gem about his new game store and Finn about his narrating. He got into a long discussion with Tristan about the ins and outs of medieval castles and historical architecture, which slightly stunned me because it didn't seem like something Ilias would be interested in until I remembered the way he'd talked about exploring various cities and finding the parts where the ancient intersected with the new.

It made me appreciate just how amazing Ilias was. Heat flared in my chest, and the previous swirl of emotions picked up again.

It was probably too soon to tell Ilias how I was feeling, especially if he still had things to work through. But I didn't want to lose him either. It was a balancing act—a tightrope for me to walk between going too hard and not telling Ilias anything.

And I'd never had much luck with tightropes.


After lunch, we headed back to Mum and Miranda's house for a couple of hours for a cup of tea and a piece of cake. Ilias and I didn't have to be at our next hotel until tomorrow at lunchtime, so we had a rare afternoon off.

Which was mostly because I'd asked Marcus and

Vanessa ever so sweetly to make it so. I spent enough time away as it was. I didn't want to literally just come for lunch and rush off again.

We'd needed a place to crash for the night, and Lewis and Jason had offered to let us stay with them in Lincoln since they were the only ones who'd known about our relationship.

Mum had seemed pleased when I said I was sticking around for the rest of the afternoon, and I sat on the sofa next to Ilias with Mum on another sofa opposite us while Miranda made tea in the kitchen. The house seemed quiet without the usual chaos of my siblings running around, and I wondered whether my mums relished the peace and quiet or resented it.

"I'm sorry I didn't get to talk to you much at lunch," Mum said. She'd swapped her low heels for a pair of old, fluffy slippers as soon as we'd come in, and the contrast between them and her smart, navy dress made me smile. "You were all the way down at the opposite end, and I kept getting snared in conversation."

"That's what happens when you're the birthday girl. You're the centre of attention."

I grinned and Mum rolled her eyes fondly. "Well, I'm glad it's over with. And I'm glad Lewis didn't make a fuss. I was half expecting some enormous surprise party."

"Lewis knows you'd hate that," I said. "You said small, so he went small."

"He's a good boy," Miranda said, sweeping in holding a tray of mugs, her many bangles jangling. "And it was nice of him to bring Jason too."

"We're getting quite the full house," Mum said as she accepted a floral mug. "Next time, we'll have to make Jules bring her girlfriend. You'd like her."

"Is that Chantelle? Finn's friend?"

"Yes. Did Jules finally admit it, then? I haven't pushed her, but it's clear something is going on."

"Sort of. Under duress," I said with a wry chuckle. "She's nervous because of Chantelle's daughter. I think Finn said her name was Kelsey?"

"Her heart's in the right place," said Ilias. His fingers were resting against my thigh, solid and comfortable. The perfect point of connection. "And relationships aren't straightforward most of the time. Everyone has... baggage."

"Yeah, they do." I reached down and placed my hand over his, squeezing it gently. "I guess they'll just have to talk it out."

"They will," Miranda said softly, offering me a mug patterned with sunflowers. "It's a good thing she's thinking it through though. You never want to force unstable situations on children. Not if you can help it." She gave me a gentle smile, and I nodded.

Miranda and I had always had an odd relationship, not mean or strained but distant. I think it was because I hadn't wanted her when I was a child, and she'd never forced a relationship upon me.

It had been hard at times, watching Finn and Jules accept her as their other parent because they couldn't remember anything else, but I'd never kicked up a stink, and I loved them too much to cause a fuss because then they might get hurt, and even as a kid, I'd never wanted that.

Even if I'd wished they remembered our dad.

But Finn had been too little, and Jules's memories of him were fragments at best. Mum and Miranda had never stopped me from talking about Dad, and they'd kept photos of him on the mantelpiece and shared their memories of him, but it had never quite filled the ache in my heart.

Hearing Finn and Jules call Miranda "Mum" had always stung until I'd realised it didn't take away from my dad. It was just what made sense to them. And I couldn't hold a ghost over their head because I wanted things to be different.

Miranda had never treated us differently, and she'd always loved us in the same way she loved Richard, Eli, and Lewis. The same way my mum loved her children. Miranda made my mum happy, and that was all I wanted because I couldn't stand the idea of my mum being miserable and alone.

By the time I'd arrived at that place of grudging acceptance and understanding, I hadn't known how to reach out, and Miranda had never pushed. I was grateful for it, but sometimes I wished things were different. I just didn't know how to change it.

Maybe one day, when this trip was over, I'd come back and sit down with her, and we could talk things out. Ilias had said open communication was the basis of all healthy relationships, and perhaps it was time for me to truly put my past to rest.

I didn't think I'd ever get to a place where I'd call Miranda "Mum", but perhaps we could be better friends. I thought I'd like that.

"So, Ilias," Mum said, clearly sensing it was time for a topic change. "Oscar says you're a wonderful photographer, and he sent us some of your photos from Hawaii. How did you get started with that? Also, I have to ask, but do tell me if I'm being too pushy, if you're ever up this way, would you consider coming into my school and talking to our photography club? I know they'd love to talk to you. They're a bright bunch."

"Mum's a school librarian," I said. "And when she finally retires, the whole school is going to cry."

"Of course!" Ilias said with a bright smile. "That sounds fun. Just give me some dates, and I'll see when I'm free."

"Wonderful," Mum said, beaming at him. She took a sip of her tea. "So tell us about you."

# CHAPTER TWENTY-TWO

*Oscar*

"Fuck, fuck, fuck! Why, Mario, why?" The blue Nintendo Switch controller vibrated in my hand as I watched Mario plummet to his death off the side of the platform for the third time in as many minutes. Next to me, Finn chuckled as his Princess Peach avatar twirled her parasol in satisfaction.

"You are really not good at this game," Finn said as the clock ran out and the screen once again declared him the winner. We were sitting on one of the plush sofas in Lewis's living room, playing Super Smash Bros. on his Switch.

It was mid-morning on Monday, and Finn had come round to hang out for a couple of hours before Ilias and I had to get back in the car. I appreciated getting to spend time with him, just chilling out and playing video games like we had as kids.

What I didn't appreciate was getting my ass handed to me over and over again by my baby brother.

"I'm really not," I conceded. "But one day, I'll beat you."

Finn grinned and raised an eyebrow. "Really?"

"Yes, really."

"I could just let you win if you really need your ego stroked that much."

"Ha, ha. Don't be a dick," I said. "And who put extra spark in your coffee this morning?"

Finn shrugged. "I don't know."

I hummed but didn't say anything. I knew Finn had stayed at Gem's last night, and I knew his relationship with the Scotsman was starting to bring my brother out of his shell a little.

Although, considering what I'd found out about my brother a couple of months ago, I wasn't sure I wanted to know where the more confident side of Finn came from.

Finding out my quiet, shy baby brother, who'd never say boo to a goose, was secretly running an anonymous audio porn blog had been more than a little eye opening. He'd sworn us all to secrecy, which I'd stuck by, but I hadn't been able to look at him the same way since. Not that I was horrified, more that I'd realized Finn really was all grown up.

It had reminded me that everyone had secrets. And they weren't always ones people wanted to share.

"Ilias seems nice," Finn said, leaving the screen on set-up rather than starting another match.

"He is." I glanced around. Ilias was in the kitchen with Jason, chatting about work.

For a moment, I wondered if I should tell Finn about the worry that had started bubbling away in my stomach last night. I'd spent hours staring up at the ceiling of Lewis's spare room, wondering if I was imagining things or if my fears were justified.

"But?" Finn asked. He turned to me, scrutinising my expression. "What's wrong?"

"Nothing's wrong."

"There is." He pointed at my face. "Your nose is twitching. It's your tell."

I grabbed my nose. "I don't have a tell."

"You do, but maybe I only notice because I know you so well. You hide yours better than Jules." He gave me a small smile. "You don't have to tell me if you don't want to, but if there is something bothering you, I'll always be here to listen. You know I won't judge you."

"Okay." I craned my neck to check that Ilias was still in the kitchen. "You have to promise not to say anything."

"I won't," Finn said. "Why don't we go and grab a coffee so you don't have to whisper?"

"Er, sure."

"Come on." Finn stood up. "We can get pastries for everyone else too. Ilias will be fine here for a few minutes."

I nodded and flicked off the Switch.

Ten minutes later, Finn and I were walking along Lincoln's cobbled streets towards a little bakery at the top of the hill. There was hardly a cloud in the sky, making it the perfect late-spring day. Since it was a Monday, there weren't many people around. Finn was companionably silent, waiting for me to start speaking.

I didn't know where to begin, and eventually the first words out of my mouth were, "I think he's going to run."

Finn gave me a quizzical glance but said nothing.

"I don't mean he's going to physically run away, but I'm worried he's going to withdraw." I sighed, pausing for a second to turn and look out over the city laid out before us. "Ilias lost someone... his fiancé, when he was quite young. And he says he's gotten over it, but I don't think that is something you ever really get over. I know he hasn't been in a serious relationship since, and I think it scares him. He said he'd talk to me if he was worried, but..."

"But you're afraid he won't, that his fear will take over and he'll break away before you even get the chance to talk about it," Finn said.

"Yeah, something like that. I know I've lost people too, but nothing in the same category as that. And I'm scared I'm going to lose Ilias."

"You really like him, don't you?"

"I do. I don't know if this is love or something else, but I can't imagine my life without him in it."

"Then talk to him," Finn said, putting his hand on my arm. "Like you said, the pain of losing someone never really goes away. It's still there, even if we wish it wasn't. You know that relationship, that loss, is always going to be a part of who Ilias is. You just have to let him know you'll be there for him and that you know your relationship with him doesn't replace the one he lost. I'm going to assume you're not going to make Ilias pretend the other man never existed?"

"God no, I'm not a complete dickhead." I was shocked he'd even suggest it.

"Then tell him that. Tell him all this. Let him know you care about him, that you want to be with him, and that you understand if he sometimes gets sad or if he wants to talk about his fiancé. He might not want to, but I think if you give him the option, it'll help. It's just being open with him. Don't make the mistake of trying to find the best time or hoping it'll all work out for the best without actually doing anything. That... that leads to problems," Finn said as he looked down at the floor. "If you want this relationship, you have to plant your feet and let him know where you stand."

I nodded. Finn had always had great insight, more than people often gave him credit for. He didn't always apply that insight to his own life, but nobody was perfect. There was just one tiny nagging thought left, burrowing into my mind.

"And what if I say all that, and he runs anyway?"

"Then you know he wasn't right for you, and he's not ready. But I think you'll be surprised. It might be painful for him, but I think you'll get there. When I was watching him yesterday..." He trailed off and gave me an encouraging smile. "Don't give up on this too easily, and don't give up on him."

We turned and continued walking up the street, and all I could do was hope Finn was right.

· · ·

When we got back to Lewis's house forty minutes later, Ilias was still at the kitchen table chatting to Jason. They'd been joined by Lewis, who was looking at something on his laptop screen and marking something in the large diary spread out next to him. It was a riot of colours, stickers, and Post-it notes, but I assumed it made sense to him.

"We're back," I said. "And we brought pastries."

Finn and I had stopped at a little bakery and coffee shop at the top of Steep Hill and enjoyed a quick drink before grabbing a large selection box of freshly made pastries to bring back. I put the box on the table and pulled it open.

Ilias hummed appreciatively as he reached for a large Nordic knott filled with custard and blueberries.

"I knew there was a reason I liked you," he said with a grin before taking an enormous bite. I chuckled and took another of the knotts, leaning over to press a kiss to his cheek.

"Ilias was just giving us some ideas for places to explore," Lewis said, "and telling us more about the series you pitched to *The Traveller*. I knew your Hawaii trip was part of a whole LGBTQ+ holiday feature, but I didn't realise it was the first series like this they'd done. That's awesome. Why didn't you tell us?"

"I don't know," I said with a shrug. "It didn't seem like a big deal. They'd have done one eventually."

"Nope, I don't buy that," Lewis said. He gave me one of his patented Lewis stares, the one that made his clients reconsider their life choices. "You knew it was important, and you knew it needed to happen, so you made it so.

Don't be so modest. You should learn to celebrate your achievements."

I gave him a mock salute, still holding half my pastry. "Yes, sir." Beside me, Finn snorted. I turned to him and grinned. "Anything to add?"

"No. But Lewis does make a good point. You've told me in the past that you only pitch things you're interested in, and I know Eli's asked you for recommendations for him and Tristan, so I think you know it's a big deal. You just don't want us to make a fuss."

"Why is it," I grumbled, "that you always manage to hit the nail on the head?"

"I'm good at reading people," Finn said.

"You just need to learn to take your own advice," I said.

"Yes, well, this conversation isn't about me." Finn's face flushed, and he reached across me to retrieve a chocolate babka from the box.

"Where will you be off to next?" Jason asked. "Do you get to choose, or do they just send you?"

"Depends. I had to submit some suggestions and my reasoning behind the destinations, but it'll be up to the magazine where I go. It'll depend on what they think fits the brand, where we can get press trips, what other features they've got coming up. Stuff like that."

"Wherever it is," Ilias said, having finished demolishing his pastry, "I hope it's warm. And doesn't rain."

"Noted. I'll ask Marcus to send us to Thailand during monsoon season or to some Scandinavian ice hotel."

"See, you say that, but you'd have to suffer through them with me, and we'd both end up miserable."

"I'd ask for separate rooms," I said. "And lock the door."

"That's not going to stop me," Ilias laughed. "You'd have to fly out and back with me. And this is a couple's article, so we're supposed to spend time together."

"No monsoon season, then." I chuckled. My heart swelled in my chest as I looked down at him—the beautiful man with custard on his lip and an enormous heart that seemed so full of life.

Finn had asked me if I loved Ilias, and I'd said I wasn't sure, that it was too early to tell. But looking at him now, I knew that was a lie. Early or not, I loved him.

Now all I had to do was show him that and hope it was enough.

# CHAPTER TWENTY-THREE

*Ilias*

"Good afternoon, welcome to Heather Sands. Are you checking in?" the impeccably dressed young man behind the reception desk asked as we approached, and the details quickly rolled off Oscar's tongue since they were the same ones he'd been repeating for several weeks.

While the receptionist confirmed everything, I glanced around the entrance hall of the boutique hotel, which was right on the Yorkshire coast, taking it all in without really seeing any of it.

My mind was already elsewhere.

I was trying to put it down to the fact that it had been an intense couple of days, tacked onto a long couple of weeks. We were just over halfway through our list of hotels, with just the north of England and Scotland left to do, and I was starting to feel the effects of all the travelling.

But deep in my heart, I knew it was more than that.

Meeting Oscar's family and having those intense moments of connection with him had stirred up long-dormant emotions and reclusive fears I couldn't push away. There was a new weight resting on my chest—a monstrous fear that somehow I was going to lose Oscar the same way I'd lost Daniele.

Logically, I knew the chances of that scenario reoccurring were slim to none, but that didn't stop the fear from whispering in my ear that I was destined to be alone. That in ten years, I'd have nothing more than scant memories of both of them and be left wondering whether they'd even existed at all.

That was the hardest part. The one thing I was terrified to admit—that as heavy as my grief was, the weight of my doubt was worse.

It was hard to confess, even to myself, that I hardly remembered Daniele anymore. My memories were like broken shards of glass that got cloudier with each passing day.

"Ilias?" Oscar asked, putting his hand on my shoulder and snapping me out of my thoughts. "You okay? Ready to go?"

"Yes." I gave him a smile that even I knew was fake. "Let's go put everything upstairs, then we can explore."

Oscar frowned at me but said nothing. He reached for his bag and waited for me to follow him towards the stairs. I cursed internally because the one thing I hadn't wanted was for Oscar to catch on to the fact that I wasn't feeling myself, not that I was really trying to hide it.

I both desperately wanted and utterly hated the idea of

him asking me what was wrong. The two sides of myself were at war, and I wasn't sure which part was going to win. With anyone else I'd have buried my fear so deep it wouldn't have been able to surface for another thousand years, but with him...

I thought back to that night in Hawaii when I'd first told him about Daniele and we'd talked about a possible relationship. Oscar had made me promise to tell him when I was scared, and I wanted to honour that, even if the idea made me want to run screaming for the hills.

"We're just in here," Oscar said. He'd stopped so suddenly I'd nearly walked into the back of him, and it was only at that point I realised we'd climbed three flights of stairs. I really was working on autopilot.

He clicked the key card into the lock and pushed the door open. "After you."

"Thanks." I stepped through the door, expecting another nice hotel room similar to the other ones we'd stayed in. Except, apparently, Heather Sands was determined to outdo their competition.

"Fucking hell," I said. "Are you sure we've got the right room?"

"Yeah." Oscar looked at the little card in his hand, then back at the door. "302. This place is pretty small, so it's hard to get lost." He glanced up, and I saw the exact moment he realised what I meant. I stifled a laugh.

"I'm pretty sure they've given us a suite."

"Shit. This is bigger than my flat."

The room was gorgeous; an enormous, open space with a

soft, plush-looking sofa, coffee table, desk, and television at the front and large windows overlooking the sea on the far wall. An enormous bed made up with white sheets and deep purple cushions stood on a raised area to my right, and while it wasn't a four-poster, it did look ridiculously comfortable.

There were large wardrobes in the same dark wood as the rest of the furniture, and through a door to my right I saw a bathroom and the edge of what looked like a claw-footed bath. The whole space oozed boutique charm and elegance, and for a moment I forgot about everything that had been bothering me.

"Okay," I said as I let go of the handle of my suitcase. "This place is getting good marks on the Verrati index."

Oscar chuckled. "But there isn't a four-poster."

"True, but look at how big that bed is." I climbed up the step and walked around the bed, glancing out the window. "And the view is gorgeous. I could walk around naked in here and nobody could see me."

"Hmm, I like that idea," Oscar said. He was watching me with a wicked smile, and it made my heart flutter like a bird desperate to take flight. "But does it squeak? That's the true test, right?"

"Only one way to find out." I let myself flop backwards onto the bed, listening for any tell-tale groans, but all I heard was the flump of my body onto the sheets, and the soft *whoomp* of the decorative cushions toppling onto me. Apparently, I had caused a pillow avalanche.

"No squeaking," I said as I bounced my body up and down a few times to make sure. "But I'm not sure if they should lose marks for the number of pillows. I could have suffocated."

As if to accentuate my point, another cushion landed on my face. I didn't make any attempt to move it. I was having too much fun with the ridiculous moment. "See? I could die here."

I heard Oscar laughing and the sound of his feet on the carpet. Then the cushion was lifted and the dark purple filling my vision was replaced with his face. He leant down and pressed a soft kiss to my lips.

"Ta-da, you've been rescued."

"Such heroics," I said, trying not to laugh. "How will I ever repay you?"

"I'm sure you'll think of something." He leant down and kissed me again. My hands came up to encircle his neck, pulling him down onto the bed with me. I wanted to lose myself in his kisses, his touch, his body. I wanted to get out of my head and leave my fears behind.

But with every press of his mouth, all I could think about was that I didn't want this to end. That I didn't want to wake up one morning not knowing what the touch of his lips felt like, haunted by only memories.

"Ilias?" Oscar asked. He pulled away and sat up, looking down at me with an expression filled with concern. "What's going on?"

"It's nothing. I'm just tired."

"Please." He put his hand on my chest, right above my heart. I knew he'd be able to feel how hard it was pounding. "Don't shut me out. Talk to me."

"Seriously, it's nothing. Just leave it. Please." I knew

everything I was saying was wrong, but I didn't know how to make it right. Talking to him was easy in principle, but harder to execute in reality.

"No." His tone was gentle, but there was a firm edge to it that caught me by surprise. "Please, Ilias. We made a deal. We promised we'd talk to each other."

"We promised we'd try," I said. "There's a difference there."

"Don't do that. It's not fair." He frowned, and it made my chest ache because I hated seeing him like that. "Come on, talk to me. I promise I'll listen, and I promise I won't judge you. Is this…" He hesitated, and I knew what he was going to ask before he said it, but it didn't make the words hurt any less. "Is this about Daniele?"

And there it was. The one question I couldn't avoid without lying to him outright. I was trapped.

"Yes," I said quietly, my voice shaking. "It is."

Then without warning, I started to cry.

My emotions consumed me, dark and raw and desperate to be fed. Tears flooded down my cheeks as my body shook and my breathing became rushed and ragged. I hadn't cried like that in years, but it was like I'd opened a valve, and it was all flooding out faster than I could control.

Oscar was muttering soft words above me, making soothing sounds as his hand caressed my shoulder. In the back of my mind, I realised I'd curled onto my side, hugging my knees to my chest like it would make me disappear.

I didn't know how long I cried because time seemed to slip away. But eventually, I felt my body calm, and I took a deep, shuddering breath. It felt like the first one I'd drawn in a lifetime.

It was like I'd been washed up on the shore after a storm, and behind me the sea was calm with only the edges of the ruffled waves showing any indication there had been disruption.

"I'm sorry," I said. My voice was hoarse and broken.

"Don't be." Oscar leant down and pressed a soft kiss to my temple. I realised he was stretched out on the bed next to me, propped on the mountain of pillows. I shuffled slightly so I could rest my head in his lap, and his fingers carded through my hair as I let out another deep breath. "Do you want to talk about it?"

"No. Not really." I stared down at Oscar's feet and realised he'd taken his shoes off. His socks had colourful triangles printed all over them. "But I probably should."

"You don't have to if you're not ready."

"I don't think I ever will be," I said.

"Nobody ever is I don't think. But I'm here. I promise I'm not going anywhere." Oscar's words were like a soothing balm on my soul. I nodded.

"I know. Logically, I do anyway. It's just..." I sighed. If there was one thing I hated more than anything else it was feeling vulnerable. It felt like all my nerves had been exposed and every moment was agony.

"Are you scared I'm going to run away?" Oscar asked. "Or do you think I'm trying to replace Daniele?"

"No, it's not that." The second option had never even crossed my mind if I was honest. I'd never seen the two as mutually exclusive, and perhaps that was because I wasn't sure whether Daniele and I would ever have made it that far.

"I'm scared I'm going to lose you too," I said eventually. "I know the chance of history repeating itself is very low, but all I can think about is how much I don't want to lose you. The fear is paralysing me because all I can think about is being in the same situation in ten years' time except I'm haunted by two ghosts instead of one. I know it's ridiculous—"

"It's not ridiculous," Oscar said. "You went through something awful, something that I wouldn't wish upon anybody."

"Thanks." I smiled weakly, but I was still looking at Oscar's feet. The triangles were red, orange, blue, and green. In the back of my mind, I was trying to count them. "Do you know the worst part? Apart from nobody else knowing."

"What?"

"It's that I hardly remember him anymore. And I feel like such a shit person for that. All I can remember are fragments: the sound of his laughter, the shape of his smile, how much he loved pistachio gelato. They're all just pieces, and I can't remember how to put them together anymore. If I didn't have pictures, I'd have forgotten what he looked like."

I held my breath, waiting for Oscar to tell me what a horrible person I was. It was like waiting for an axe to fall.

"You're not a shit person," he said softly. "You're human. People forget, and it's okay. I know it's not the same, but I can barely remember my dad. I don't even know if half my memories of him are real or not or if they're just stories I've been told or things I've imagined. It hurts, and I wish it was different, but it's not something I can change. You can't punish yourself for being human."

"Do you know the worst part?" My voice was barely above a whisper. "Sometimes, I don't wish it was different. I mean, I wish Daniele hadn't died, but that's because death is shit, and he wasn't even twenty. But... I don't even know if we'd still have been married. I was in love with the idea of him, rather than the idea of being married to him. I guess it's more the hindsight of growing up, but we barely knew each other, and I'm so different now.

"It might have worked. I mean my nonna ran away and married my grandad at seventeen, and they'd only spoken like three times, and they've been married for over sixty years. But I don't think we'd have been the same. And I feel guilty about that... that Daniele died for something that might not have lasted more than six months."

With every word, it felt like I was draining some long-festering wound in my chest that I'd refused to acknowledge. The pain was almost unbearable, but by the time I'd reached the end, I somehow felt better for it.

"I understand," said Oscar. "But you can't beat yourself up for that. At the time, you wanted to marry him. You loved him, and you believed in your relationship. That means something, I promise. The years might have changed your perspective, but they don't change how you felt at the time. You loved him, and Daniele knew that. And that's the most important thing."

"You think so?" I felt like a child looking for some kind of desperate reassurance.

"I do." His fingers continued to card through my hair, and I felt my eyelids starting to droop. My emotional outburst had left me feeling utterly exhausted. I wasn't usually an afternoon nap person, but today might have to be an exception.

"Just for the record," Oscar continued. "I'm not going anywhere. I know you said you're afraid of losing me, and I understand that. But I want you to know I'll be here for as long as you want me."

I nodded, shifting my position slightly and draping my hand over his thigh. As long as I wanted him... that sounded nice.

As sleep dragged me under, I wondered if forever would be possible.

# CHAPTER TWENTY-FOUR

*Ilias*

WHEN I AWOKE, I remembered why I hated taking naps so much. My mouth felt like something had died in it, my head was pounding, and I was groggy as fuck.

I felt worse than the time I'd woken up hungover after spending the night before doing endless rounds of the strangest shots the bar had on offer. I didn't think I'd even been asleep for that long, given that it was still relatively light.

I tried to sit up, opening and closing my mouth in the hope that it would stop my tongue from feeling fuzzy. It did not.

"Hey," Oscar said. He was stretched out on the bed next to me, and I realised that while I'd rolled off him during my nap, neither of us had gone far from each other. "How're you feeling?"

"Honestly? Like shit. But that's because I took a nap,

and now I feel like I've been asleep for a thousand years. Never let me take a nap again. Unless we're on a plane, but those don't count." I stretched and looked at my watch. It was only half four. "How long was I out?"

"Half? Three-quarters of an hour? Not too long." He gave me a soft smile, and it kindled the warmth in my heart. This time the fear was dimmer. It wasn't gone, not completely, but it wasn't as frightening as it had been—like it had been revealed as a small toy casting a monstrous shadow.

I'd never be able to get rid of it, but with Oscar beside me, holding my hand, I wasn't afraid of it anymore. I could learn to live with it.

"Did you watch me sleep?" I asked with a grin. Oscar shook his head, but his smile didn't fade.

"Sort of, but mostly I just answered emails."

"Exciting." I shuffled up the bed to sit next to him, leaning over for a kiss. "Thanks. For taking care of me. And making me talk it out."

"You're welcome." He kissed me again, his hand coming up to cup my jaw. "I was afraid you were going to run."

"I probably would have."

I melted into his touch, enjoying the closeness. Heat flared in my chest, and I ran my hand up Oscar's thigh. He let out a soft moan. God, I wanted to do so many delicious, dirty things to him. We'd had a lot of fun over the past few weeks, but we'd never gotten as far as anal. There had been an infinite number of hand and blow jobs, and some very sexy frotting one morning when desire had taken over as soon as we'd woken up.

"What do you want?" I asked. I would always let Oscar take the lead because there was something about making him happy that made my heart sing. "You can have anything you want from me."

He rolled me over, slotting himself between my legs. "Are you sure? You just went through something very emotional. I don't want to take advantage of you."

If I was the sort of person who swooned, I would have swooned. But I wasn't, so I didn't. But I did melt a little farther into the bed.

"I am. I want you, Oscar. You mean everything to me. I need you. Please."

Oscar leant down and kissed me, sliding his tongue inside my mouth. "Can I fuck you? Please. I want to be inside you."

I groaned as desire shot through me. "Yes. Yep. Definitely. Absolutely. I am one hundred percent on board with that. Get me naked and get your dick inside me now."

Oscar chuckled. "No, we're not rushing. I want to take this slowly."

"Seriously?" I raised one eyebrow, but inside my chest, I swooned. Just a little.

"Yes. I like this thing called romance. Have you ever heard of it?"

"Hmm," I said, screwing up my face and trying to stop myself from laughing. "Maybe. Sounds fake though."

"Nope, this is real." He kissed my forehead. "You are

incredible, Ilias Verrati, and I want to show you that. I want to make you feel everything you give to me."

"I..."

"If you even consider telling me you're not worth it or that you're not special, so help me God, I will push you out of bed right now."

"I retract my thoughts," I said. I couldn't remember the last time anyone had wanted to do anything romantic for me. Well, anyone except Oscar. He was a romantic through and through.

It was incredibly and wonderfully him.

"Good."

"I do have one non-romantic question though. Do you have lube and condoms? Because as fun as the idea of you fucking me is, I'm not into pain, and yeah, spit as lube is a thing, but it's not my thing."

"I've got both," Oscar said. There was a wry smile playing across his mouth as he spoke. I thought back to the prickly man I'd gone to Hawaii with and wondered what had changed.

In the past, I'd have said he finally got a good dicking, but since I was the one in bed with him, I knew it was more than that. But he stole my thoughts away with a lingering kiss before he climbed off the bed and headed for his suitcase.

"How devious," I teased. "When did you get these?"

Oscar shrugged. "This morning. I made a quick stop when Finn and I went to get pastries."

"You took your brother with you to get condoms?"

"He waited outside. Finn is a gentleman," Oscar said as

he threw the bottle onto the bed and unwrapped the box of condoms, dropping the plastic wrapper into the bin before walking back over to the bed. He put the box down and slowly peeled off his jumper.

I grinned, reaching for my own shirt, desperate to move things along.

"No touching," Oscar said. "I want to do that."

"I can't even take off my clothes?"

"No." He smiled serenely and unbuttoned his shirt, dropping it onto the floor before pulling off his jeans. "You're mine, and I want to spoil you. You just agreed to romance, remember?"

"I didn't realise it would mean I couldn't get naked." I stared at Oscar, who stood in front of me in just a pair of tight, navy boxers that clung to every part of him. "Although, I'm not complaining about this."

Oscar rolled his eyes and climbed onto the bed, bracketing me with his body and leaning down for a kiss, heat blazing in his eyes. "Shut up."

He nipped at my lip and pressed his tongue into my mouth, setting my blood on fire with every touch. His fingers reached for my shirt, popping open each button as he trailed kisses down my neck. He pushed my shirt over my shoulders, both of us sitting up for a second so I could pull it off and throw it somewhere. I'd find it later.

Oscar put his hand on my chest, gently guiding me back down to the bed. His lips were hot against my skin as he picked up where he'd left off, trailing kisses across my collarbone and down towards my nipples. I groaned as he kissed them, laving them with his tongue.

It felt good, but it wasn't enough. I desperately needed more.

"More... Please, Oscar. Touch me."

"I am touching you," he said, giving me a sly smile as he pressed slow kisses down my stomach.

"That's not... Fuck, that's not what I mean."

"You really need to learn patience."

"Patience is for other people."

Oscar chuckled. "You're so demanding."

He undid my belt and flicked open my jeans, relieving some of the pressure on my aching cock. He tugged my jeans down, and I lifted my hips so he could slide them off. Oscar tossed the jeans onto the floor and caressed my inner thigh.

"I'm desperate," I said. "There's a difference."

"Poor you. I'll have to do something about that." There was a hint of something in his voice I hadn't heard before. It sounded almost possessive. Whatever it was, it was hot as fuck.

He lowered his head between my legs, running his lips up my inner thigh until he reached my groin. He trailed more achingly soft kisses up my straining cock until he reached the waistband of my boxers. I thought he might tease me again, but instead, he just pulled them down and threw them out of the way.

"You're so gorgeous," he murmured. Any response I'd considered giving was cut off when he flicked his tongue over the head of my cock, licking up the drops of precum gathering there.

Oscar's hand stroked my thigh, his fingers sliding closer

to my ass as he took my cock into his mouth. I groaned as pleasure flooded me, and somewhere I heard the click of a bottle.

Oscar's slick fingers brushed against the sensitive skin of my hole, making me gasp. My hips bucked, pushing my cock deeper into his mouth. I'd have felt guilty for gagging him if Oscar hadn't swallowed around me and kept going.

He was going to be the fucking death of me.

"Yes," I said as he pushed one finger slowly inside me. "More! Please, Oscar, more."

"Patience," he said, releasing my cock with a slick pop. I glanced down my body towards him. He looked so fucking gorgeous—tousled hair, slick, red lips, and eyes full of heat.

He gently thrust his finger in and out, curling it to rub against my prostate. The pressure was deliciously teasing, and I tipped my head back and closed my eyes, letting it wash over me.

Oscar worked another finger into me, then a third, and by the time that happened I was a desperate mess in the middle of the bed who was *this* close to pinning him to the bed and riding his cock into oblivion. I could barely even string a sentence together.

"Oscar," I whined. "Please. I need you." I'd been going for demanding, but my voice failed me.

His fingers slowly eased out of me, and I sighed. I heard the rustle of the box of condoms and a single thought lit up my brain, making me sit bolt upright. Oscar raised an eyebrow at me.

"You okay?"

"Yeah, but I've... You..." I gestured at him. At some

point he'd lost his underwear, and my eyes were drawn to the flushed head of his hard cock. "I haven't reciprocated in any way. Like, I should at least suck your dick."

"It's fine," Oscar said. He leant down to give me a kiss, condom in hand. "I don't need anything, and I won't think you're selfish. Let me spoil you."

I frowned and opened my mouth, but Oscar just put his other hand on my chest and pushed me back down. "Don't argue with me. Just let me take care of you. Please."

"Okay." I nodded, watching as he rolled the condom onto his perfect cock. "But later, I'm getting my mouth on you. It'll be my turn to spoil you."

"If you insist." Oscar positioned himself between my spread thighs.

Any thoughts I'd had about continuing the conversation disappeared as he pressed his cock slowly inside me. There was a touch of sweet burn as I stretched around him, but fuck did he feel good inside me.

I moaned his name as I tilted my head up to beg for a kiss. Oscar obliged, kissing me sweetly as he pushed his cock deeper.

"Fuck, you feel so good," I said against his lips, his breath mingling with mine.

"You do too. You're perfect, Ilias." He continued to kiss me as he began to rock his hips. His cock brushed over my prostate as he pulled out slowly, then thrust back in at the same torturous pace.

At first, I thought he was teasing me, but I knew that wasn't Oscar's style. He just wanted to take me apart achingly slowly until there was nothing left of me but atoms, and then he'd piece me back together with gentle kisses and soft words.

I wrapped my arms around him, trailing my fingers up and down his spine, lifting my hips and wrapping my legs around him to pull him in deeper as he fucked me slowly. It was so different from all the sex I'd ever had, and it made the experience a thousand times more intense. All I could do was give in to it and surrender to Oscar's touch.

"Touch yourself," Oscar whispered as he thrust in deep and slow, his cock caressing my prostate. "I want to watch you come."

Slipping my hand between us, I gasped as my fingers grasped my weeping dick. It was almost like I'd been shocked. "It's... Fuck, it's too much. It's too much."

"Does it feel good though?" Oscar's voice was soft, his whispered words sending shivers across my skin. "Can you come for me?"

"Y-yeah, I can." I stroked my cock, broken sounds escaping my lips as the pleasure sent me higher and higher.

Oscar seemed determined to hit my sweet spot with every move he made, and it would be torturous if it didn't feel so fucking good. Heat and pressure were starting to build in my spine and my gut, and I felt my muscles starting to tremble.

"I'm... fuck, I'm getting close."

"That's it. I want you to come for me. Can you do that?" He kissed me again, his whole presence enveloping me and flooding my senses. "Come for me, baby."

I jerked my cock faster, gripping myself tightly as Oscar's cock rubbed over my prostate, and that was all it took. My orgasm overtook me, and I came with a yell, painting our skin with my cum. I felt nothing but absolute bliss and the press of Oscar's lips against mine. He was still fucking me, but he'd changed the angle and sped up his thrusts, and I knew he was chasing his own release.

"Yes," I groaned, trailing kisses down his neck. "I want it. I want you to come. Please, Oscar. Give it to me."

Oscar moaned, his eyes closing and mouth falling open. It was such a beautiful sight I wanted to try to remember it forever.

He thrust deep inside me again and again until he came with a deep groan. He buried his face in my neck as his cock pulsed inside me, his chest heaving, and all I could hear was the sound of our hearts racing.

# CHAPTER TWENTY-FIVE

*Oscar*

"What do you want to do now?" I asked as I brushed a stray strand of hair out of Ilias's face.

We were lying side by side in bed, under the covers this time, having crawled in after cleaning up and dumping the remaining excess cushions on the floor. I didn't actually feel like doing much except lying there until it was time to go down for dinner.

"I don't mind," Ilias said. He looked so relaxed. He wasn't the put-together person everyone usually saw, and it made me so grateful I got to see him that way. "We could stay here, just veg for a bit? Or we could go down to the beach? Walk along the sea? I don't think it's far. Depends how energetic you feel."

"I kinda like the idea of staying here," I said. "But the sea does sound nice."

"We could get fish and chips. I haven't had fish and chips for ages."

"Didn't you have some in Devon last week?" I grinned, and Ilias scoffed.

"That was posh hotel fish and chips. I mean, like, proper chip shop fish and chips."

I thought for a second. We were supposed to be having dinner in the hotel's restaurant because one of the requirements for the article was that we test out the food. We couldn't recommend somewhere with shit food to our readers, no matter how beautiful the rooms were. But fish and chips by the sea did sound good.

"How about we have dinner here tonight because I have to eat here at least once, and I know we have a table reserved, but tomorrow, we can have a poke around the town and get fish and chips before we head off?"

Ilias screwed up his face for a second like he was thinking hard before breaking out into a grin. "As long as I get fish and chips, I'll be happy." He kissed me again. "Come on, let's go for a walk now."

"But I thought we were staying in bed?"

"Nope, I want to go and scout out chip shops. And I'd like to actually leave the hotel once today. I've spent most of the day either in a car, a house, or a hotel. I need some fresh air."

Ilias made a fair point. I had to give him that. "Fine. Let's go."

I hauled myself out of bed and collected my clothes, pulling them on while trying to watch Ilias. He really was gorgeous, and I wanted to while away hours in bed with him—not necessarily making love but just being together.

When he was dressed, he shoved the room key into his jacket pocket along with his phone, then reached for my hand. I smiled and slipped my fingers into his. Ilias grinned, and my heart flooded with emotion.

It was good to see him smile again after our earlier conversation. The fear and guilt in his voice and expression had almost broken me, and I'd just wanted to scoop him up in my arms and take his pain away. I'd never be able to truly understand what he'd been through, but I hoped what I could offer would be enough.

I could see now why he'd gravitated to hook-ups and flings—relationships that required no emotional connection, despite how obvious it was that he craved them. The more time we spent together, the more I realised how much Ilias loved to be near me.

It wasn't just his barnacle approach to sleep but the way he wanted to hold my hand when we walked together, the way he would rest his hand on my thigh when we were in the car, and the way he would press a soft kiss to my face just because.

I'd told Ilias I wasn't going anywhere, and I'd meant it. I just needed to make my feelings clear.

Because wherever he was in the world, that was where I wanted to be.

"By the way," Ilias said as we headed down the stairs, "did you hear back from Marcus yet about the rest of the destinations you pitched?"

"Not yet. I think they're still deciding."

"Any way you can get him to hurry up? I need another holiday."

"Doesn't this count as one?"

Ilias shrugged. "Sort of, but it's been very intense with all the travelling. I just want somewhere I can lie on a beach for a week."

I snorted. "How much lying on a beach did you actually do in Hawaii?"

"Fine, I want somewhere I can lie on a beach if I want to. I want the option to be there."

We walked through reception and out into the evening sunlight. The sun hung low in the sky, bathing the sea in a spectacular riot of colour. The hotel was at one end of a horseshoe bay, and from outside the hotel we could see the pretty, seaside town of Heather Bay spread out in front of us. High on the hills on the opposite side of the bay stood what looked like a castle, and I made a mental note to see if Ilias was up for exploring it tomorrow.

"You could lie on the beach here," I said, gesturing at the wide strip of dark sand and the row of colourful beach huts that lined the beach. "Might be a little chilly though."

"I am definitely not wearing skimpy swimwear in this weather," Ilias said with a dramatic shudder. "It's May in Yorkshire. It's hardly Santorini. And there aren't any cute beach boys to bring me drinks and snacks."

"That reminds me, I pitched Santorini as one of the European locations. It's picturesque, warm, and it's some-where my sister desperately wants to visit."

"So you want to go there first to piss her off?" Ilias

asked. "I've met your sister. She's not one to be messed with."

"No! I'm going there to test it out." I laughed at Ilias's expression. I didn't think he believed me. "It's the truth. I want to find somewhere nice that I can recommend to her and Chantelle."

"You better make sure it's child friendly, then," Ilias said. "Not just with some shitty, half-assed kids club either."

"Oh, please. You think *The Traveller* is going to recommend somewhere with crap childcare? How else will we appeal to the yummy mummies who want the feel of a family holiday without actually having to spend time with their children."

"One day," Ilias said with a wry smile, "I'm going to take you to one of my family events and turn you loose. You'd go down a storm."

"You just want to watch me cause chaos."

"Yes, because it'll be spectacular. I'm going to introduce you to my auntie Tonia. You'll hate her. I'm going to bring popcorn."

I shook my head and rolled my eyes fondly. The idea of attending one of Ilias's family functions both fascinated and horrified me. Based on the stories I'd heard, they sounded like a soap opera playing out in miniature in the span of two or three hours.

I'd always thought my family was intense, but Ilias's took it to a whole new level.

We'd reached the steps to go down to the beach. In the light of the setting sun, the beach huts in front of us were bathed in a fiery glow. There were quite a few people pottering along the sand with children and dogs, and to our left, the line of shops and restaurants that made up the front was still busy with people.

"Which way do you want to go?" I asked as we came to a stop. "Want to walk along the front and then come back via the beach? Or beach first?"

"Let's go beach first." Ilias squeezed my hand tighter and began to steer me towards the stone steps. The tide was quite far out, leaving a wide stretch of sand that curved around the bay. We'd tried to get out and explore all the towns and beaches we'd stayed near, even if the weather had been shit, but there was something about this beach that felt different.

Maybe it was because Ilias and I had gotten everything out in the open. There was no longer a shadow hanging over our relationship, just the acceptance that things weren't always going to be simple.

We both knew things weren't going to be magically fixed with a single conversation. Ilias's fears wouldn't suddenly disappear with a click of my fingers, even if I wished they would. It was going to take time, and I was going to be there every step of the way.

"What are you thinking about?" Ilias asked as we walked. There was a breeze coming off the sea that ruffled his hair and made him look gorgeously rumpled.

"Not much," I said. "Just about you and me. And how pretty it is here."

"It is lovely." Ilias paused for a second to watch a large, soggy-looking golden retriever chase a ball into the water.

The air was filled with the cawing of seabirds, the barking of dogs, and the shrieking of happy children mixed with the sound of the waves. "It must get busy in the summer though."

I nodded. "I reckon so. It's very picturesque." I looked up at the rows of houses I could see winding their way up into the hills above the bay. "I wonder how many of those are Airbnbs or holiday homes."

Ilias frowned. "Honestly, I hope not many of them. You hear all these stories about locals getting priced out of places when they get popular with holidaymakers—like how landlords prioritise making quick cash off tourists rather than letting to local tenants. And forget even trying to buy."

"Sometimes I wonder whether my job is a bad thing," I said as we started to walk again. "I love travelling, and I love being able to show different places to people, but sometimes I wonder whether the cost is too high."

"It's tricky because so many places rely on tourism. A bad season can make or break a local economy. But you're right that it can also exploit people and make things harder for locals. If half the houses in a place are holiday lets, it just creates ghost towns out of season. There's no community and no care. If people can't afford to live there, then the things that tourists want or rely on aren't going to be available because there's nobody around to run them. Places get drained of life and beauty, the things that attracted people in the first place. It's a vicious circle."

Ilias squeezed my hand and continued. "I don't think it makes you a bad person though or your job an inherently bad one. People are always going to want to travel, and if you weren't writing these articles then someone else would be. You're aware of the issues, or you try to be, and I think that's a good first step."

"Thanks," I said.

"Besides, it's not as if you're jetting off to Dubai every week on a private jet and posting from some luxury hotel."

"I mean, I probably wouldn't be allowed in."

"Me either, but that wasn't my point." He nudged me, and I grinned. "My point was, you're not trying to be some shitty travel influencer or something. You want people to explore the world, but you want the same opportunities for everyone, and you want people to be aware of their impact."

He pulled me to a stop and twisted me around so he could kiss me.

"We're having some very serious conversations today," he added, and I felt him smiling against my mouth. "We should talk about something fun instead!"

"Any suggestions?"

"No. All I can think about is fish and chips."

I laughed, and we continued walking. "I do have one thing to say though."

"What?"

"Don't you have a travel Instagram? Doesn't that make you some sort of travel influencer?"

Ilias gasped playfully. "Oh no, you've discovered my secret."

"You've never hidden it," I said. I'd never gone looking for his account, but he'd mentioned it a couple of times offhandedly in Hawaii, so I'd assumed it was something he ran with care.

"At least you didn't call me a shitty travel influencer. And for the record, I'm not. I'm a delight!"

"I wouldn't know."

"Wait, you don't follow me?" Ilias asked, and it was all I could do not to laugh at the extreme level of faux outrage in his tone. "That is a heinous crime and must be rectified right now. Come on, get your phone out."

He reached for my back pocket and tried to extract my phone, except he seemed more interested in grabbing my butt than actually retrieving the device.

"Fine, fine. Stop pawing at me."

"I wasn't. I was getting your phone."

"Really?" I hummed suspiciously as I pulled up Instagram. "What's your account name?"

I followed Ilias's instructions and pulled up his account. I knew his grid was going to be beautiful, so seeing the stunning array of photographs didn't surprise me. What did catch me off guard was the number of followers he had.

"You have half a million followers?"

"Yes," Ilias said gleefully. "Didn't you know?"

"Er, no."

"So you've never casually stalked me on the internet?"

"Mostly just on Twitter," I said. "It felt weird to do more."

"It wouldn't have been weird. It's not like you'd have told me."

I turned to look at him, and I saw his smile getting

bigger. There was a devious edge to it that I hadn't seen before, and I got the feeling I was missing something.

"Also," Ilias continued, "I can't believe you didn't follow me when we started dating. How rude! I feel like I should throw some sort of diva strop about it."

I laughed. "You can if you want."

"Nah, that'll just prove your point about me being a shitty travel influencer."

"I never said shitty!" I exclaimed, and now Ilias was laughing too. "You're putting words in my mouth."

"I can put something else in your mouth if you want."

"Thanks, you've just ruined it," I said with a snort.

"Hey, I never said *what* I'd put in your mouth. You were the one who immediately thought of my dick. I could have been suggesting candy floss for all you know."

"Were you going to suggest that?" I raised my eyebrow, and Ilias shrugged.

"Maybe. Now you'll never know." He leant in to give me a teasing kiss, then pulled me towards the steps at the other end of the beach.

"Come on," he said as I let my feet follow him. "I'm getting hungry, and if we don't go back now, I'm going to raid all these fish and chip shops."

# CHAPTER TWENTY-SIX

*Ilias*

"Do you think you can manage not to get us lost today?" I asked teasingly as we climbed into the car to head up towards Hareford House, the castle on the cliffs above Heather Bay. We didn't have long to explore, but I wanted to get out in the fresh air before the next leg of our journey.

"You can drive if you want," Oscar said, giving me a withering look.

"No thanks. It's your turn."

"You just don't want to be the one who gets lost," Oscar muttered as he turned the car on. "You know all we have to do is follow the signs? We probably could have walked."

"Probably, but it's also meant to rain, and I don't fancy getting soaked and spending the rest of the day looking like a drowned rat. Especially since we have to drive up to Northumberland this afternoon."

"Okay, you have a point there."

"Only five more hotels to go, then we're done," I said. "I never thought I'd be glad to see the back of luxury hotels, but I'm quite looking forward to a few nights in London."

"I think it's just been the intensity. We haven't really been able to settle anywhere." He pulled the car onto the main road and began to follow the signs out of town.

"Exactly! Although, it's given me a list of places I want to go back to." I peered out the window at the small shops and terraced houses, wishing I had more time to have a nosy.

Out of all the places we'd stayed, Heather Bay was the one that intrigued me most. The narrow, cobbled streets that wound their way up the hills seemed like they'd be a treasure trove of shops, cafés, and restaurants.

"Like here," I continued. "I haven't done nearly enough poking around."

"We'll have to come back, then," Oscar said. "Take a long weekend at some point."

There was something in the casual way he'd suggested us taking a non-work trip together that pulled me up short. If I'd been walking, I would have stopped dead in my tracks.

Travelling was our life, and Oscar was casually just slotting me into his plans like it was nothing. I wasn't even sure if Heather Bay was somewhere he'd wanted to revisit, but he'd suggested it because I did want to come back.

The slow realisation that had been building deep beneath the surface of my emotions bobbed to the surface, but this time, they didn't come with a parasitic attachment of fear.

Oscar and I were building something together—a relationship that had a real chance. And while I would always miss Daniele and what we might have had, it didn't mean I had to spend the rest of my life alone. I just had to take each day as it came and build memories with the man next to me.

We followed the winding road up towards Hareford House, and turned onto the long, tree-lined drive between two large stone pillars. As we parked the car, I got hints of a gorgeous view over the bay, even with clouds starting to gather across the horizon.

"Do you want to go into the house?" Oscar asked. "Or do you just want to walk around the grounds?"

"We could see how much a ticket is. But maybe start with the grounds in case it starts pissing it down, then we can take shelter." Even though it was May, there was still a sharp breeze blowing in off the sea, and it sent a shiver running down my spine.

As I pulled on my jacket, wishing I had something warmer, a fat drop of rain landed on the back of my neck quickly followed by several more.

"Why must it always fucking rain in this country?!" I shook my head. "I just want some bloody sunshine."

Oscar laughed and pulled an umbrella off the back seat, casually popping it open and ushering me under it as we began to walk towards the visitor entrance. "Now you've said that we're going to get three months of unending, baking heat and humidity."

"And I'll complain about that too," I said, trying not to laugh. "Because we don't have any bloody air conditioning.

Heat is only acceptable when I have a pool, cocktails, and something cold to lie under."

The rain was coming down heavier now, and our pace increased, feet crunching on the gravel.

"This is going to ruin your fish and chips on the beach for lunch idea," Oscar said. He had to raise his voice for me to hear him over the drumming of the rain on the umbrella.

"Fish and chips in the car?" I asked, hopping on one foot to avoid a rapidly forming puddle. The view of the bay had been quickly obscured by the incoming clouds, giving the whole place an eerie vibe.

"Don't you think that'll make the car smell?"

"I don't care as long as I get fish and chips! We can air it out later."

Oscar laughed, his fingers finding mine and pulling me close. We were suddenly nose to nose, and the world shrank to just the two of us under an enormous umbrella.

And I suddenly knew, with complete clarity, that I wanted to spend every day having adventures with this man. Because I loved him.

I loved him more utterly and completely than I'd ever loved anyone.

Oscar had taken the pieces of me that I'd tried to hide and pretend weren't broken and had started to glue them back together, unfazed by the fact that he had no guidelines to go on. He hadn't had to fix my broken heart, but he had done it anyway whether by accident or by choice.

Oscar had allowed me to love again.

My free hand reached out towards him, tentatively brushing his cheek.

"Are you okay?" he asked, frowning.

"Yes." I nodded. "I just realised something though."

"What?"

"That I love you," I said, holding my breath like I was waiting at the top of a rollercoaster, waiting for the drop. "I hope that's okay."

"It's more than okay." Oscar smiled and tilted his head. His lips were virtually touching mine. "I love you too."

Then he kissed me, and I knew I'd never forget that moment for as long as I lived.

As pretty as Hareford House was, I hardly remembered a moment of our tour. My mind was still lingering on the man holding my hand, and the three simple words that had changed everything.

I'd never expected to fall in love again, and I certainly hadn't expected to fall for a prickly travel journalist who'd asked me to be his fake boyfriend.

But that was love, I supposed. It happened when you least expected it.

"What are you thinking about?" Oscar asked. We were driving again, zipping up towards Northumberland in the afternoon sunshine. The rain had cleared not long after we'd left Heather Bay, and despite his minor protestations about lingering smells, Oscar had still given in to my demands for a fish and chip lunch by the sea.

"You," I said. "Just thinking about how strange fate is."

"Oh?"

"I never really thought I'd fall in love again. I thought it was for other people. But then you came along and caught me off guard." I shrugged. "I just wasn't expecting it."

"Is that a bad thing? Do you not want to love me?" Oscar sounded concerned, and I winced.

"No, fuck no, nothing like that! I just meant that it surprised me. *You* surprised me but not in a bad way. I think that's why I fell for you. You were so immune to my charms at first, and you intrigued me. I wanted to know what made you tick."

"What did you find?" Oscar asked. When I turned to look at him, he was grinning.

"A grumpy journalist who actually cares very deeply, even if he won't let many people see it. And someone who has the most basic taste in cookies I've ever met."

"Oh my God, this again! Peanut butter and chocolate is not a basic choice. It's a classic. You're just pretentious."

"Pretentious?" I laughed.

"Yes! You're a cookie snob."

"Then I'll never buy you cookies again."

"You've never bought me cookies to begin with," Oscar said pointedly.

"Fine," I said, picking my phone up from where it had been resting in the middle console. I'd been intending to find a cookie bakery in London I could drag Oscar to the minute we got home to prove my point, but I was distracted by the string of messages from my family. "Oh joy."

"What's wrong?"

"It's just my family." I flicked open the messages and rolled my eyes. "They somehow found out I had a boyfriend. I guess Dominic ratted me out, even though I just called you my friend, so now they're playing twenty questions. Oh, and they're asking if I'm going to be bringing you to my cousin's wedding, even though it's not until next year." I sighed. "And now you think I'm really fucking weird or not committed because I told my brother you're my friend, and you're probably thinking about how to get rid of me because I just told you all the ridiculous shit my family's pulling."

"First of all," Oscar said, putting his hand on my thigh in that comforting way he always did. "I don't think you're not committed. I understand why you did it, considering you know what they're like. And I'm not going anywhere. To be honest, I kind of expected this. You've told me enough stories to prepare me. So if you want me to come with you to your cousin's wedding, I will. And we can even have some kind of code word, and I can swoop in and rescue you if they try to overwhelm you."

"Seriously? You'd do that?" I stared at him. "You realise me taking you would be like throwing prime rib into a lion's den?"

"I mean, you've met my family."

"Yeah, but your family is actually reasonable."

Oscar laughed. "Only to some people."

I grinned and shook my head, starting to tap out some limited responses. They were mostly just limited variations of me politely telling people to fuck off, which they'd probably all bitch about thoroughly, but I didn't care. I had a boyfriend who loved me, and that was all that mattered.

"I do just have one request though," Oscar said. "Can

we start the meet and greets in small doses? I'd rather leave with all my limbs attached."

I laughed. "Fine, if you insist. You can meet Dominic and Louisa first. We can go out for dinner or something. My brother owes me big time for squealing, so I'm going to demand dinner, at least, as compensation for emotional damage."

"Emotional damage?"

"Yeah," I said, looking at the unending stream of messages and GIFs. Someone really needed to take all my aunts', uncles', and cousins' phones away. "For having to look at this shit. Oh my God, my uncle is now asking gay relationship questions. I'm out!"

I forwarded the message to Dominic with a snide comment about needing repayment for dealing with this shit, then locked my phone. I'd deal with the rest of them later.

"So... where were we?" I asked with a wry smile, knowing exactly where we'd left off.

"Not sure," Oscar said. "But I've just seen a sign for some services. Fancy a break? I'll get you snacks."

"Are you trying to distract me with food?"

"Is it working?" He grinned and pulled into the lane for the exit.

"I suppose. But just this once."

"I'll take it."

I smiled to myself and turned my phone over in my hand. This amount of happiness would probably have felt overwhelming six months ago, but now it just felt normal. And I hoped that never changed.

# CHAPTER TWENTY-SEVEN

*Oscar*

"Okay, have you made a decision?" Ilias asked from where he was stretched out on the bed in my studio flat wearing one of my old t-shirts and a pair of boxers. It was very distracting.

"I think so," I said, trying to focus on my laptop and the list in front of me. We were trying to narrow the seaside hotels down to the top ten for the article, but it was proving to be a challenge. "What about you?"

"I'm not the one writing the article. I'm not sure why I'm getting a say."

"Would you really not want me to ask your opinion?" I raised an eyebrow, and Ilias grinned with faux innocence. "You just don't want to make a decision."

"I liked them all! I'm not sure why Marcus would have us review fifteen hotels if the list was only for ten. Why not just pick ten for us to check out and then if one of them sucked we could have looked for another option?"

Ilias had a point, but there wasn't really anything I could do about it now, considering we'd already stayed at all of them.

"Come on, you have to ditch at least one. Which was your least favourite?"

"I don't know," Ilias said, rolling over onto his stomach. It gave me the perfect view of his ass, and I wondered if he was trying to distract me. I frowned as Ilias casually rolled his hips from side to side.

He was definitely trying to distract me.

"Which one scored lowest on the Verrati index?" I asked, determined to try to focus on the task at hand. For now at least.

I hadn't expected Ilias to stick around so much once we'd gotten back to London. I'd been expecting things to go back to the way they'd been before we'd left on our seaside adventure, but instead, Ilias had practically moved into my studio with only one or two quick jaunts back to his brother's house for extra clothes.

I hadn't said anything about it to him because I didn't want him to think I didn't want him there. I did. It just amused me how quickly things had progressed between us. But I'd always believed there was no set timeline for these things. Every relationship moved at a different pace, and it just depended on what was right for the participants.

"The second Kent one," Ilias said. He was flicking through a notebook that was filled with random scribblings. "It was nice, but the decor was a bit dated, and the food could have been better."

"Agreed. I think *nice* is the best word I can think of to describe it."

"And nice is not what we're going for."

"Exactly. Madelyn Rossi does not do *nice*," I said, marking the hotel name in red on my list. "One down, four to go."

"You have to pick next. It's only fair."

I hummed in agreement and scrolled through my notes, trying to watch Ilias out of the corner of my eye. He was rolling his hips again, his skin-tight, white boxer briefs highlighting the perfect curve of his ass. His t-shirt had started to ride up, showing off a strip of tanned skin at the base of his spine. I didn't know why he was still wearing the t-shirt to be honest.

"Stop that," I said without looking at him.

"Stop what?"

"Trying to distract me."

"Me? Distract you? I'm not doing anything." I heard the teasing note in his voice and scoffed.

"Yeah, sure."

"Trust me, if I was trying to distract you, I'd be going for something far less subtle," Ilias said, and I knew he was trying to bait me.

I wasn't going to give in. But my mouth had other ideas.

"Like?" I asked, still not looking up.

"I thought we were supposed to be working?"

"We are." Not that I was actually focusing on my notes.

I'd read the same sentence five times in the last thirty seconds.

"Then choose another hotel," Ilias said.

I chewed my lip, trying to force my distracted brain to make a decision. "What about the Suffolk one?"

"I liked that one."

"As much as the others?" I turned my head to look at him and instantly realised I'd made a mistake.

Ilias had removed his t-shirt and was now stretched out on his side facing me, giving me a perfect view of his tanned chest and the dark trail of hair leading down into his boxers... which were clinging to his half-hard cock.

Ilias saw me looking and reached down to adjust his dick, his eyes locked with mine.

"The bed squeaked," I said, forcing the words out. "Remember?"

"That's true."

"And the room was quite cramped."

"It was," Ilias said as he palmed himself through the front of his underwear. I couldn't take my eyes off him, and all my points about work evaporated.

"So, er... that one is out then?"

"Agreed."

I marked it in red. "Do you want to choose another one?"

Ilias chuckled. "Do you?"

"Not really," I said.

"I thought you didn't want to get distracted?" Ilias teased. "I thought you wanted to get this done."

"Fuck it. We can finish it later." I closed the laptop and stood, striding over to the bed. It took me barely five steps.

Ilias grinned up at me, but I didn't give him a chance to say anything before I leant down and claimed his mouth in a hungry kiss. Ilias moaned as I used my knee to push his thighs apart, climbing onto the bed and blanketing his body with mine.

"You're wearing too many clothes," Ilias said against my mouth.

I sat up and pulled my t-shirt off before realising I'd need to stand up to shuck off my jeans and underwear. I had no idea how people ever managed to make getting undressed look sexy because I always found it awkward as fuck.

Ilias was watching me with gleaming eyes. As my gaze met his, he grasped his waistband and slowly pulled his boxers down, revealing his flushed cock.

A low growl escaped my chest as I reached for him, my bed groaning underneath us as I pinned him to the mattress, his body hot and hard underneath me. His erection rubbed against mine, the friction sending a delicious wave of pleasure through me.

Our lips met over and over, his tongue pushing into my mouth and making me melt. I just wanted to keep him in my bed and bring him to orgasm over and over until he was utterly spent. I'd do anything to make Ilias happy, to show him just how much he meant to me.

"Mmm, more," he muttered, his fingers tangling in my hair and pulling me closer. He ground his hips up again. I nipped his lip and made him gasp before starting to trail kisses down his neck, knowing how much it made him squirm.

I worked my mouth down his body, teasing the hard nubs of his nipples with my tongue and my teeth but not lingering. I didn't have the patience to drag this out.

"Fuck, oh fuck!" Ilias cried as I wrapped my lips around the leaking head of his cock. His hands were on my head, anchoring himself as I swallowed him down. One of my hands trailed down the inside of his thigh, pushing his legs wider, while my other hand reached for my own cock, giving myself some slow strokes as I sucked him.

I pulled off his cock with a slick pop, leaving Ilias wanting more. He whined and moaned, his hands trying to pull me back to him.

"No," I said with a hoarse chuckle, moving my mouth lower and pressing a kiss to his taint. "I'm not sucking your cock again."

"What are you—fuck!"

I smirked as I answered his unanswered question with my tongue, swiping it across the musky, furled skin of his hole. Ilias's hips practically jack-knifed off the bed. I licked and sucked on the sensitive skin, working him open while he writhed in pleasure.

Ilias ground his hips down, riding my tongue, and I let him take what he wanted from me.

"Here," Ilias said, tapping my head with something solid. I lifted up to look at him, drinking in his flushed skin and wanton expression before realising he was trying to hand me a bottle of lube. I grinned.

"Did you want something?" I asked.

"No. I want you to paint the fucking *Mona Lisa* with it."

I snorted and took the bottle, pouring some onto my fingers. "Might be a bit difficult with lube."

"Ha-fucking-ha. Just—fuck! Oh fuck, yes!" Ilias's snark melted into moans as I slowly pressed my finger into him.

"Like that?" I asked, curling my finger to tease his prostate.

"Y-yes. More."

I worked another finger into him, stretching him open while my other hand reached underneath my body to jack my cock. "Do you want a third?"

"No," Ilias said. "I want you to fuck me."

I pulled my fingers out of him and got my knees underneath me, unwrapping the condom Ilias had thrown onto the bed next to me. He grinned at me and flipped himself over onto his hands and knees, looking at me over his shoulder with expectation.

"God, you're so fucking perfect," I said as I dripped more lube on his hole and slicked up my cock. Ilias moaned as I tapped my dick against him.

"Oh fuck, give it to me." Ilias groaned as I pushed slowly inside him. His ass was hot and tight, squeezing my cock and pulling me in deeper.

I gripped his hips tightly, planting one foot on the bed to give me more leverage as I bottomed out. Ilias let out another moan, then looked at me over his shoulder.

"Fuck me, Oscar."

I didn't need any further encouragement. I pulled Ilias onto my cock and began to fuck him hard and fast, giving in to my desperate need for him. Ilias cried out as I pounded him, pressing back onto me.

"Yes! Just like that. Fucking yes... Harder..." Ilias dropped his head and shoulders down, allowing me to go impossibly deep.

Desire consumed me. I wasn't sure where it had come from, but maybe it had always been there just waiting to be unleashed. I couldn't get enough of Ilias.

At this rate, we were never going to get anything done because all I wanted to do was spend my time worshipping him and turning him into a rapturous, begging mess in the middle of my bed.

"Touch yourself," I said. "I want to feel you come. Want to hear you."

"Yes... You, fuck, you like it when I'm loud, don't you?"

"Yes. Love hearing you. Love knowing I'm doing that to you."

Ilias groaned, and I heard the wet slap of skin on skin as he began to jerk himself. It sent pleasure spinning through me, and I gripped his hips so hard I almost worried he'd bruise.

I pounded into him, angling myself so I could tag his prostate with every drag of my cock. I knew I'd gotten it right when Ilias cried out in desperation.

I felt my orgasm bearing down on me, and I knew there was nothing I could do to stop it.

"Ilias..." I growled. "I'm close."

"Me too. Fuck! I'm gonna... gonna come."

Ilias cried out, his ass tightening around me as I thrust in deep sending me spinning over the edge alongside him. I let out a deep groan as my orgasm shook my body, releasing all the pent-up tension I'd been starting to feel throughout the afternoon.

I hadn't even realised I'd been frustrated until then.

"Mmm, that was fun," Ilias said from underneath me, twisting his head to look up at me with a satisfied smile spreading across his face. "We should do that again."

He stretched out his arms and sank farther into the bed. I gently pulled out and released his hips, watching him spread out like an oversized cat and sigh happily.

"Do you feel better now?"

"What do you mean?" I climbed off the bed, disposing of the condom in my bathroom bin.

"You were getting frustrated," Ilias said, rolling onto his back, still gloriously naked, his spent cock resting against his hip. "With work. I thought you could do with a distraction."

"So you *were* trying to distract me!" I flopped down onto the bed next to him and gave him a soft kiss. Ilias shot me a withering look and a fond smile.

"It helped though, didn't it?"

"I suppose."

"Really? You suppose? You didn't just take out all your frustrations on my ass?"

"I'm sorry. Did I hurt you?"

"Of course not." Ilias snuggled into me and kissed me again. He looked utterly gorgeous all rumpled and relaxed. He looked like mine. "I liked it, and if I hadn't, I'd have said something."

He wrapped his arms around me, pinning me in place. I

kissed the top of his head, his sweet vanilla and peach smell filling my senses.

"You do realise I still have to finish the list?" I didn't want to get up again or go back to work, but Marcus was expecting a draft of the article by Wednesday morning, and it was already Monday afternoon.

I only had to write a couple hundred words about each place, but distilling the hotel, the local area, and the experience down to something short and catchy was my idea of a nightmare.

It was more like writing sales copy than a review. I had a tendency to wax lyrical and focus on the things that interested me rather than what would interest *The Traveller*'s readership. It was something I was still working on, which was partly why I suspected Marcus had given me this assignment—because it would give me a chance to practice.

I was still expecting my draft to be returned by the end of the week covered in notes and tracked changes.

Ilias muttered something I didn't catch, then said. "Fine. But we're doing it from here. Your top ten, off the top of your head. And if you can do it in under two minutes, I'll give you a blow job later. Go."

I chuckled. "Fine... Right... Heather Bay, that was nice, August House..."

# CHAPTER TWENTY-EIGHT

*Ilias*

I GRIPPED Oscar's hand tightly as we climbed out of the Uber and onto the pavement outside Dominic's house, my heart drumming against my ribs. I had no idea why I was so nervous to have dinner with my brother and Louisa, but it felt like I was about to be interrogated by MI5.

Not that I was going to let that happen. Dominic had some serious explaining to do about why he'd ratted me out to everyone.

The interrogator was about to become the interrogated.

"Breathe," Oscar said as we stepped up to the familiar, polished black front door. "It's going to be okay. It's just your brother and his wife, not your entire family. We can do this."

"Easy for you to say," I muttered. "Your family is charming. I just don't understand why we couldn't have just gone to a restaurant instead? Why did they insist on making dinner?"

"Because they wanted to be nice?"

"I bet it's because Dominic wants to pin me down and ask me awkward questions. Although, his plan would have worked better in a restaurant because I wouldn't yell at him in public." I reached for the door handle, then wondered if I should knock.

My living situation had been a little weird for the past couple of weeks, and I'd half moved out of Dominic's and into Oscar's studio without really talking to either of them about it.

When we'd gotten back from our seaside tour, I hadn't wanted to go back to sleeping alone, so I'd decided not to. The first night I'd gone back to Oscar's to relax and unwind, and when we'd ended up in bed, it had felt totally natural to stay there.

And after that, I hadn't wanted to leave.

I'd made a few quick trips back to Dominic's for clothes and to see Teddy, Nico, and the twins, but I'd always gone back to Oscar's afterwards. His studio was tiny and a little cramped with two of us living in it, but it felt more like home than Dominic's house ever had.

The decision about the door was taken away from me when it swung open to reveal a glamorously dressed Louisa and a beaming Teddy in a pair of blue and orange pyjamas patterned with sharks in swim trunks.

"Uncle Ilias!" Teddy cried as he leapt at me, a beaming smile on his face. "I missed you. You haven't been here in forever."

"I'm sorry, buddy," I said, scooping him up into my arms and giving him a squeeze. "I've been busy with work."

Teddy frowned and looked at Oscar, then back at me. "Can we go see the sharks this weekend, please?"

"Sure." I didn't have anything else planned, and I owed him. Teddy was used to having me around virtually all the time, and in the space of a month, I'd practically up and left, and that wasn't fair to him. "We can go tomorrow. For the whole day. As long as your mum says yes."

I looked at Louisa, and she nodded. "You can go with Uncle Ilias. But you have to go and do your teeth now, then go to bed. Okay? Go ask your dad if he'll read you a story while I finish making dinner."

"Okay." Teddy gave me a kiss and wiggled out of my arms. "Bye! See you tomorrow."

I watched him run towards the kitchen, his feet thudding on the wooden floor. I grinned and turned to Oscar, who was hovering politely behind me.

"So that's Teddy, and this is my sister-in-law, Louisa," I said with a casual wave of my hand. "Louisa, this is my Oscar. Shit, I mean, my boyfriend, Oscar."

"Lovely to meet you," Oscar said as he reached out to shake Louisa's hand.

"So nice to meet you too. Finally." Louisa shot me a wry smile. "Come on through. Dinner is nearly ready. Let me get you some drinks. I've got some nibbles too."

"You're hungry, right?" I whispered to Oscar as we followed Louisa through to the living room, which seemed to have been tidied to within an inch of its life.

I wondered what form of bribery had been offered to Nico to put his elaborate train-scapes away.

"Er, yeah. You said Louisa likes to cook."

"It's her hobby," I said. I'd told Oscar to come hungry, but I wondered if we had different definitions because if Louisa decided she was making dinner, she was likely going all out.

And to prove my point, Louisa chose that moment to stroll through the living room door with an enormous charcuterie board in hand. It looked absolutely gorgeous.

It also looked like an entire meal for four on a wooden slab the size of a tree trunk.

"Lou, is this your idea of nibbles?" I asked, staring at the immense selection of fruit, cheese, olives, cured meats, and crackers. "What have you made for dinner?"

Louisa shrugged and reached for a bottle of red wine that had been left to breathe on the sideboard. "Nothing fancy. Just some burrata and tomatoes to start, herb crusted lamb racks, and Nonna's tiramisu."

"I love how that's your definition of nothing fancy," I said.

"It sounds wonderful," Oscar said, and I rolled my eyes and grinned at him.

"Don't be such a suck-up."

"You don't have to have any if you don't want," Louisa said with a teasing smile as she passed me a glass of wine.

"I never said I didn't want any. I just said that my equivalent of a simple dinner is very different than yours, but that is definitely not a bad thing."

"Can you cook?" Oscar asked with a wry smile. "I never asked."

"Excuse me. What do you think I've been doing for the past two weeks? I made you carbonara! And moussaka. They didn't just appear in your kitchen."

"You did." Oscar put an arm around me and pressed a kiss to my temple. "And they were delicious, but my point stands that technically I never asked if you could cook, you just took over my kitchen."

"That's because your range of meals seems to be limited to bad student food and whatever takes your fancy on Deliveroo," I said with a raised eyebrow.

I saw Louisa watching us with a curious smile, then I realised she'd never seen me with a boyfriend before, so this had to be a totally alien experience for her. I didn't think I acted that differently with Oscar, but maybe I did.

"That's only mostly true. I can make a good roast dinner. But that's about it."

"Seriously? You can make a full roast dinner, but you can't make pasta?"

"To be fair," said Dominic as he strolled through the living room door. "Not everyone had an Italian nonna insisting they learn to cook and making them practice every summer from the age of six. Most people just buy pasta." He gave Oscar an easy smile and stuck out his hand. "Hi, I'm Dominic. You must be Oscar."

"It's nice to meet you," Oscar said as he shook Dominic's outstretched hand.

Dominic took the glass of wine Louisa handed him and gestured for us to take a seat on the nearest sofa, which was oddly free of teddies and baby toys. "How was your trip? I've hardly seen you since you got back."

"Sorry, I've been busy," I said, perching on the edge of the sofa. I'd only been gone a few weeks, but already, I felt out of place at Dominic's. "Also, I'm not sure if I've forgiven you for ratting me out to everyone. How did you even know?"

"I didn't," Dominic said, looking at Louisa with a frown. "Neither of us did. I wouldn't do that to you. I promise."

"Then who told?"

"I don't know." He thought for a second. "Wait, hang on. I know." He sighed. "You went out for dinner a couple of weeks ago, right? And you bumped into Henry Lu?"

"Yeah," I said slowly. "Henry's brother Jason is dating Oscar's brother Lewis. But I don't see how that's relevant?"

"Tonia's cousin's sister-in-law was there having dinner too, and I reckon she must have seen the two of you."

I sighed and rolled my eyes. "How the fuck did she recognise us? Does Auntie Tonia just send all her friends and distant relatives my picture?"

"I have no clue," said Dominic. "But that's my best guess. Mum mentioned it to me last week, and that's all I can think of. I'm sorry."

"Not your fault," I said, taking a sip of my wine and wondering how quickly I could get drunk. The enormous charcuterie board sat on the coffee table between us, which was also oddly clean. I was used to seeing it covered in at least one set of sticky fingerprints. "I'm adding another strike to my mental list next to Auntie Tonia's name."

"I'm surprised you still have room," Oscar said. "Based on what you've told me."

"God, that woman is insufferable," Dominic said.

"Agreed," I said. "But I'm not going to talk about her. Mostly because we'll be here all night, and I'll just get so fucking frustrated that I'll break something. So to answer your earlier question, the trip was good. Intense though. Lots of driving."

"You started in Cornwall, right?" Louisa asked. She'd sat down next to Dominic on the sofa opposite us, and I was forever grateful she'd taken me up on my subject change.

"Yeah, down in Fowey at this place called August House. It was really lovely, although we didn't get to see much of the town because of the rain."

"We're looking at heading down there in the autumn, maybe while Teddy's on half-term," Dominic said. "Wrap up warm, let Teddy and Nico run along the beach, give them a change of scenery."

"It's a beautiful part of the world," Oscar said.

Dominic nodded and reached for the board, picking up a few bits. "I've never been, but it would be nice to have a family holiday just the six of us if we can find somewhere."

"Are you still going to Italy this summer?" I asked quietly.

"Yeah," Dominic said. "Are you coming? Nonna and Grandad would love to see you again."

"Maybe. It'll depend on work and whether I can spend time with Auntie Tonia without strangling her."

"Italy?" Oscar asked, looking at me with a raised

eyebrow, and I saw him putting several things together very quickly.

"Yeah, it's a family tradition," I said. "Everyone on my mum's side spends the summer with Nonna and Grandad. We used to go for a couple of weeks every year. Everyone still does actually. I just... haven't been in a while because of work."

Oscar nodded. "That makes sense."

"Have you got much booked in for the summer?" Dominic asked. He was frowning and looking between Oscar and me as if he knew he was missing something. I didn't think Dominic knew about Daniele. I'd certainly never told him, and I didn't think Zoë would have tattled on me.

"Potentially," I said. "We're still waiting to get the go-ahead on the next trips in Oscar's LGBTQ+ holiday series, and the dates for those will depend on what's available. And I've got a few more things in the works."

Dominic nodded but didn't press further, and the conversation moved on. I wasn't sure why I felt awkward, but I did. I'd been out to Italy several times since everything had happened because there was no way my family would have let me go ten years without visiting my grandparents.

The first time had been hell, the second time I'd just been numb, and by the third trip I'd started to process everything and didn't feel so hollow.

But I'd been on an emotional rollercoaster recently, and falling in love with Oscar had made me vulnerable in ways I'd never expected. I didn't think I'd be able to cope with a week in the place where I'd lost my first love while my family interrogated my second. I knew they'd spend the whole time picking over Oscar like vultures on a carcass, and the whole idea made me weirdly nauseous.

Maybe it would be a good idea to go back to my therapist for a while, just to talk all of this shit out so I could finally move on. Or something like that.

The rest of dinner was fabulous, and it was actually fun to spend time with my brother outside of him being a parent. I'd forgotten how fun he could be when he partially removed the stick from his butt.

By the time Louisa rolled out the tiramisu, I thought I was going to burst, but I still managed a few mouthfuls because it was too good to resist.

"I can send you home with some if you want," Louisa said as I forlornly eyed the dish. "We're not going to eat it all."

"Home?" I asked, turning over the word on my tongue.

"Sorry, is it too soon to say that? I wasn't sure if you were still living here? We've not really talked about it." She winced. "And now I've put my foot in it. Sorry."

"It's fine." I looked at Oscar, trying to judge his expression. I reached for his hand under the table, and he gave me an easy smile.

"I mean, my flat isn't much, but you're welcome to stay there with me if you want."

"I'd like that," I said, my heart almost overflowing with emotion. "I don't have a lot of stuff, so I won't take up much space."

"There isn't much space to begin with." Oscar squeezed my hand. "But it will do."

"Yeah," I said. "It's a good start." I leant over and kissed him, not caring that my brother was sitting right there.

When we parted, Dominic was giving me that strange expression again like he was happy but concerned.

I was going to have to talk to him, this time alone. And I got my chance ten minutes later when he shooed Louisa and Oscar out of the kitchen so he could load the dishwasher.

I lingered by the counter under the pretence of making coffee, even though both Louisa and Oscar had declined, and I didn't think caffeine would do me much good this late at night. Because I apparently cared about that shit now that I had a man to curl up against and fall asleep with.

"So... what's with the face?" I asked as Dominic stacked plates in the dishwasher. He frowned.

"What face?"

"The one you were making when Oscar and I were talking about being together. Do you not like him? Am I going to get a lecture about moving too quickly?"

"No, it's not that." Dominic's voice was quiet. He sighed and slotted some cutlery into the plastic holder. "I just... I never thought I'd get to see you happy again. Not like this. Ever since Daniele..."

He trailed off, and I stared at him.

"What do you mean?"

"It's okay," he said quickly. "Nobody told me, and it's not like the whole family knows. Just me, and Louisa, and Mum."

"H-how?" The news had staggered me, and I almost felt dizzy. Dominic strode over and put his arm around me.

"Anthony's wedding," Dominic said. "I heard you crying with Zoë. I, er, I wanted to say something, but I didn't know what. I didn't want you to get mad at me for overhearing, but you just sounded so... devastated. And I realised nobody had really asked you about Daniele after it happened, and I just... didn't know what to do. I didn't say anything and decided I'd be there if you ever wanted to tell me."

"Oh... That was nearly nine years ago, Dom."

"I know. And I'm not upset you didn't tell me. Truly, I'm not. I know our family is shit at keeping secrets. That's why Louisa and I didn't tell anyone she was pregnant with Teddy until she was about to pop because I knew as soon as I told anyone except Mum and Dad, everyone would know in two minutes." He squeezed me gently, and for the first time in a long time he just felt like my brother, not someone trying to be more.

"So the face is because you're happy for me? Sad for me?"

"Relieved, I guess? And happy. You always projected this carefree, careless air about you, and I never knew if you were really happy or not, and I never wanted to ask because then I'd have to admit I knew your secret," Dominic said. "Which, logically, is kind of fucked up. But that's how we do things here apparently."

I chuckled. "Isn't that the Verrati family motto? Share at your peril. Emotions are a family affair. Relationships are family decisions."

Dominic snorted. "And that is why I'm reading every parenting advice thing I can get my hands on so my sons don't become emotionally damaged by our relatives."

"Good luck with that," I said. "I thought all families were supposed to give you a healthy supply of emotional trauma?"

"No, I think that's just ours."

I smiled and shook my head. "You know, I actually like hanging out with you when you're like this. Less drill sergeant, more normal man in his very, very late thirties."

"Don't fucking remind me." Dominic groaned, releasing me and going back to the dishwasher. "I don't feel like I should be turning forty."

"Are you going to have a party?"

"Depends on whether I get a choice in the matter," he said. "I think I just want to do a nice dinner party. Immediate family only. Go to a nice restaurant, have some good food, that sort of thing."

I thought for a second, then I remembered Raphael's. I wondered if they did private hire because the restaurant would be the perfect size for my parents, my brothers and their families, Oscar and me.

My heart fluttered at the realisation that I was automatically including Oscar. I knew things were getting serious between us pretty quickly, but I didn't want to change that.

I knew what I wanted, and it was him.

"You know, I might actually know somewhere," I said.

"Great. Send me the details."

We stood in semi-silence for a moment, just the sound of clanking plates filling the room.

"Hey," Dominic said as he shoved a washing tablet into the dishwasher and closed the door. "I mean it. I'm really glad you're happy—genuinely happy. You deserve it. And I promise, I won't share any details. But you will have to introduce him to a couple of people if you want to bring him to my not-forty-fortieth."

I grinned. "Thanks. I'll hold you to that. Or I'll promise Teddy you'll take him swimming with sharks for his sixteenth."

"Come on," Dominic said with a wry smile. "You and I both know you'll be doing that anyway."

# CHAPTER TWENTY-NINE

*Oscar*

BEING BACK in Madelyn Rossi's office, watching as she poured over the layouts for the next issue on her desk, was a slightly eerie experience. I didn't think I'd be back there so soon, and while I probably should have been pleased Madelyn was taking an interest in me and my work, it felt more like I'd been summoned for execution.

"So," Madelyn said eventually, sitting back in her chair and picking up the cup of coffee her assistant had just delivered. I noticed her mug had dachshunds on it. They were all wearing bowties. "How was Hawaii? Did you and Mr. Verrati enjoy the St. West?"

"Yes, it was beautiful. The whole island is absolutely stunning, and everyone was so welcoming. I'd definitely recommend it."

"Good. Your article says much the same, but it's nice to hear your enthusiasm in person. I'm glad you and Mr.

Verrati had time to connect." She looked at me over the rim of her glasses, and I saw a wry smile playing across her lips as she sipped her coffee.

A sudden jolt of fear struck my chest, and I wondered if she knew I'd lied to her. Icy horror slid down my spine, one vertebra at a time, freezing me to the spot.

I didn't know how she'd found out, but this was Madelyn Rossi.

She knew everything.

"You can relax," Madelyn said. "I'm not going to punish you for lying to me about being in a relationship. I realised it was rather presumptuous of me to assume."

"N-no, it's fine."

"I was rather impressed by your ability to think on your feet, I must say. I wondered how long it would take you to come clean, but apparently that isn't necessary anymore?"

"Er, no?" I tried to process everything Madelyn had just said, forcing my brain to work through her words despite the fact that it was screaming at me to run. There was no running from this though. "We're actually together now."

"I thought so." She nodded. "I saw you two outside the office yesterday."

"Sorry," I said. Ilias had come to meet me for lunch, dragging me out to a nearby ramen bar to grab something to eat. He'd kissed me goodbye when he'd walked me back. Right in front of the building.

"You don't need to apologise for kissing your boyfriend," Madelyn said as she sipped her coffee again. "I am rather interested in how it all occurred, but you don't need to tell me. I'm not here to pry into your private life."

I let out a small sigh of relief because I wasn't sure I'd be able to recount the entire thing to Madelyn without sounding like a complete banana.

"But please don't lie to me again, Mr. Moore. I'd rather we were just honest with each other. I've found it makes things a lot easier. Although some people might disagree. Then again, they tend to be the sort of people who don't like honesty."

"Okay," I said. "I can do that."

"Good." Madelyn gave me a pleased smile, and I realised the reason so many people were terrified of her was because you knew absolutely where you stood with her. Madelyn knew everything and pulled no punches. If she didn't like something, she was going to tell you, and I could see why some people felt threatened by that.

I liked it though. She might be hard to please, but at least I'd always know if I was doing a good job. There wouldn't be any bullshit to wade through, and that would make things a hell of a lot easier.

"Let's talk about the rest of the series," Madelyn said, setting down her mug and looking at a notebook next to her. "Marcus sent me your list of suggestions, and we think starting with New Zealand, Thailand, and Santorini, will work nicely with my plans for the rest of the year. We'll get Mr. Verrati on a freelance contract for the rest of the series as well."

"I'm sorry, did you say starting?" I hadn't meant to interrupt her, but that word had latched itself onto my brain and was now flashing bright, neon yellow.

"Yes, I did." Madelyn looked at me, her expression serious. "I think you're a good writer, and I think Mr. Verrati is a good photographer. You clearly work well together, so I'd like you to do more. Also, our sister magazine, *Your Wedding*, is looking for some new travel content from a diverse perspective. They have a new editor, and she's looking to diversify the content away from heterosexual couples with an unlimited budget. We had a very interesting meeting last week, and your name came up. Obviously, your contract is with *The Traveller*, but if you would be open to some cross-over work, Jane would be very keen to have you."

I blinked several times, then realised I needed to answer. "Er, sure. It sounds interesting. Can I get some more details about what they're looking for?"

It wasn't an opportunity I was going to say no to, especially because it meant that I'd get to help make a positive change. I'd never picked up a wedding magazine in my life, so I had no idea what they'd want content-wise, but I imagined it wouldn't be too different from what I'd written for Marcus.

"Of course. I'll get Marcus to arrange a meeting between you, Jane, and himself to discuss things further. I'd like Marcus to be kept in the loop since he's your direct manager, and I don't want Jane pinching you. If you have any problems, do let me know. I realise these situations can get political, even if we're all trying to play nicely," Madelyn said as she scribbled a note to herself. "How does that all sound?"

"That's great. Thank you."

"Good. I'm glad we're in agreement."

I realised I was being dismissed, so I said goodbye and hurried out. As soon as the door closed behind me, I let out a long breath.

I looked at my watch and realised it was nearly twelve. As I walked back to the desk where I'd left my stuff, I pulled out my phone and fired off a text to Ilias to see if he was free for lunch. I wasn't completely convinced I hadn't just hallucinated that meeting, and I needed someone to talk it out with.

Thirty minutes later, I emerged from the office building where *The Traveller* and some of its sister brands were housed to find Ilias standing in the sunshine. My heart soared when I saw him, and I instantly pulled him in for a kiss.

"Hello," he said. "You're in a good mood. What happened?"

"I'm not entirely sure. I had a meeting with Madelyn, then things got a bit weird." We turned and started walking down the street. There was a little bakery not far from the office that did good sandwiches and would be perfect for our impromptu lunch date.

Ilias slipped his hand into mine. "Weird how?"

"Turned out she knew I was lying about not having a boyfriend when I pitched the Hawaii project. She was just waiting for me to come clean," I said, shaking my head. "I'm not sure how she knew, and I'm not sure I want to know."

"Shit. What did she say?"

"Just that she doesn't want me to lie to her again, which

is fair enough. And she seemed pleased that things had worked out for us."

"Okay, yeah, I can see why that was weird," Ilias said. "Do you think Marcus ratted you out?"

"Maybe? But I thought I'd kept it a secret from him too." I frowned.

Ultimately, it didn't matter how Madelyn had found out because it didn't change things in the long run. I was tempted to ask Marcus, but if he didn't know I'd lied, then I'd be admitting it to him as well, and the less people who knew, the better.

"Anyway," I continued, "she and Marcus have agreed to the next three locations for the series, and she wanted to know if we'd be interested in doing some work for *Your Wedding* because apparently the new editor wants more diverse content."

"Seriously? That's awesome! Congratulations." He squeezed my hand and nudged my shoulder.

"Thanks, and I'd keep an eye on your emails because you're going to be offered freelance photography contracts for all three projects."

"I'd hope so," Ilias said with a wry chuckle. "Otherwise why would I want to travel with you?"

I snorted.

"Where are we going, by the way? You didn't say."

"New Zealand, Thailand, and Santorini. Not sure in which order, but those are the three we're starting with," I said.

"Perfect. I'll pack my teeniest, tiniest swimwear just for

you." Ilias pulled on my hand to slow me down and leant over to give me a kiss. "I have good news too."

"Yeah?"

"I found a little studio for rent. It's out in Battersea, so it's a bit of a trek, but it's a great space, pretty cheap to rent, and the owner said she's happy for me to do whatever I want as long as it's legal," Ilias said as we continued walking.

"I've been writing up some plans and getting a website thrown together, but I'm thinking of offering personal and family photography with an emphasis on queer people and families, making it a safe, happy place for them to come and get photos done. Y'know headshots, portraits, that sort of thing."

"That's amazing. Seriously, it is."

"You think so?" Ilias asked, and I heard the uncertainty in his voice.

I knew he'd been looking at doing some studio work as a way to pay his bills and give him some financial stability, but over the past week, he'd really thrown himself into the idea after we'd discussed moving in together.

We both knew my studio flat wouldn't do us forever because it would be like permanently living in a hotel room, but it was so expensive to rent in London that we'd both need to have solid income to get anywhere bigger. Ilias had floated the studio idea past me before, and I'd woken up on Saturday morning to find him sitting next to me in bed, tapping away on his laptop and making notes.

Apparently, when Ilias wanted something to happen, he made it happen pretty quickly.

"I do," I said. "You're great with people, and I know you'll make everyone feel comfortable. You take amazing photos, and you said yourself this will still leave you with the flexibility to travel."

"It's going to have to," Ilias said with a chuckle. "I'm not turning down a free trip to Santorini from Madelyn Rossi. Especially not after you lied to her!"

We'd reached the bakery, and the tables and chairs outside were already full of people.

"She put me on the spot. What was I supposed to do?"

"I'm glad she did," Ilias said, turning to me with a warm smile and eyes full of adoration. "Because if you hadn't lied, I wouldn't have gotten this, and that would have sucked. Because you're the best thing that's ever happened to me, Oscar, and I love you more than anything."

"I love you too." I pulled him in for a soft kiss. "You're the best lie I've ever told, and you make me so happy I could burst."

"You're the sweetest." He grinned at me. "But enough sap. I'm starving, and apparently, I have to actually do work shit this afternoon, so I need energy. Come on, you owe me lunch."

He pulled me towards the door of the bakery so fast I almost lost my balance. We both laughed, and I realised I couldn't wait to have more adventures with Ilias, big and small.

Because life was made up of a million adventures, and I wanted every one to be with him.

# CHAPTER THIRTY

*Ilias*

"You know, you can let go of me," Oscar muttered sleepily, his body shifting underneath mine.

"But I'm comfy," I said, snuggling deeper into his neck. I knew it was morning because I could already see the light around the edges of the curtains of our hotel room, but I couldn't be bothered to find out the actual time. "Besides, you love me being on top of you."

Oscar chuckled hoarsely. "Yeah, but not when you're strangling me."

I sighed and slightly released my hold on him. "Better?"

"A bit." He reached his arm across and began trailing his fingers lazily down the bottom of my spine. "It's a good thing our room has air con, or I'd have kicked you off me in the night. I hope we don't get a hot summer at home, or I'm going to fucking melt."

"Charming," I said, blowing a raspberry on his collarbone to express my feelings. It was childish but funny, and Oscar made an undignified sound in response. "Don't worry, I overheat very easily, so I'll probably try to push you out of bed so I can starfish in the middle and stay cool."

"I'm going to get us a fan and put it on your side of the bed, then maybe you'll stay there."

"Honestly, it sounds like you don't want me in bed with you at all." I ran one finger lazily across his chest to toy with his nipple, watching it harden under my touch.

Oscar rolled me over, pinning me to the bed and looking down at me with a raised eyebrow and a half smile.

"That's definitely not true. I just don't want to sweat to death as a result of being koala-ed by you every night. But if it's the price I have to pay to have you in bed with me, I'd pay it a hundred times over."

"I'm not sure if that's sweet or gross," I said, "but we'll go with sweet."

He kissed me softly, his body pressing against me as we made out. There was no rush or desperate need because we had all the time in the world. The hotel we'd been sent to in Santorini was designed for relaxing, and although we had a few things on our itinerary, our main job was to make the most of the facilities.

And I counted our bedroom as one of the most important ones.

My arms snaked around Oscar's neck, pulling him closer. I felt his cock starting to get hard against mine, and I groaned at the sweet burst of friction. Our bodies entwined as we moved on the bed so we were lying side by side, our legs tangled together as our hands and mouths explored.

Need was starting to burn under my skin, but I wanted something more than a quick, hard fuck. Mostly because that required energy, and it was too early for that sort of exuberance.

"I love you," Oscar said as he leant back for a moment, his eyes roaming over my face. "You're so gorgeous. I'm so lucky you're mine."

"I'm lucky too." I kissed him again. "I love you so much."

Oscar's kisses grew more heated as his hands slid down my spine and squeezed my ass, pulling me tightly against him. I moaned as he ground against me. My hips bucked, searching for more. An idea slid into my mind, and I rolled in Oscar's arms, pressing my ass back against him. I stuck my hand under the pillow, trying to find the bottle of lube we'd used yesterday.

"Fuck my thighs," I said as I passed Oscar the lube and tilted my head back for a kiss. I didn't have the patience for him to work me open, and this was a good enough solution.

Oscar clicked open the lube, and I felt his hand slide between us to slick up his cock. I squeezed my thighs tightly as he slipped his cock between them and groaned as it brushed along my taint and nudged the back of my balls. Oscar's hand, still wet with lube, gripped my hip to pull me closer.

His movements were slow and deliberate, and he trailed kisses down my neck and nipped at my shoulder. I lost myself in the hazy pleasure that surrounded us, gasping as Oscar reached down to grasp my cock.

"Yes... like that. I want..." But I couldn't put into words what I wanted. The feelings were too big and too complicated to be summed up in simple words.

"Tell me," Oscar murmured as he slowly stroked my cock at the same leisurely pace he was thrusting between my thighs.

"Everything," I said. "I want everything with you."

"Good. Because I want everything too."

We moved together slowly, letting ourselves become lost in each other until everything became too much. I spilled over Oscar's hand with a broken moan, and not long after he painted my thighs with his release.

It was the perfect way to begin another day together.

Sometime later, we piled into the enormous, waterfall shower, then walked out to the terrace with mugs of fresh coffee from the machine in our room because the hotel was *that* fancy.

Our room was set into one of the cliffs overlooking the sparkling sea that was so bright and beautiful it almost didn't look real. I could see why so many people wanted to come to Santorini. It was utterly picture perfect.

"What do you want to do today?" I asked, putting my arm around Oscar's waist and leaning against his shoulder.

"Breakfast will be finishing soon," Oscar said. "I vote we start with that. Then maybe we can venture into the village and explore?"

"I like that plan. But first, I want to take a photo." I

pulled my phone out of the pocket of my shorts and swiped my thumb across the screen.

"Of the view?"

"Of us!" I poked his arm until he turned and we had the incredible landscape behind us. It wouldn't be the most perfectly Instagrammable photo ever, but I didn't care. This was for me, not anyone else. "I realised I don't actually have a lot of photos of us together, and I want more."

Oscar grumbled, but he was grinning as I lifted my phone up, trying to get the perfect angle. Oscar was barely an inch taller than me, so that helped a little. I tapped the button a couple of times, then dissolved into laughter at Oscar's expression.

"Stop pulling faces," I said. "Don't be a dick."

I held the phone up again, and Oscar pressed a kiss to the side of my head as I did. When I tapped on the screen to view the pictures, I smiled, my heart fluttering in my chest.

There was me, smiling, and Oscar kissing me, the pair of us framed by blue skies, low white walls, and the glimmer of the sea. It was the most utterly beautiful photo I'd ever seen and so perfectly us.

"That's cute," Oscar said as he looked over my shoulder. "Send it to me?"

"It is. We're adorable as fuck." I sent the photo to Oscar, set it as my background, and slid my phone back into my pocket. "We should start one of those couples' Instagrams. We'd make a mint. I mean, who wouldn't want to look at our cute as fuck faces in beautiful places?"

I was ninety percent joking because, although it sort of sounded like a fun idea, I knew how much work those accounts were. It also meant letting people into our relationship and putting it under a microscope for people to judge and speculate about. It really wasn't for everyone.

But a tiny part of me wanted to do it just because I wanted to show Oscar off to the world.

"Seriously?" Oscar asked with a half smile and raised eyebrow.

"Maybe? I was mostly joking." I grabbed his hand. "Come on. Let's go get breakfast."

We ate on a terrace overlooking the sea under the shade of an enormous umbrella as the morning breeze caressed my skin. It felt like one of those deliciously lazy mornings, the sort I'd be happy to repeat regularly. It reminded me how lovely my life was because, despite all the hustle and the stress, I got to have days like this: sitting in the sun on a beautiful Greek island at a five-star hotel with the man of my dreams.

It was the sort of thing most people would kill for.

Oscar was sipping orange juice and looking at something on his phone. "Here," he said, sliding it across the table. "What do you think?"

It had Instagram open, showing a new, blank profile for TwoRainbowTravellers.

I raised an eyebrow, unsure what I was seeing. "Is this..."

"It's for us if you want it. I know you said you were joking, but I want to have all sorts of adventures with you Ilias, big and small. And even if we keep it locked and just for ourselves and our friends, I want us to have a record of all the places we go together. Of all the things we do.

Because you are my greatest adventure, and I want to remember every second of it."

"I… I…" I was too stunned to speak, but it felt like my heart was two seconds away from exploding. Oscar was the sweetest man I'd ever met, and I'd never understand why he'd chosen me, but I wasn't going to question it.

"Yes," I said. "Let's do it. Let's share it with everyone. It can be like your articles for *The Traveller*—only an Instagram version. We can show people where they can travel if they're queer, and we can celebrate that. The world can always use a little bit more queer joy."

I interlaced our fingers across the table. Oscar reached for his phone and pulled up the photo I'd sent him. "You'll have to write the caption."

"You're the writer," I said with a laugh as I took the phone.

"Yeah, but you're the one who's good at social media."

"I'll have to teach you." I tapped something out on the screen, added some hashtags, and tagged my own account so I could share it later. Then I hit Post. "There we go. Done."

"Perfect," Oscar said, taking his phone back. He smiled wryly. "How long do you think it'll be until one of our families finds it?"

"An hour? Maybe two? Depends on when I share it on my story. Oooh, you'll have to give me the login details so I can add it to my phone too."

"I will but later." He stood up and offered me his hand. "Fancy a stroll? We can get your camera. Maybe find somewhere for a late lunch?"

I stood and took his hand, feeling the warmth and weight of it against mine. "It's like you read my mind."

We headed out of the restaurant, making a quick stop at our room so I could grab my camera bag before we headed out into the sunshine.

Off on another adventure.

# EPILOGUE

## SIXTEEN MONTHS LATER

*Oscar*

"YOU KNOW, this is the first wedding in ages that I've been excited to go to," Ilias said as we stepped inside the enormous, old mill Eli and Tristan had chosen as their wedding venue.

It was a dramatic, four-story building that combined a stripped back, industrial feel with clever, cosy touches like large, squishy sofas in the open, downstairs area. There were two bold floral arrangements on either side of a sign welcoming us and asking us to turn our phones off. I assumed their friend Leo had done the flowers.

"Is that because you don't think you're going to be interrogated?"

"Yes. Your family is charming, and they love me. They're not going to spend the whole day demanding to know when it'll be our turn and casually mentioning that

I'm not getting any younger. I'm not a fucking punnet of strawberries! I'm not going mouldy."

I laughed, the sound bouncing off the walls. "Mouldy strawberries?"

"I don't want to be a rotten tomato, so strawberries it is."

"I think I've missed something here," Lewis said, popping up next to me with Jason in tow. It was almost strange seeing Lewis in a suit instead of his usual pastel shorts, long socks, and vest top combination.

"Ilias was just saying how much he's looking forward to the wedding," I said with a wry smile. Lewis frowned, but as he opened his mouth to ask another question, I distracted him by asking, "Is it true there's a variety show this evening?"

"Apparently," Lewis said. "I offered to help organise it, but Eli wanted it to be a surprise. I don't even know who's performing."

Behind him, Jason's lip twitched, and my eyes widened. Jason put a finger to his mouth, glancing down at his husband. I grinned because that was going to be adorable and there was a definite chance Lewis was going to cry.

"See? Best wedding ever, and it hasn't even started," Ilias said. "And I don't have to go to church and listen to some old windbag go on and on." He saw Lewis shoot him a questioning look and grinned. "Most of my family is vaguely Catholic, so I've had to sit through fourteen Catholic weddings, and let me tell you, there are so many better things to do with your life."

"I know you gave me shit for not having a fucking

wedding," Lewis said wryly, "but at least I didn't make you sit through that."

"Still don't think you have much of a leg to stand on," I said. Lewis and Jason had surprised us all by getting married in secret and inviting us to a "birthday party" that turned out to be a wedding celebration. None of us had seen it coming, and Miranda had nearly fainted in shock.

"Eh, the parents forgave me, so it's fine. Plus, Richard and Eli have had big weddings."

"And there's Jules's next year," Jason added.

"Exactly!"

"Did I hear my name?" Jules asked, strolling through the mill door looking dapper as always, her fiancée Chantelle next to her and Chantelle's daughter, Kelsey, behind them.

"Yeah," Lewis said. "We were just talking about your wedding."

"Gah, don't remind me," Chantelle said with a laugh. "Bane of my life right now that is. Still trying to find a photographer."

"Seriously?" Lewis gave Jules a pointed stare. "Why didn't you say? I know someone."

"You do?" Jules asked. I didn't know why she was surprised. Lewis knew everyone.

"Yeah, Bastian. He's a friend of Edward's. He does cosplay photography on the side, but his main business is weddings. I'll get you his details."

"We should have just hired you to plan the bloody thing," Jules said.

"I'm not a wedding planner."

"You'd be good at it though," Finn said quietly, sliding quietly up to us, hand-in-hand with Gem.

"Nah, I couldn't deal with people being dicks. I'd throw cake at someone."

"Wouldn't recommend it," Ilias said with a shake of his head. "Especially not if it's fruit cake. It hurts when it hits you in the back of the head."

"How do you know that?" I asked, and Ilias shrugged.

"Remind me to tell you about my cousin Ernesto's wedding one day."

"One day being during dinner," Lewis said. "I want to know too."

"Don't you all look dapper." We turned en masse to see one of the grooms coming through a door in the far wall. Tristan looked very handsome in a sharply tailored black suit, and I knew Eli was going to burst the moment he saw him. Even though they were two wildly different people, I'd never met a pair of opposites more suited to each other.

"The invitation said black tie, and Eli sent us all a very detailed message about the sort of vibe he was going for," Finn said. "I don't think any of us were going to risk dressing down."

I chuckled. Eli's message had been so long it had been virtually impossible to read, but we'd all sort of expected it. Eli was the dramatic one in our family, and none of us had expected his wedding to be casual.

"He's also been interrogating us about our wardrobe choices for months," Gem muttered with a dry chuckle.

"Shouldn't you be upstairs?" I asked, glancing around the room, then back at Tristan. More guests were starting to arrive, and the space was filling up with excited chatter. "We can get everyone in place."

Eli and Tristan weren't having a formal wedding party because they hadn't wanted to choose who went where, especially because Eli's family-and-friends list was a lot bigger than Tristan's. Instead, we'd all promised to act as helpers, just without the whole standing at the altar part.

Ilias and I headed upstairs to the ceremony space on the top floor, which had a high, vaulted metal ceiling. The aisle was lined with jars filled with large, black candles, and there was a dramatic arrangement of hanging flowers over the end where the ceremony would take place. As guests started to arrive, we helped direct them and pointed out a stack of programmes and a basket of tissues for them to help themselves too.

Everyone had taken the glamorous dress code to heart and was dressed to the nines, but it was also gloriously queer, and I loved it.

"We should sit down," Ilias said, coming up to me as the last few guests slotted into place. "Come on, I've got us some seats saved."

He led me to two seats near the front, just behind my mum and Miranda. Next to us was Eli's best friend, Orlando, and his two partners. Orlando looked about two seconds from bursting into tears, and the two men on either side of him were holding his hands tightly.

"You okay?" I asked, and Orlando nodded.

"Think so. I just can't believe he's getting married." He shook his head. "Now he can stop worrying about it."

"Has he been annoying?"

"That's the polite word for it," Orlando said as he began to give me a very quick rundown on Eli's wedding planning shenanigans.

It didn't take long for the ceremony to get under way, and we all stood as the music swelled softly. Tristan appeared first, walking down the aisle with his sister. He looked so nervous that I thought he might pass out. My fingers found Ilias's and he squeezed my hand. The music rose, and I turned my head again to look down the aisle for Eli.

Then I gasped because, even though I'd expected dramatic, Eli was something else.

His suit was also black, but the jacket was longer with a pinched in waist, almost like it was corseted. There were dramatic golden epaulettes on his shoulders, and behind him flowed a magnificent cape of black and gold that shimmered as he walked. It was so utterly Eli that I couldn't have imagined him wearing anything different.

Beside me, Orlando had started crying, and one of his partner's handed him a handkerchief.

"Wow," Ilias said. "Your family does weddings in style."

The ceremony was beautiful, and everyone shed a few tears. Afterwards, we all went downstairs for drinks and nibbles. Evening had already drawn in, and there were candles burning everywhere.

"I knew your brother had a flair for the dramatic," Ilias said, sipping a glass of wine. "But this is tasteful, fun dramatic. Also, I've never been to a Halloween wedding, so that's extra cool."

"Are we applying the Verrati index to weddings now?" I asked.

"I haven't before, but maybe we should. We'll have to use my family's weddings as a baseline because if we use this one, we're fucked."

"Eli is rather extra."

"I am indeed," Eli said, appearing beside me. He was still wearing his cape, although he had scooped it over one arm so it didn't get trodden on.

"And we wouldn't have it any other way," I said as I pulled him into a hug and kissed his cheek. "I'm so happy for you. You look amazing."

"Thanks. The endless arguments with Edward over the cape were clearly worth it." He grinned. "Have you seen the cake? It's bigger than Kelsey. And it's got four different flavours because we couldn't choose."

"I will definitely need a piece of each," said Ilias. "Especially if it's not fruit."

Eli pulled a face, and Ilias laughed. We chatted for a while before Eli got pulled away, leaving Ilias and me alone. We strolled outside onto the terrace where hundreds of fairy lights cast a fantastical glow over the space. There were a few other people out there, including a couple of Americans Eli had befriended during a drag tour in Tennessee, but since it was already quite cold, most of the guests were staying inside.

It was nice to have a moment that was just the two of us in the chaos of the rest of the day.

"So," I said, "having fun?"

"I am. But mostly because I'm here with you." Ilias

smiled at me fondly, the fairy lights giving him an almost magical halo. "Everything is fun when I'm with you."

"Everything?"

"Everything." He kissed me softly. "I love you, Oscar. You make my life so perfect, I can't imagine it being any different."

"I love you too." I pulled him close to me, cupping his jaw with my hand. "Truly, Ilias, you are everything to me."

We stood there together for a few minutes more before we went back inside to join the party.

And I knew, for the rest of my life, I'd always remember how perfect Ilias looked that night because he was my always and my everything.

My oh-so perfect adventure.

*The End*

# ACKNOWLEDGMENTS

As I write this, I'm struck by the realisation that this is the end of another series, and brings the Baker-Moore family saga to a close, at least for now. I've absolutely loved writing every member of this family, and Oscar and Ilias were the perfect people to finish up with.

As always, I am indebted to a fantastic group of people who continue to help and support me.

To Charity, who supported me through the drafting process when it dissolved into just vibes. You are the best PA and friend I could ask for.

To Carly, for continuing to encourage me and for helping me with Oscar.

To Susie, for polishing my words to within an inch of their life.

To Crystal Lacy, for answering my endless questions about Hawaii and tourism. I am very grateful for your help and patience.

To Toby, Noah, and Jayne for cheering me on every day as I write.

To Natasha, for the gorgeous cover.

To Lori and Rosie, for being my final pairs of eyes.

To Dan, who I know will bring these words to life in the most wonderful way.

To my husband for always supporting me, and helping me to believe in myself.

And last, but never least, to you, my fabulous readers. Whether I'm new to you or you've been here since the start, I am grateful for you love and support.

If you enjoyed *Oh So Oscar*, please consider leaving a review. Reviews are invaluable for indie authors, and may help other readers find this book.

Until next time.

Love,
Charlie x

## ALSO BY CHARLIE NOVAK

Final Score

The Off the Pitch Short Collection

Off the Pitch: The Complete Collection (Boxset)

STANDALONES

Screens Apart

SHORT STORIES

One More Night

Twenty-Two Years (Newsletter Exclusive)

Snow Way In Hell

AUDIOBOOKS

Always Eli

Finding Finn

Natural Twenty

Charisma Check

Proficiency Bonus

Strawberry Kisses

Summer Kisses

*For a regularly updated list, please visit:*

*charlienovak.com/books*

*charlienovak.com/audiobooks*

# CHARLIE NOVAK

Charlie lives in England with her husband and two cheeky dogs. She spends most of her days wrangling other people's words in her day job and then trying to force her own onto the page in the evening.

She loves cute stories with a healthy dollop of fluff, plenty of delicious sex, and happily ever afters — because the world needs more of them.

Charlie has very little spare time, but what she does have she fills with baking, Dungeons and Dragons, reading and many other nerdy pursuits. She also thinks that everyone should have at least one favourite dinosaur...

Website: charlienovak.com
Facebook Group: Charlie's Angels
*For day-to-day-musings, giveaways and teasers.*

Plus sign up for her newsletter for bonus scenes, new releases and extras.

facebook.com / charlienovakauthor

twitter.com / charlienwrites

instagram.com / charlienwrites

bookbub.com / profile / charlie-novak

amazon.com / author / charlienovak

Printed in Great Britain
by Amazon